INVITE ME IN

CONJURING FASCINATION SERIES

INVITE ME IN

JM PAQUETTE

For those willing to take another chance
and invite someone in

CONTENTS

BONUS STORY
CALL ME FORTH

CHAPTER 1

SYLVIA

"**W**ELCOME TO VIKING TIMES," THE TEENAGER BEHIND the counter drones, "where all of your fantasies come to life." He glances up from his monitor long enough to snatch the ticket Sylvia has laid on the counter, sliding it angrily beneath the scanner—

Brrm!

—then frowns as the machine fails to recognize her ticket barcode. The printed page has been folded and refolded in a dozen directions, evidence of Sylvia's indecision about coming to the show tonight.

Slowly, oh so slowly, he drags his judgy gaze up to meet hers, his eyes practically shouting, *How dare you hand me this battered piece of paper, expecting me to accept this crap after enduring hours of customer service hell?*

Sylvia looks down at the counter, then casually over her shoulder, scanning the small crowd behind her. No one seems particularly interested in her exchange, the next couple in line more entertained by one another

1

than anything else, and she turns back to the clerk with an apologetic smile.

His annoyed gaze doesn't leave hers as he smooths the paper on the counter edge and carefully slides it back under the scanner. This time, the machine beeps, and his eyes flick toward the computer screen.

"Reservation for two," he says, looking back at where she stands, very much alone, on the other side of the counter. "Is your companion meeting you here?"

Sylvia shuffles nervously. *Why did I agree to come to this stupid show in the first place?* She knows her best friend Miriam meant well when she gifted the tickets for Sylvia's birthday, even when she insisted Sylvia go anyway despite Adam not being in the picture.

Get out of the house, Miriam had said. *Who knows? Maybe you'll meet some sexy Viking and bear him many children!*

It had seemed like a good idea at the time. But now, standing in front of this surly teenager working the front counter, very aware of the line forming behind her, Sylvia isn't so sure anymore.

"No," she murmurs, tucking a strand of blonde hair behind her ear and leaning forward a little. "No one is meeting me here." She clears her throat, aiming her words so only he can hear her. "It's just *me.*"

"We don't offer refunds for online ticket purchases," the teen says loudly, clearly preparing for her to start an argument. The name tag pinned to his black polo says "Jimmy."

"I don't want a refund," Sylvia says quickly. "I'll just leave the seat empty ... if that's okay."

Jimmy sighs, shaking his head. "Whatever you want, lady. Just tell your server you don't need the second plate." The printer beeps and a long receipt slides out. Jimmy grabs it, and in one smooth motion, he tears the bottom part, removes the sticker with a set of numbers on it, then jams it on the back of two small red and silver flags.

Sylvia silently accepts the receipt and flags he slides across to her. "Congratulations. You're a Mulranian," he tells her. "Follow the red and silver signs." Sylvia almost steps away, but the clerk catches her. "Don't forget your helmet!" Jimmy says with forced cheer, plopping a plastic horned helmet onto her head. He hands her a second one. "You paid for two, so here."

Sylvia pushes the helmet back from her forehead, adjusting the awkward weight, the plastic edges snagging on her long hair. Just as she shoves the extra helmet into her purse, she swears she can feel eyes boring holes into her back, watching her walk down the hallway marked by red and silver flags like Jimmy the clerk had instructed. She resists the urge to look over her shoulder.

Get it together, Copland. You're just being paranoid.

Another bored teenager catches her at the next doorway. This time, a girl jammed in a low-cut peasant dress with a fake brown bodice and stitched on belt wears a blonde wig with two long braids framing her chest. *I see how it is,* Sylvia observes. *The guys get to wear regular clothes while the girls have to wear that. I bet the women in the show all wear string bikinis!*

The girl nods at Sylvia as she approaches. "Welcome to Team Mulranian," she recites, gesturing for Sylvia to hand over her flags. She checks the back for a number.

"27 and 28," the girl reads, then looks up at Sylvia. "You waiting for someone?"

Sylvia shakes her head again, biting her lip. "Just me," she repeats.

"Cool," the girl says. "Watch your step." She heads into the main area, a wide-open space designed to mimic a tent interior: cloth walls and a large pole in the center. The tables form several semi-circles around fake fire pits, each seat facing the open expanse of dirt where the main show will take place. Five levels of tables ring half the space across from the performance area, each level holding four tables, and Sylvia follows the girl down to the very bottom level, just above the ground. The tables seat six, and the girl points to the two seats in the middle. "That's you," the girl says. "Water, tea, or wine?"

"Umm," Sylvia says, taking her seat at the still empty table. "Wine," she decides.

The hostess-turned-server glances at the empty seat. "You get two glasses. You want them both at the same time?"

Sylvia sinks into herself, wilting under the server's gaze. "Sure," she replies before she can change her mind. She doesn't normally drink, but tonight, she needs the extra help to survive the entire night—*alone*.

The girl nods, turning with a flourish of skirts as she heads back, ascending the steps.

Sylvia removes her purse, setting it on the empty chair to her left, when the extra helmet slides out. *Seriously? I should just leave this on a table somewhere.* She tries to jam the damn thing back inside her black bag when her own helmet slides forward on her head again, and a voice speaks behind her.

"Excuse me—is this seat taken?"

4

Sylvia looks up at a handsome blond man with bright blue eyes. The helmet slides back again, almost falling off her head. She holds it in place while she stares at him. He isn't wearing a helmet, his hair falling perfectly around his face. "Um." She fumbles with her purse, sliding it back onto her lap, a plastic horn jamming her in the gut. "No?"

"Great!" He smiles warmly, then a woman joins him, her manicured hand grasping his shoulder. "Would you mind scooting to the end? We're actually a foursome." He gestures toward the other shockingly beautiful couple behind him.

"No, I don't mind," Sylvia mumbles, something sinking in her chest as she claims the pair of seats at the end of the table. She leaves the seat on the end empty, settling herself into her new chair, deliberately avoiding the pitying looks of her table companions.

Sylvia leans forward, trailing a finger along the red and silver tablecloth draped over her table. The material isn't fancy, but it's still nice enough, the seams well made. She looks up at the matching banner strung overhead, then down at the symbol lining the low wall separating the tables from the performance area. The design matches her designated flags, save for the stylized black dragon at the banner's center. Looking back up the stairs, she sees each table in this section has the same colors.

To her left is another area draped in brown and black but with a stylized horse instead of a black dragon. To her right is a section of blue and gold with two axes crossed over a warhammer, followed by black and green with a huge bird.

More people start to trickle in, the murmur of voices growing louder as the room fills to full capacity.

The young server returns with two silver plastic mugs of red wine, eyebrows creasing as she sees the new couple sitting in Sylvia's previous seat, then steps over to set them before Sylvia. She thanks the girl with a nod. Spending her own days waiting tables at Abe's Diner downtown has taught her to appreciate the work of others in the service industry, and she reminds herself to leave a ridiculous tip.

Sylvia takes a longer sip of her wine than intended, hoping the alcohol kicks in soon. She keeps her face angled away from the other couples at the table, though she can feel their curious glances on her now and then. She studies the room instead, using her few history classes at the community college to assess the decor. She always did love Viking stuff—it was why Miriam had gotten her tickets in the first place.

The tents are probably accurate, given that Vikings has become a generic term for various Germanic tribes everywhere from the fourth to the tenth century. Sylvia frowns, recalling Professor Ball's face as he recited tales of those barbarians with delight, relishing the details of battles and treaties, weapons and armor, and marriages of convenience. The fact that the professor hadn't been hard to look at probably explained why she retained so much of that class.

Always a sucker for a pretty face... though it did actually help me that time. She had gotten her Associates a year ago with decent enough grades, but that class was her only A. School wasn't her strength, not enough to justify more classes, not when she could work instead.

Sylvia lifts her flag, studying the layout of the colors and comparing it to the large banner hanging a few feet in front of her table. She initially dismissed the flag as junk, but staring at the intertwining colors, she notices her small flag contains the same stylized dragon, the creature subtly outlined in silver against the red. Scanning the room, she sees that the other flags have similar subtlety—a black horse, gold weapons, and a green bird. Viking Times may be a cheesy tourist trap, but someone with an eye for design was involved in the layout. Sylvia has never been to one of these shows before, but she's heard about them. A tiny thrill of excitement runs through her at being so close to the ground where the action will play out.

She may not thank Miriam for her gift by the end of the night, but at least she isn't angry anymore. *Besides*, she tells herself, *Vikings are always half-naked on TV. Maybe I can enjoy some eye candy along with my wine.* She takes another long pull from her cup, surprised to see that she has almost finished it already. Shaking her head, she lifts it again, draining the contents in a long gulp, then swaps it for the full cup.

The server comes by, hauling a large tray, sets up over the fake fire pit in front of the table, and starts handing out bowls of yellow broth and flat bread. "Vegetable soup and barley bread!" the girl announces. "Enjoy *nattmal*!" She leans in to whisper to the table. "Night meal," she translates with a wink, then heads back up the stairs.

Sylvia is surprised to find she enjoys the soup and simple bread. She expected something super salty and processed, but the food is surprisingly plain. *More accuracy*, she thinks. *Whoever set this up did their homework.*

Sylvia has finished her second cup of wine and her food when the server returns, whisking the bowls away. She glances at Sylvia's empty cup before she leaves.

A few moments later, she returns with another tray full of food, this time turkey legs wrapped in tin foil that she sets on everyone's plate. "Mutton!" she announces cheerily. "Actually turkey," she whispers, then plunks down another plastic cup of wine before Sylvia. "I thought you could use this," she says with a wink.

Sylvia nods gratefully, reminding herself again to leave a great tip.

She takes a few bites of the turkey leg, then puts it down. She's never been a huge fan of turkey, and while the meat isn't terrible, it's not her favorite. She is filled up with wine and soup, and she wonders, *Should I hit the restroom before the actual show begins?* Scooting her chair back, she tries to stand, but the room tilts dangerously, and she sits back down hard.

I guess I'm really not used to the wine!

Slowly, she rises to her feet again. But this time, the world doesn't move. *Maybe I should bring my purse... never mind.* With the extra helmet inside, it's bulky now. If someone wants to steal it, they are welcome to the few measly dollars inside. Ignoring her tablemates, who seem engrossed in a quiet conversation with one another, she heads carefully up the stairs in search of the restroom. Another server dressed in the same peasant dress points to a long hallway on the right, and Sylvia heads down it.

She is about to push the door open when it suddenly jerks inward, and a tall red-headed man steps out.

"Oh!" Sylvia exclaims, stepping out of his way. "I'm sorry!"

"No reason to be sorry," he says in a friendly voice, a small smile on his lips as he looks her over. Sylvia almost looks down at herself, the simple black skirt that swishes around her ankles, the blue tank top under a plain sweater, but stops herself just in time. She glances at the sign above the door.

"I thought this was the ladies?" she asks, frowning. She tries not to notice how handsome the stranger is, focusing instead on what he's doing coming out of the ladies' bathroom. His slightly flushed face is clean-shaven beneath the shock of shoulder-length red hair, broad shoulders hidden by a black t-shirt and legs encased in dark jeans.

OhmygodJamieFraser, her drunk mind shouts.

"So it is," he replies casually, backing up to hold the door open for her. "Allow me." For a second, he seems to glow, skin otherworldly, eyes golden, but then it is gone, and he's just a normal, handsome man again.

Too much wine. It's almost like he's...

"Allow you to what?" It's only after he frowns that she realizes she has spoken aloud. "I'm sorry," she says again, feeling her cheeks redden. "I'll just go now."

"Very well," he says, gesturing her through the door.

Sylvia ducks under his arm, trying to ignore the sudden rush of her pulse as she passes near him. "Thanks," she mumbles. She doesn't look back until she hears the door shut. The stranger is gone. She enters the sink area to find it occupied by a single woman. Sylvia uses the stall, and when she emerges, the woman is still standing in the same place, staring at her reflection, a hand resting on the side of her neck.

Sylvia meets her gaze in the mirror, wondering if the stranger is alright, and the woman smiles dreamily at her. Rinsing her hands, Sylvia turns off the water and reaches for a paper towel. "Everything okay?" she asks the woman.

"Of course," the woman replies, pulling her hand away from her neck and washing her hands slowly. "I'm fine."

"Okay," Sylvia replies, watching as the woman seems to remember where she is. Her movements speed up, then she is drying her hands on the way out the door.

Weird, Sylvia thinks. *Apparently, I'm not the only one who can't handle my wine.*

CHAPTER 2

THEO

WHEN THEODORE MULDAVIAN SPIES THE WOMAN ENTER the bathroom alone, he immediately heads in that direction. The warnings of his friends echo in his ears, but he is running late tonight, and he doesn't have enough time to find a snack beyond the walls of their joint venture. A quick glance around assures him that neither Oren nor Harald are around, and he knows Grace will already be backstage prepping the few last-minute details.

What they don't know won't hurt them, he decides. It's true that he doesn't go on stage for a little while yet, but it's not quite enough time to go for a proper hunt. Of course, it's his own fault; he is basically addicted to that silly plants and zombie game on his phone, playing round after round when he should have been heading here.

Or hunting.

But it was a special level! How could I resist such temptation? Vampires aren't generally known for our restraint. And I was already impulsive when I was alive, so this is nothing new.

Besides, this isn't even a risk. The woman is alone in the bathroom. No doubt she will be glad to see me—they always are.

No one will notice him following her inside. He makes sure of it, cloaking his movement in the small illusion magic that allows him to pass beneath human notice. Theo doesn't enjoy all of the facets of his vampirism, like the fact that sunlight will burn him alive or that reflective surfaces don't show his form, but he definitely likes his ability to hide himself in plain sight. As long as he doesn't draw attention with large movements or noise, no humans will notice him or recall his presence there. It certainly makes feeding easier.

Theo likes things easy.

Slipping into the ladies' bathroom, he peeks under the doors to make sure no one else is in the room. His prey steps out of her stall, a small gasp escaping as she sees him there. Theo lowers his defenses, letting her see him as he truly is, and her momentary shock fades, replaced by wonder and a slow-burning lust. She takes a step toward him, wrapping her small hands around the back of his neck, threading her fingers through his shoulder-length red hair.

"You," she murmurs, stepping onto her tiptoes, capturing his mouth with hers in a soft kiss. Theo allows her to caress him, allows himself to be kissed, knowing that this moment of desire will be what she remembers of their encounter, snatches recalled in dreams later on. When she breaks the kiss, pausing for breath, Theo runs his mouth along her jawline, moving to the soft spot of her neck, to the pulse that beats there, where the blood beneath sings to him.

He bites quickly, taking care to drink every drop of blood. He doesn't like leaving messes, especially when he's feeding on the fly like this. He is vaguely aware of the humans beyond the door, a handful milling about in the store near the front doors, a few determined employees moving purposefully from the tables to the kitchens and back again.

None seem inclined to come this way, another feature of his vampire magic, and he allows himself to sink into the moment, absorbing her pleasure and her blood. He can dip into her memories if he chooses, but he doesn't, preferring to keep their encounter brief and impersonal. She is nice enough to look at, but he doesn't think she is someone he wants to actually talk to.

It's been a long time since he met a human that he wants to have a conversation with. Besides Grace, the assistant he excludes from his judgements regarding modern humans, Theo hasn't met an interesting human in decades, maybe centuries.

The thought finishes crossing his mind, then he senses her, a woman coming closer, seemingly oblivious of his keep-away magic. He finishes quickly, sealing the wound with his saliva. He checks to make sure he hasn't left any blood anywhere, then gently places the woman's hand on her neck and moves her so she stands at the sink. By the time she regains her senses, the wound will be healed, and she will think she zoned out in front of the mirror.

He moves to the door, licking his lips and sucking his teeth to make sure no evidence remains, and he gets there just in time to open the door and surprise the blonde woman standing there.

"Oh!" she says, stepping back. "I'm sorry!"

He stares at her, trying to determine how she ignored his defensive barrier. She isn't a vampire—he can sense others of the blood when they are this close. A quick once over shows simple clothes—modest black skirt over sensible boots, simple tank top covered by a button-down sweater. He scans her hands, seeing only small human fingers and delicate wrists. Not a demon. *Maybe she's a witch?*

"No reason to be sorry," he replies, turning on the charm. Instead of throwing herself at him and pushing them both back into the bathroom as he expects, the woman glances up, checking the sign above the doorway.

"I thought this was the ladies?" she asks with a small frown.

"So it is," he agrees, backing up to hold the door open for her. "Allow me." He pushes her mind again, but she just stares at him, a shy smile on her lips.

How is she resisting me? A longer look reveals nothing, but he does notice how divine she smells, a light scent that makes him want to press himself against her, licking her skin, teasing himself with the blood so close beneath the surface. *I must have her,* he decides. *But not now. Soon. After the show, I will find her.*

I have to find her.

The ferocity of the thought is a surprise, a rush of desire spinning through him.

"Allow you to what?" she murmurs, and Theo narrows his eyes. *Who is this girl?* "I'm sorry," she blurts, staring at the floor. "I'll just go now."

"Very well," Theo tells her. *For now.*

"Thanks," she mumbles, ducking under his arm and disappearing into the bathroom. He lets the door close and hurries down the hallway, slipping through the door marked "Employees Only." He runs through the conversation again as he wanders to his dressing room. The girl's face etches itself into his mind, and he thinks of her smell. He isn't paying attention to his surroundings and looks up in surprise when Oren taps him on the shoulder to get his attention.

Oren is ready for the show, dressed in the leather pants and vest he favored back when they were boys running raids across the river. Never a fan of the heavy armor the rest of them used, Oren was fast, relying on his dexterity and speed to get him out of tricky situations—or his bigger friends, of course. The tattoo marking his membership in the tribe is visible on his pale chest, and he still wears the long silver chain with the small locket around his neck, though Theo knows that the silver burns his vampire skin. Beneath his shaggy dark hair, the back of Oren's neck is lined with thin scars, evidence of his eternal devotion to a woman he could never have. Morena was a long time ago now. Theo keeps hoping that one day Oren will show up without the necklace, a sign that he has finally let her go.

Not yet, he thinks, staring at the pink skin around Oren's neck and chest. *But there's hope.*

If it were her, would you let her go? His inner voice is quiet, and he tries to pretend not to picture the mysterious blonde from the bathroom.

No. I would not.

Theo shakes his head, unaccustomed to such thoughts, such demanding desires. "You ready for tonight?" Theo asks, distracting himself.

"To let Harald beat me again?" Oren laughs, shrugging. "You know how he is."

"It's his turn," Theo says.

"You know Grace will win," Oren tells him. "Lady Astrid *always* wins."

Theo chuckles, thinking of his assistant's face when he first proposed Viking Times three years ago. "I'll do it," she had said, "but only if I get to fight."

"Of course," he had told her, knowing her showmanship would pull everything together.

"And I get to win. Every night." He agreed, and Grace's character always won, no matter which champion defeated the others.

"You're late," Oren comments, running a hand through his hair.

"Plenty of time," Theo tells him. "I don't even show up until after your fight."

"Let me guess," Oren says, walking down the hall and ducking into his dressing room two doors away from Theo's. He returns swinging his staff, the old weapon a favorite in Oren's repertoire. "You were killing zombies again."

Theo shrugs, busted. "I just can't beat the damn beach level!" he exclaims. "I watched videos and everything. Damn fishermen just keep dragging my plants into the water."

Oren shakes his head. "And to think you were supposed to be our thane." He frowns at his friend. "We never would have survived it." Theo snorts, thinking that none of them *had* actually survived it. "Did you see the crowd tonight?"

Theo shakes his head. "No, I was busy in the—I just got here." He catches himself just in time. Oren hates when Theo feeds on the property. "How is it?"

"More like who," Oren says, shaking his head. "Vannetti is here."

"The Vig? Where?" Theo's focus returns immediately, the girl sliding out of his thoughts. Vannetti represents the Klaviger, the group that loosely oversees all vampires in the New World. They aren't Volturi or Camarilla—more like self-appointed hall monitors making sure that no vampires risked exposing them to the humans by doing something stupid, like a show featuring former Vikings fighting with real swords. Theo had made their case for Viking Times three years ago, and they had been approved with the understanding that their fights would be believably human and their show utterly mundane. Besides a small percentage of the profits in exchange for clearing away a lot of red tape, the Klaviger left them alone.

Why would they drop in now? Vannetti must want something.

"Your section, down in front." Oren looks up, hearing the crowd shift, knowing his cue to enter is coming soon. "He's not alone, either."

Theo scowls. "Let me guess: Gabrielle is with him."

Oren nods. "Your favorite."

"Thanks for the warning. I will make myself scarce after the show."

"You know, if you'd just let her have you, she'd be over it and leave you alone."

Sighing, Theo tugs his shirt off and reaches for his costume. "Never. That woman is crazy. I want no part of that."

Oren shakes his head, walking away down the hallway, voice trailing after him, "She'll steal your virtue one day, Theo. We won't always be here to protect you!"

Theo frowns, pulling the gray cotton shirt down over his head and shaking his hair free. The girl's face swims across his mind again.

Now that one, he thinks, reaching for his belt, *I would let her steal my virtue any day*.

CHAPTER 3

SYLVIA

SYLVIA RETURNS TO HER SEAT JUST IN TIME. A SMALL silver dish of what looks like mousse sits in front of her, and she takes a small bite, relishing the hazelnut flavor that explodes on her tongue. *This might be legit,* she thinks, recalling a bonus quiz question about the only nut available to Vikings.

The lights dim, and she leans forward, caught up in the moment. A bright spotlight focuses on the far side of the arena, and a woman steps out from behind the "tent wall" curtain. She is tall with a dark pixie cut, and her gray fur bikini shows off a body made for more than show. Dark tattoos line her legs and arms, and a belt around her waist holds a sword at her hip. She carries a microphone with an ease that speaks of long practice.

"Welcome, earls and peasants, to Viking Times!" she announces. She is met by a small cheer and more than a few catcalls, and she flashes a bright smile. *This woman loves her job.*

"Now, a few rules before we get started," she says, reciting how there is absolutely no photography allowed during the show. "It spooks the guys," she whispers into the mic with a grin. "And while you may be surrounded by plastic on your table," she slides the blade free from the scabbard at her hip, twisting it so it glints in the spotlight, "we are using real weapons, and we don't want anyone getting distracted. I may want to kill them to claim the title of thane, but I need a fair fight—I can't have anyone doubting my skills, thinking my victory was the result of unhappy chance!" She pauses, seeming to scan the room.

"Now, let's get acquainted." She runs quickly to stand before the brown and black banner with the horse to Sylvia's left. "The Eorlings!" she cries, and a cheer follows from the people sitting at those tables. "Fast like the horses of old!"

She moves over to stand a few feet in front of Sylvia's section, and though she is clearly performing a speech she must give during each performance, Sylvia is excited despite herself. "The Mulranians!" the woman announces. "Fierce as the mythical dragons!" Sylvia cheers with her section, caught up in the moment, and waves her red and silver flag like her tablemates.

The woman moves again to Sylvia's right. "The Gunvalds!" she shouts. "Strong as the Viking warriors of old!" The blue and gold section erupts in cheers.

The woman moves to the final section of green and black, but her pace is slower now. "Finally," she says, "my favorite section." There are boos and hisses from the other tables, but the woman continues, speaking only to the far section. "You must be wondering my name," she tells them. "Allow me to introduce myself: Astrid Adabjorg!" she shouts. "And my section, the Bjorgs! Cunning like the falcon!" This section cheers the loudest of everyone, and the woman jumps back to the center of the arena.

Her knee-high leather boots have fur lining that peeks out around the laces. Sylvia loves boots of all kinds. *I wonder where Astrid found those. They look authentic.*

"Enough about me," Astrid says. "I know what you're really here for, especially you ladies." She winks, then spreads her hands wide, sword raised high to the ceiling. "I give you the reigning Gunvald champion: Harald!" The lights come on as the curtain pushes aside, and a blond man in a leather loincloth emerges, muscles gleaming in the overhead lights. A huge tattoo covers his chest, a geometric design that Sylvia wants to study closer.

Just for historical accuracy, she tells herself. *Nothing to do with those insane pecs.*

He holds two axes over his head, encouraging the crowd as they yell and cheer. He wears a leather harness across his shoulders, the straps holding a large warhammer on his back, and he tugs it free with ease, suddenly juggling all three weapons in a display of grace and skill.

"And his challenger," Astrid continues. "The Eorling fighter Oren!"

Another man exits the curtain wearing more clothes than the champion. Leather pants and vest cover his lean form, but Sylvia can see the edges of tattoos across his chest. She appreciates his limber strength in the way he moves, casually spinning a wooden staff in both hands. His dark hair is longer than his muscle-bound opponent, shaggy in that easy sexy way Sylvia appreciates.

She takes another sip of wine, then settles in to enjoy the show.

The two men face off, Harald settling the war-hammer on his back and holding an axe in each hand as Oren steps slowly from side to side, staff resting lightly in both hands. Sylvia doesn't see the moment when the fight begins; it seems like one moment they are standing still, and the next they are spinning around one another. Harald swings both axes in a wide arc, and Oren steps in quickly, blocking the swing with the staff against Harald's forearms. Without stopping, he spins around Harald to stand behind him, staff following him to whip overhand and swing down for Harald's head. The big man steps aside just in time, and the staff lands on the ground in an explosion of dirt.

The crowd cheers as Harald turns to face his foe, axes ready for another attack. Oren turns just in time to avoid an axe to the face, then uses his staff to smack one of Harald's hands. An axe goes flying through the air, landing with a thump near the wall in front of Sylvia.

With one weapon each, the two face off again. Sylvia thinks that Oren's speed will allow him to win, but then Harald simply reaches out and grabs hold of the smaller man's arm. Oren tries to free himself but isn't able. The Gunvald section erupts in a wild roar of approval as Harald uses the grip to jerk Oren this way and that. Harald finally tugs the smaller man for-ward, and Oren's feet slide out from under him. Harald releases him as he lands on his back in the dirt. Just as Harald is about to bury the axe in his chest, Oren drags his staff across his body in defense. The loud crack of the weapons' collision echoes through the room. The Eorlings explode in approval, then Oren is scooting back out of reach, regaining his feet.

He pauses for a second, then begins breathing heavily, as if suddenly remembering that he's been working hard for long minutes. The two seem about to start fighting again, but Astrid steps into the circle of light illuminating their fight. She takes a long look at Oren, then turns to the audience, "I think poor Oren over there needs a break." Her comment is met with whoops from the Gunvald tables and boos from the Eorlings. Oren shakes his head, accepting the criticism with a shrug.

"What do you expect?" he asks, his voice cheerful. "The man is a beast!"

"You mean Champion," Harald retorts in a deep voice, tossing his head back in laughter. "I know you can't beat me in face-to-face combat. Not with that little stick!"

"It's definitely not little," Oren quips, holding the staff above his head. The crowd laughs, and Oren continues. "And I only need one weapon," Oren looks over at Harald's axe laying in the dirt, "and I manage to hold onto it the whole time." He strolls lazily toward the axe and picks it up. Turning, he winks at Sylvia before strutting back to where Harald stands.

The big man lifts a hand overhead to retrieve his warhammer. "You'll find I have plenty of weapons at hand," Harald says.

"Let's ask the crowd," Astrid says, turning to face the Eorlings. "What do you think? Did Oren defeat the champion?"

The Eorlings cheer, but it is half-hearted. They know he didn't really win the fight.

"I appreciate your honesty," Astrid tells them, then turns to face the Gunvalds. "And you? Did your Champion defend his title?"

The Gunvalds explode in a loud cheer, and Oren bows, accepting his defeat. He returns the axe to Harald with a flourish, then moves to stand behind Astrid. Sylvia turns her attention back to her wine as the banter continues, waiting to see who else will join the fray. For a moment, she recalls the red-headed man from the bathroom. He hadn't been dressed for the show, but he could have just arrived. His scruffy cheeks and long hair would fit right in with the group in the arena. She glances down at her flags, silver and red. *Perhaps he is the Mulranian?*

Astrid begins speaking again, but Sylvia only catches the end of what she says, "—new challenger, the Mulranian!" The ten flap parts, and out steps her Jamie Fraser from the bathroom. He wears a light gray shirt with the sleeves rolled up to reveal strong forearms with dark lines of tattoos disappearing beneath the fabric. His wrists are wrapped in dark leather cords. Dark pants hug his delicious thighs, disappearing into black leather boots. His shirt is interrupted by a wide leather belt holding a broadsword at one hip. Sylvia's eyes focus on the necklaces he wears, visible through the low V-neck of his shirt: a thin choker of brown leather beneath a thick silver torc, and a string of multi-colored beads on a leather thong that hangs low on his bare chest, the bottom hidden beneath the shirt.

Astrid is still talking, but Sylvia doesn't hear it, transfixed by the man she had been so close to almost an hour ago. Despite the lighting and the fact that she knows he can't possibly see her amid the sea of faces in the crowd, she is sure that he is looking right at her. He slightly dips his chin, an acknowledgement of sorts, before joining the conversation.

"—and fight your Champion!" Astrid finishes her announcement, then steps aside with Oren.

The Mulranian draws his sword with a smooth motion that speaks of long practice, a grin crossing his face as he and Harald circle one another. The redhead is not as large as the Champion, but he isn't lean like Oren, a steady strength obvious in the easy way he holds the large sword. Sylvia sits up in her chair, leaning forward a little, wine forgotten. Her tablemates give her curious glances, but she ignores them.

The fight begins without a sound, each man moving suddenly. Harald's axes spark as they meet the Mulranian's sword, the big man moving faster than Sylvia expected. The clash of metal is loud, echoing in the open space, and the crowd cheers in waves of approval. The Champion is big and strong, but the newcomer is strong and slightly faster, scoring hits that knock Harald's axes aside. Sylvia snickers as the Champion loses the second axe, recalling Oren's criticism. Harald's face is red as he draws the warhammer. His movements may be slower, but he swings the hammer with devastating strength, the clash forcing the redhead to one knee.

Her hero is about to go down beneath the onslaught, but then Oren leaps into the fray again, staff sweeping Harald's legs out from under him. Astrid steps neatly aside as the three warriors begin to fight, weapons swinging wildly. The crowd cheers as Oren executes a perfect leap over Harald's head to land behind him. Her tablemates grumble in surprise as Sylvia squints, searching the ceiling for the wires that must allow him to perform such a feat. Seeing none, she increases her judgement of Viking Times. Not only were they somewhat historically accurate, but they also had a great choreographer and special effects team as well.

Oren is the first to go down, catching a blow from the warhammer on his chin. He lays on his back in the dirt, unmoving. The redhead goes toe-to-toe with the Champion, but the big man, finally out of strength, falls back, warhammer sagging in front of him. The Mulranian spies an opening and takes it, knocking the weapon out of Harald's hands. The bigger man steps back, hands raised, clearly defeated.

Astrid returns to the center of the arena. "Nicely done, Mulranian!" she cheers the victor.

"I assume this makes me the new Champion," the Mulranian replies as the crowd roars. Sylvia joins in, letting out a whoop that feels far better than she anticipated. Delighted, she lets out another one, joy filling her.

"Champions defeat *everyone* on the field," Astrid says, moving a few feet away from him, "and I believe you are not the last one standing."

Sylvia laughs as Astrid draws her sword to a loud screech from the women in the audience, and the two face off in a fight that is much more choreographed but still lovely to watch as Astrid leaps here and there. Her movements are believable, unlike the men who lay on the ground. They moved like magic. Astrid is good, but not like them. Still, a few swings and clangs of metal, then Astrid holds the tip of her blade to the redhead's throat. He kneels in defeat, drops his sword, and raises his hands.

"I yield, Mistress," he says. The Bjorgs go wild, whistling and whooping in victory. Sylvia claps, adding more noise to the celebration.

"As you should," Astrid says, moving her sword away from the redhead and sheathing it in one motion. She reaches out a hand to lift him to his feet. "You know what happens now," she says with a wink.

"I do?" the redhead replies, eagerness mixed with hopefulness in his tone.

"Of course you do," Astrid says, letting the crowd enjoy the moment. "We feast!" she says triumphantly. The tent flaps open, and two men in costume carry out a long wooden table. Astrid helps the fallen fighters up as the men return with two long benches, placing them along the back of the table so the feasters will face the audience.

"Now," Astrid says, turning back to the crowd. "Let it not be said that this thane does not share with her people." She looks at the men. "Bring me some worthy companions!"

Harold steps forward first, entering the stands and returning with a young girl of about ten years old on his arm. The child is thrilled to accompany him on the dirt.

Sylvia looks up in time to see the redhead approach her section. He is looking above her, clearly spotting his mark, but then his gaze flicks to her. She is acutely aware of his presence, just like when she walked by him at the bathroom, and she feels the moment his body turns to her instead of his intended target.

Her tablemates stare at them both as he approaches her. "My lady?" the Mulranian asks, taking her hand gently and kissing it. "Would you accompany me?"

"Uhh," Sylvia manages, then shoots to her feet, not wanting him to let go of her. She stumbles awkwardly away from her chair, joining him on the arena floor in a daze, aware of nothing beyond his hand on hers. Her Viking turns his head to his left, mouthing something, and Sylvia turns to follow his gaze. Oren, who has been making his way to a lovely dark-haired woman in the second row, immediately shifts his attention to the young boy sitting a few chairs down. He bows, taking the child's hand and leading him to the table.

Sylvia follows the redhead to the table in the center of the arena, glad she always wears boots as her feet sink a little into the loose dirt. Anyone wearing heels on this would lose them.

She allows herself to be seated on the end of the bench, scooting down enough to make room for her warrior beside her. There is some shuffling behind her, and she glances down the table to see the young girl and boy being seated beside one another. A professional photographer has entered the arena, his traditional Viking clothing clashing with the camera in his hand, but he is efficient as he takes a picture of the two kids. None of the warriors pose in the shot, which Sylvia thinks is odd for a marketing ploy, but not as strange as when the photographer raises an eyebrow at her companion. The redhead shakes his head once, the movement sharp and clear, and the photographer moves on to snap a few pictures of Astrid and her audience member instead. The man drapes an awkward arm around Astrid's shoulders, clearly excited and unnerved to be on the arena floor.

Sylvia risks a glance at her Viking, taking in the small details of his pale shirt, the tiny buttons that she couldn't see from her seat, the very real look of his necklaces, especially the torc. She assumed some of it was fake, but sitting next to him, she isn't so sure.

One thing she is sure about is her attraction. She feels it in her chest, warmth from more than just wine building in her skin as she breathes in his scent. She expects him to smell sweaty after all that fighting, but instead, there is something else, something she can't identify but wants to curl up inside forever.

I don't know what's happening to me, Sylvia thinks, *and I don't care. Just let me stay next to him for a little bit longer.*

He seems just as transfixed with her as she is with him, and it occurs to her that she doesn't know his name. The others were introduced by name and clan, but he is simply the Mulranian, the dragon.

My dragon, she thinks simply. *Mine.*

Something long slumbering inside her comes to life, and fierce longing fills her. She wants it to be the wine. The logical voice in her head, the one that always barges in and destroys possible moments of intimacy, remains silent for the first time since she was fourteen. But she's been drunk before, and even alcohol doesn't cause this reaction, the sudden craving in her to touch him, to slide her fingers along his skin.

She feels something growing, a power she can't name any more than she can identify the scent, but she lets herself fall into it.

A hand touches her shoulder, and she glances up, the moment broken. Oren stares down at her, a friendly smile on his face as his mouth opens to speak.

He is cut off as the redhead near Sylvia snarls, her Viking leaping from the bench to shove Oren back. There is a gasp of surprise as Oren pushes back, shock on his face as he forces the Mulranian aside. The redhead moves fast, faster than Sylvia can track, then the two men are up on the tabletop, fighting.

At first, Sylvia thinks it is more of the show. The wide-eyed glee of the children down the bench certainly suggests it is. But something about the sounds of their fight, the tense expressions that they didn't have during the rest of the show, makes Sylvia think otherwise. Oren is moving fast, ducking around the Mulranian's fists. Neither man has drawn a weapon, the fight quick and dirty with feet and fists.

Sylvia glances quickly to her left, trying to catch Astrid's eye. The woman has been running the show. If this isn't planned, her face will show it. Sylvia catches the very end of wide eyes on Astrid's face, then the woman is leaping back from the table, dragging her audience member with her just in time for him to avoid a kick to the face.

A quick glance to her right allows Sylvia to catch Harald's movement as his hands grip the end of the table and lift it quickly, the jerk bouncing both Oren and the redhead off balance for a split second. Oren steps away from the Mulranian's reach, and without pausing, the redhead leaps off the table, grabs Sylvia around the waist, and tosses her over his shoulder. Her plastic helmet bounces to the floor as he carries her out of the arena and through the tent flap.

She hears Astrid's voice through the thick curtain. "There you have it! The Mulranian has claimed his prize!" The crowd cheers again, and Astrid keeps talking, but Sylvia doesn't hear what she says as her Viking carries her away. Sylvia presses her hands against the broad back beneath her, the skin warm but not hot as she expected after that last fight.

"Um…" she says after a long moment. Her kidnapper continues hurrying through the back area, carrying her down long hallways with spotty lighting. Sylvia sees the concrete floor in bursts of light as they move. She is very aware of her arms draping down his back, her hands bumping into the firm muscles of his backside with each step. She has the overwhelming urge to cup her hands and squeeze the next time she touches him, and she yanks her hands up, bracing her elbows against his shoulder, horrified at her desire. Of course, he has tossed her over his shoulder like some Viking prize of old, but she should at least try to maintain some level of propriety. Sylvia isn't one to throw herself at random strangers, even sexy ones who look like Scottish highlanders.

"Excuse me?" she tries when it becomes clear he has no intention of putting her down any time soon.

The steady gait slows.

He's back, a voice inside her whispers.

Back? From where?

Sylvia frowns. She has a history of encounters with people with mental illness, people who had lost touch with reality. She doesn't want to think this man is like them, but experience has been a brutal tutor in her life. And he has practically kidnapped her.

But that moment at the table comes back, that sense of connection and belonging.

He couldn't be like those people, the voice insists.

What people? The logical part of her mind is back. *You mean people who try to summon demons with your blood and friends who run right off the edge of cliffs?*

Stop it. Don't think about that night.

"Put me down," she commands, the words bursting out as a thin thread of panic slinks up her spine at the resurfacing memories.

At her words, the man pauses. His hands are gentle as he first lifts her up, then puts her on her feet before him. The way he moves her is odd. She would have expected him to let her slide down to her feet. Instead, he just deadlifts her entire weight and moves her to the ground. She doesn't think he is strong enough for that, but she abandons the thought. There are far more pressing matters.

"Thank you," she says formally. Glancing around, she sees that they are in a small dressing room. The redhead steps back from her, hands going up in front of his body. Sylvia looks up to his face, not surprised to see the shock there.

"I..." he begins, but the sound just fades. He shakes his head once, hard, as if to clear it. "I'm so sorry," he says, firmer this time. "Did I hurt you?"

Sylvia looks down at herself, straightens her sweater, smooths her skirt, and runs a hand through her hair. "I'm fine," she assures him. Looking back at the small room, she surveys the weapons leaning against the wall, the discarded leather armor piled on a chair in the corner, and in the far back of the room, resting on a shelf, a battered Viking helmet. "Seriously?" she asks, walking over to it and completely forgetting her circumstances. "Is that real?"

"The helmet?" he asks, following her. "Kind of."

"What does that mean?" she asks, bending down to look at it. The metal is worn, the rivets smooth, rough leather hammered into place around the rim. "Can I touch it?"

"As you would," he says, the words odd but clearly giving permission as he reaches over her shoulder to grab it. She is acutely aware of his body near hers again, that same sudden rush of attraction spiraling through her, and he plops the helmet into her hands. It is heavier than she expects. She flips it over, studying the inside, happy to escape the moment by focusing on the helmet instead. She had a brief love affair with artifacts when she worked for the museum one summer, and she has a memory for details. "Aren't you going to ask me about horns?" he says.

She looks at him, noting that the wild man who arrived with her has vanished, replaced by the charming friendly fighter she'd met in the bathroom. She reminds herself not to forget, knowing that a man who could snap like that once could do it again.

"Vikings didn't actually wear horned helmets," she tells him, glad to show off her knowledge and break the odd tension in the room. "That's all propaganda by the Romans and other historians. The Vikings made them look bad, so they embellished the details to make them seem larger than life somehow." She pauses, chuckling. "In some versions, Vikings can fly too." She flips over the helmet, admiring the craftsmanship. It's definitely old, museum-quality old. "I'd love to hear the story behind this one," she says, setting it carefully on the shelf. Turning to face him, she frowns.

"So, you want to tell me what happened out there?" she asks.

The man steps back from her, hands straight against his sides, distance creeping over his face. He refuses to meet her eyes, looking everywhere else in the small room but at her. "What do you mean?" he asks, keeping his voice neutral.

"You know what I mean," she replies. "Or do you end every show by carrying off audience members to your dressing room?"

"Maybe we do," he says, finally looking at her. "Some women would be thrilled for a chance to meet me back-stage." A haughty note has entered his voice. Sylvia is simultaneously attracted to and annoyed with him.

"I bet," Sylvia snaps, recalling the woman in the bathroom staring dazedly at her reflection. The Mulranian definitely has an effect on women. Even her.

Standing there, she can feel the pull between them, and she forces herself to focus, ignoring the attraction the same way she has learned to deal with her panic attacks. *If I don't think about it*, she tells herself, *it will pass over me quickly. Focusing on the feeling only drags it out.*

She yanks her attention away from her body, staring at him instead, at the beautiful mystery man who has kidnapped her like some Viking warrior in a raid. "But judging by the looks on your friends' faces, this wasn't part of the show." She bites her lip, distracting herself from the low heat building in her belly as she stands near him. The conflicting pull of fear and attraction is exhausting, but she pushes through it. "Nicely done, by the way. You made it look natural... eventually."

He raises an eyebrow at her praise. "Thanks for the glowing review."

"I enjoyed the show," she tells him honestly. "Very cool fighting. But it was practiced." She shakes her head. "That last bit on the table—that was not. You were trying to hurt each other."

"How can you tell?" he asks. "Are you a choreographer? A master fighter?"

Sylvia shakes her head. "No. But I know people. And Oren was surprised when you attacked him." She pauses, reviewing the order of events in her head. "You freaked out ... and right after he touched me." She cocks her head, arms crossing protectively in front of her body. "Was that the trigger?"

The redhead says nothing for a moment, staring at her. The heat builds again, the slow pull inside her, and she returns the gaze. Something about Theo brightens, a subtle shift in his honey skin, eyes wild, tugging her into him. For a moment, she nearly loses her balance, her entire body swaying in his direction, but then she rallies, pulling herself back from some invisible ledge. Now it is her turn to shake her head.

"What the fuck is going on here?" she asks in a strange, slow, muddled voice. *Is there something wrong with my voice or my ears?* She narrows her eyes at him. "What are you doing to me?"

"Who are you?" he asks in a deep, persuasive voice.

"Sylvia," she replies, the word jerking out of her without her permission. *Great. Just tell him your address next so he can properly stalk you!*

The thought frees her from whatever hold he has over her, and she uncrosses her arms, putting her hands on her hips and facing him fully as something strengthens inside her. "I don't know what's happening here, but this is fucking weird," she says, taking a step forward to stand directly in front of him, their bodies separated by inches. She can feel her heart beating heavily in her chest, her body flooding with adrenaline, and she tries to identify if this man is a threat or not. "Who are *you*?" she demands, barking the words at him.

He jerks back, surprised by the force of her words. His eyes narrow, and he looks her up and down again. A hand moves forward slowly, so slowly, raising to the level of her face. He doesn't touch her, his hand hovering an inch from her cheek as he tilts his head, considering her.

"You," he murmurs.

"Me," she agrees, her voice loud in the small room. *Me Tarzan. You Jane.* She giggles a little at the thought, and the moment ends. The Mulranian is just a man again, a beautiful one, but not undeniable. She steps sideways, moving around him and closer to the door. *It's definitely time to go.* She takes another step, and the man turns with her. He reaches out as if to grab her arm, then someone is in the doorway.

Sylvia recognizes Harald, the large man still wearing a loincloth. Up close, she can see his chest tattoo is a series of small circles inside larger triangles, an intriguing design she'd like to study. Instead of the axes he has wielded for much of the night, he holds her bulky black purse in an awkward grip.

"I believe this belongs to you," he says in a heavily accented voice that is very different from his stage persona. Sylvia thinks it's part Germanic, part Scandinavian. He holds out the bag. Sylvia takes it gratefully. "How is it, Muldavian?" he asks the man standing behind her. *I thought he was a Mulranian,* Sylvia thinks.

"It is ... odd," the redhead replies. Sylvia watches Harald's face as the two men have an entire unspoken conversation, the kind of communication that only occurs among friends after many years spent together.

"Understatement," Sylvia agrees. "So, thanks for the backstage tour ... or whatever, but I have to go." She slips forward, ducking under Harald's arm. She feels something graze her hair as she leaves, as if the man reached out to touch her again. Harald jerks his head to his left, and Sylvia sees the lit EXIT sign at the end of the hallway.

"You should go," Harald says in that same accent, bracing himself in the doorway.

"Yeah," Sylvia breathes, darting down the hall and bursting through the fire door. The night air is cool on her flushed cheeks.

She is out on the street for a few moments, catching her breath, before she orients herself and begins walking home. She considers calling a cab, but the breeze feels good on her skin, and she doesn't want to linger near this place any longer than she has to.

Just in case he comes out.

You want him to come out, a small voice inside her whispers.

Exactly, she tells it, *and I have terrible instincts. I attract awful people. I need to go home and forget this night ever happened.*

She breathes easier a few blocks away, mind still going over the details of the evening, too distracted to worry about her safety on the city streets after dark. She has crossed her purse over her shoulder bandolier-style, but she isn't watching dark spaces like she normally does, nor is she aware of the other people on the street with her.

So, when the hairy hand with huge claws reaches out of the darkness, she is completely surprised.

CHAPTER 4

THEO

THEODORE MULDAVIAN STANDS IN HIS DRESSING ROOM, trying to calm the desire racing through his veins. The girl has gone, and his blood has started to cool, but it will still be some time before he will be himself again.

"How goes it, Muldavian?" Harald repeats, his accent more pronounced as it always is when he is worried. "Are you here?"

Theo nods, inhaling deeply to clear his head—a mistake he recognizes immediately as the scent of the girl fills him. The bloodlust rushes back, stronger than before, and he closes his eyes.

"I will fetch Oren," Harald says, and Theo hears him go, his steps heavy in the hallway to Theo's sensitive hearing, though a human wouldn't have heard anything.

Yes, bring Oren, so I can crush the hand that dared to touch her.

At the thought, Theo crushes his hands into the opposite forearms, the instant pain a distraction from the voice inside.

You don't want to hurt Oren, he tells himself. *You know that.*

And the rational part of Theo does know that, knows that Oren is the one who normally talks him down during his rare moments, just as he talks Harald back from the edge the few times the big man has lost himself in the bloodfever.

Oren is the reasonable one among them. He always was, even before they were turned into vampires. Theo lets himself remember Oren as a young man, his small form forcing him to use other methods to solve arguments. He couldn't force his way through like Harald, or bluster his foes aside like Theo, but he could move fast and talk faster, and his words had gotten them out of a lot of jams over the years.

Then again, that same smart mouth had also gotten them captured and hauled halfway across the known world into the waiting arms of a vampire mistress. Moments like this made Theo wish his life had been different—but they don't come often enough to make him wish away his existence more than once a century.

Theo isn't a melodramatic person by nature. Turning vampire hadn't changed his outlook; it merely enhanced certain facets of his personality: his joy in battle, his fighting prowess, and his love for life. He knows that the bloodlust will fade, as it always does, and he just needs to get through it without killing anyone. It has been a long time since he snapped and killed a human.

But I didn't want to kill her. Sylvia, his mind supplies the name he compelled out of her before she resisted his push into her mind. *I wanted to feed from her ... and fuck her ... but there's more to this than the usual.* Theo often feeds during sex. It's easier that way. The women are distracted by pleasure and eager to dismiss any strange marks on their bodies the next day. He doesn't have to wipe their memory of the encounter, like he had to do to the woman in the bathroom before the show, though he sometimes does to avoid difficulties. Some women can't stay away after they get a taste of what he offers—and Theo has learned how to avoid stalkers.

It had been a late evening by the time he rose. He lounged in his coffin longer than necessary that evening. Cell phones and the games on them could eat up hours of the night, and sometimes Theo spends an entire night in his coffin, deciding to relax until the next sunset.

He is a traditional vampire by current pop culture standards—subject to death in sunlight and lacking a reflection—and while he loves his undead existence, spending time with the guys practicing their fighting at Viking Times, working with Astrid in her normal daytime appearance as his assistant Grace, some days, he just needs to be alone.

Sounds of footsteps in the hallway call him back to the moment, and he is relieved to find his mind clear as Oren and Harald appear in the doorway.

"How is it?" Oren asks.

Theo nods, muscles loose and rubbery in the aftermath of the bloodlust. "Better."

"So," Oren says, not waiting to get right into things, "it was the girl. Do you know her?"

Theo shakes his head. "I only met her near the bathroom—"

"Odin's tits, Theo!" Oren exclaims, eyes narrowing as he judges his old friend. "We talked about this! You can't feed on women in the bathroom before the show! Just go out and find a willing victim like the rest of us."

Theo shrugs, not bothering to correct Oren's misunderstanding. "She was perfectly willing."

"I don't doubt that," Oren snaps. "I doubt your judgement." He gestures to the room, and by extension, the entire building. "This whole thing was your crazy idea, and it's actually working. We have a good thing here, and we don't want it screwed up by people screaming vampire in the bathroom!"

"No one worries about vampires these days," Theo replies. "Vampires are sexy and cool."

"Fine," Oren agrees. "How about women screaming about attackers in the bathroom? You think that would go over better?" He snorts. "Grace is amazing at PR, but even she has limits, man." He enters the room, putting a hand on Theo's shoulder. "What's going on with you?"

Theo frowns, shrugging off Oren's touch. "Nothing. It was nothing. I'm fine."

"You nearly killed Oren in front of a crowd with women and children," Harald says quietly from the doorway. "You are not fine."

"And in front of Vannetti as well," Oren says. "You saw them sitting at the girl's table?" Harald nods. Oren looks at Theo. "You think she was with them?"

Theo shakes his head. "No. She didn't smell like them at all. I think it was just happenstance."

"Be damn unfortunate if happenstance got us shut down after your antics tonight," Oren comments. "Grace made it seem like a standard part of the show, but if Vannetti comes back again, we'll have to do it the same way with someone else."

Theo nods slowly, face miserable. "I am sorry," he apologizes to his friends. "I did not mean to screw this up for us. If there is trouble with Vannetti, let it be on my head."

"Talk to us," Oren insists quietly. "Tell us what happened. Let us help you."

Theo shakes his head, a memory of his desire for the girl rushing through him again. He shakes his head and turns around, swiping the old leather armor onto the floor and flopping down into the chair, head sinking into his hands. "I'm not sure what happened." He looks up at his friends. "I saw her and I just ... had to touch her."

"Touch her, huh?" Oren snarks. "That all?"

"I don't want to kill her," Theo whispers.

"That's good," Oren says encouragingly.

"But I need to see her again," Theo adds.

"Dude," Oren says, the only one who picks up new vernacular over the centuries, though he tends to use words for decades longer than the humans, "after your little stunt, I don't think she will want to see you."

"But there is something between us," Theo says. "Something strong." He is silent, then looks up at Oren. "Like you and Morena."

Oren sighs, eyes darkening with sorrow. "That was a very long time ago."

"I know, but I think I get it now. Sometimes, you just can't let it go."

"I let her go," Oren says quietly.

"Eventually," Harald adds, and both men look at him.

"Just because you've never fallen for anyone doesn't mean you won't someday," Oren snaps, face reddening in remembered shame.

Harald nods, letting the comment slide off like everything else as he focuses on the current issue. "What will you do?"

Theo sits up, biting his lip as he contemplates. "I have to find her, just to see what it really is."

"Don't tell me you're suddenly a believer in mate bonds," Oren says sarcastically.

"Of course not," Theo snaps. "But I believe what I'm feeling, and I think..." He frowns, eyes narrowing as if his mind is somewhere else. "I think she needs me."

"She left quickly," Harald reminds him. "She didn't need you tonight."

"Don't hunt her, man," Oren says. "Leave it be and let her go."

"Could you have let Morena go after you met her?" Theo asks.

Oren looks away. "No." He sighs heavily. "But I should have."

"It doesn't matter," Harald observes quietly, stepping into the room to place a hand on Oren's shoulder. "She would be long dead by now."

"I could have turned her," Oren says.

"Yes, but you loved her. And she wanted to live," Harald reminds him. "And in the end, she wasn't your mate."

"Apparently not." Oren sighs, looking up at the ceiling. "Why are dames so complicated?"

"I don't think this is a mate thing," Theo says, getting to his feet, "but it's definitely something." He steps past Oren and heads to the doorway, slipping around Harald. "I just want to see."

"Try to see without *her* seeing," Oren says, voice resigned.

Theo nods. He glances down at himself, then tugs the Viking shirt over his head, revealing sculpted abs and tan skin, the same body he'd had when he'd been turned centuries before. Turning back into the room, he grabs his regular shirt from the table along the wall and slides it over his head. He leans down to remove his boots, then quickly shoves his pants down his hips, revealing bare skin.

"Dude!" Oren says, shielding his eyes. "Some warning!"

"Whatever," Theo says, finding his jeans and stepping into them. He dresses quickly, sliding the same boots back on his feet. His wallet and phone go into his pocket along with the keys to the apartment he keeps in the city. "I'm going out."

"Hunting?" Harald asks.

"Maybe?" Theo replies. "Depends on who I find."

"Be careful," Harald says, stepping close to Oren and allowing Theo to pass.

"I'm always careful." Theo tosses the words over his shoulder as he heads down the hallway, following the echo of Sylvia's scent in the air.

"You're always a terrible liar!" Oren shouts, and Theo bursts through the door at a run, tracking the strange girl's scent through the night.

She is easy to find, her essence filling him as soon as he walks outside. Theo slows his pace, not wanting to actually catch up to her and scare her. He walks a few blocks, wondering why she didn't call a car service to bring her home, then realizes she must live nearby.

So close to me, he thinks. *All this time and she was right here under my nose.*

That's not all I want her under.

A small shiver runs through him at the thought, the image of Sylvia beneath him, all that blonde hair running riot around her face...

Get it together, man, he tells himself. *Keep your head. You're here to figure this out, not smother her with your need.*

A squeal catches his attention, and Theo moves faster, heading toward the noise without thought. He's heard women in trouble before, knows that surprised yelp, and while he isn't sure it's Sylvia making the sound now, a sudden jolt runs through him, the hair on his arms rising in sudden alertness, body jumping into adrenaline-fueled overdrive. He runs to the sound, the scent of Sylvia strong as he turns the last corner just in time to see a creature yank Sylvia off the street and down a dark alley.

His vampiric vision allows him to see where humans cannot, and he recognizes the shape of the demon immediately. He's seen enough demons in his long life to know the type—a Balaam, the strong, silent demons used by summoners to do their dirty work on the mortal plane. Theo has never traveled to the other realms, but he's been around long enough to know his place in this world.

Another day, he might have walked by, not wanting to get involved in the business of demons and their magician keepers. The Klaviger expressly forbids interference, not that Theo puts much stock in their rules, but he tries not to break them if he can avoid it.

It's easier to stay out of trouble. But today the Balaam demon has Sylvia, and Theo can't let her be taken, not before he figures out his connection to her.

He is still moving closer when he sees Sylvia duck out of the creature's grip. It reaches for her again, huge clawed hands lazily swiping at her shoulder, but instead of backing up, like a normal person would when caught by a monster, Sylvia moves forward, stepping close to the demon and under its reaching arm. The creature is slow to react, and before it can do anything, Sylvia flees down the alley. The demon gives chase, and Theo hovers just behind, not wanting to give away his presence just yet. He doesn't think the demon will speak—Balaam demons rarely do—but maybe he can get some clues as to who has sent the creature and what they want with Sylvia.

His girl moves fast, her bulky purse banging against her hip as she runs, fear spurring her on, but Theo can see instantly that it's pointless. The alley ends in a brick wall. Soon, she will be trapped. But instead of continuing down the alley to the end, Sylvia throws her body at the doors along the walls. The third door gives way under her weight with a sickening crunch, and she disappears into the building, a flash of blonde hair in the moonlight gone in an instant.

The demon follows a few steps behind, then Theo is through the remains of the doorway. He stands in a small entryway, open to the ceiling far above, with a staircase along the wall to his left. Sylvia has already darted up the stairs, and the demon puts its large clawed foot on the bottom step to follow.

Deciding that this has gone on long enough, Theo reaches out, grabbing the demon's hairy shoulder and yanking it back off the steps. The creature is big and strong, but slow, and Theo knows how to fight even without his sword. The Balaam gets in one decent hit, a swipe of claws that draws blood across Theo's ribs and ruins a perfectly good shirt, then Theo has his arm around its neck, pulling it to his chest. A sharp jerk snaps the bones, and after a few more weak shudders, the demon goes limp. Theo drops it, knowing what happens next. A moment later, the body shimmers, an otherworldly glow lighting up the dark space. The image burns Theo's sensitive eyes, and after he blinks a few times, the body is gone, returned to the realm from which it came. His eyesight returning, Theo glances up to see Sylvia crouched on the landing at the top of the stairs, hands gripping the spindles of the banister as she stares through them down at him. He can always hear her heart pounding, but there is another of those weird pauses where time stretches out, and it is only him and her.

The blood trailing down his chest doesn't matter.

The smell of must and decay in the abandoned building doesn't matter.

The demon he just sent home doesn't matter.

Only her eyes matter to him now, wide and blue and staring at him from between the rails, and he knows he has to go to her, to reassure her.

He takes a step toward her, his foot landing on the bottom stair, still caught up in the magnetism between them. Sylvia stands up slowly, watching as he takes another step, seeming as trapped as he is. He makes it to the top of the stairs without a sound.

Standing a few feet away from her, he notices her heavy breathing, shoulders moving with the effort, eyes still wide as she stares at him. Her pounding heart echoes in his skin.

He wants to say something, but words fail him.

He wants to touch her.

To taste her.

The thought conjures a vision, Sylvia pressed against him, her warm neck against his lips, her soul exposed in her blood as he drinks from her.

When he opens his eyes, something has shifted. Sylvia's body is wary, tense and ready to flee. Theo doesn't understand how she could know what he is thinking, but her body language has utterly changed. She has gone from willing partner to terrified victim. He reaches out a hand to touch her, knowing that he shouldn't, and at the movement, Sylvia turns, darting down the hallway in a flash of blonde hair and black skirt.

Theo stays where he is for a moment, contemplating just letting her go, but then her foot sinks deeper into the floor than it should, and he realizes that she is running too fast and too hard for the old wooden floor to handle.

She is falling through the floor.

He reacts instantly, moving to her in a flash, but her momentum has pushed her halfway through by the time he reaches her. He grabs her shoulder hard, jerking her out of the growing hole. Her purse strap snaps, the bag plummeting to the floor below. There is an awful scraping sound as her legs come back out of the floor, and he smells fresh blood, a lot of it. Quickly, he uses his other hand to grab Sylvia's waist, easily flipping and spinning her around against his body so she comes to rest with her back against one of his arms and her knees over the other. Warm blood from her legs smears across his arm, and he pulls her close.

The wounds aren't fatal. He would be able to tell. She will survive the trip home.

Home.

He doesn't know when he decided to bring her back to the apartment he uses in the city, but he is already carrying her out of the building and onto the street, setting off in that direction. He doesn't think about running, doesn't care about keeping up his human appearance, not with all the blood around them now, so he lifts off the ground as soon as he is outside, flying into the night with his prize pressed carefully against his chest.

CHAPTER 5

SYLVIA

OHMYGOD JAMIE FRASER CAN FLY.
Sylvia is held too tightly to get away, pressed hard against the Mulranian's body. Warmth floods her legs, the heat that follows many wounds, and she presses her hand hard against the puncture just above her right knee, staunching the bleeding. Pain throbs in and out, only dulled by the distraction of wind in her hair as lights from windows slide by her vision.

Her other hand is wrapped around his neck, and she holds his shirt collar in a death grip as the world drops out from beneath them both.

The Romans did say the Vikings could fly, her mind comments calmly. *Maybe this is what they meant.* She doesn't see any wings, and the smooth angle of their ascent makes their flight more magical than physical.

Magic. Of course he has magic.

Cradled in his arms, Sylvia studies her Viking's face. Red hair blows in the wind, framing honey skin, a tiny spray of freckles across his cheeks and nose, and dark brown eyes. In the building, she had been sure his eyes were light brown, glowing honey almost, but now they are dark again, milk chocolate with long lashes. He may be big and tall, and her mind may have christened him Jamie Fraser, but she knows that specific Highlander lived at least a dozen centuries after the Vikings. *Maybe he's a Saxon*, she thinks suddenly. *With that hair, maybe even a Pict.*

Seriously? The voice is a whisper. *That's what you're focusing on right now?*

Sylvia closes her eyes. The sudden darkness allows her to focus on her body, a huge mistake. Pain shoots up her legs, and she flinches. Her stomach flips dangerously as her superhero moves through the air. Biting her lip, she opens her eyes, surprised to find the man looking down at her curiously.

She stifles a groan as another bolt of pain rushes through her, this time from her right ankle. She is pretty sure she heard something pop there when he pulled her out of the floor.

"Where are you taking me?" she manages to say, looking directly up at him to avoid looking around. She isn't afraid of heights, but she really isn't in the right frame of mind to appreciate the experience at the moment.

"Home."

"Home?" she repeats. "I'm hurt. I need a hospital."

He smiles at her, and the pain in her legs fades to the background, everything in her focusing instead on his face. She wants to touch him, fingers releasing the shirt collar for a second, but her body slides a fraction in his arms, and the moment shatters. She claws at his neck, reclaiming her grip and securing herself against him again. The man raises a red eyebrow at her, then shakes his head as if facing some mystery.

"You will be fine," he tells her. "I promise you."

Sylvia opens her mouth to object, to demand he fly her to the emergency room for stitches and crutches, but the urge fades with his words. She believes him.

A small part of her decides to trust him.

You are crazy, the logical voice tells her. *You're kidnapped by a crazy flying Viking warrior. You should be freaking out.*

I will, Sylvia promises herself. *Later.*

The man flies closer to a tall building, hovering along the side and levitating up to the roof. A moment later, he lands on a rooftop patio. It's almost as big as Sylvia's entire apartment, open to the stars, and holds a single lounge chair near a sliding glass door.

The lone chair catches Sylvia's attention. *He must live here alone.* The thought is reassuring, and Sylvia doesn't want to think about why, not while she's bleeding in his arms like some victim in a horror movie.

He moves to open the door, the arm under her back shifting to curl around her waist and tuck beneath her right knee while the other reaches out to slide the door open. He doesn't use a key.

"You leave the door unlocked?" she asks, focusing again on tiny details to avoid thinking about everything else.

He chuckles. "No humans can get up here," he says, stepping inside. He leaves the door open, the cool air blowing the gauzy curtains as they enter a bedroom. He slowly sets her on the edge of the bed, grabs a handful of clothing from a dresser drawer, then disappears deeper into the apartment.

Humans, Sylvia thinks. *He said it like he isn't one.*

Clearly, her logical mind snaps back. *Or did you forget the flying part?*

Sylvia sits motionless, letting her eyes adjust to the lack of lighting. A hint of moonlight from outside streams through the open patio door, enough for her to guess at the shape of a door in the far wall next to the dresser, a bathroom or closet, and an armoire in the corner. When he doesn't return immediately, she uses the time to take stock of her body.

A darkness smudges the knuckles of her right hand, but her left palm is coated in stickiness that must be blood. She remembers using that hand to catch herself when she fell, and she probably scraped it on something. She recalls gripping the collar of his shirt with a wince. She probably ruined his shirt with her blood, though that was only part of it.

Looking down, she slides her skirt above her knees, gingerly pressing on the wound above her right knee. It has stopped bleeding, only a slow trickle running down over her scraped kneecap and around the many splinters gouging her shin. Her ankle throbs, and though she can't see the damage through her boot, she knows it will be bad. Her left leg is only slightly better—covered with splinters and long gouges, but none bleeding anymore. Sylvia doesn't want to think about how badly it will hurt to pull all of the splinters out. She tries not to imagine infection from shards of ancient building—rotting wood and rusting metal and who knows what else currently embedded in her legs.

Her heart begins to race, her pulse echoing in her ears, and Sylvia closes her eyes, focusing on slowing her breathing. *Five things I can feel,* she tells herself, her therapist's voice in her head, deciding to use her sense of touch instead of sight in the dim light. Her hands move slowly to the bed: silky sheets, rougher blanket. They drift to her legs: the cotton of her skirt, the heat of her thighs, the sticky blood covering her. *Four things I can see.* Sylvia opens her eyes, heart pounding. *The doorway we came through,* she lists, *the door he left through, the curtains, and this bed. Three things I can*—she breaks off, a sudden thought cutting her off.

His sheets.

Expensive sheets by the feel of them.

And I'm bleeding all over them. And the blanket. She shifts her weight, trying to see how much she has bled on everything, and movement jars her ankle. Pain shrieks up her leg, and she moans, panic forgotten as she breathes through the ache.

When she opens her eyes again, he is standing in front of her. His eyes seem bright again, but he has changed his clothes, wearing a new, light-colored t-shirt without any of her blood on it. Sylvia tries to stand, favoring her good ankle, and he gently touches her arm, taking her weight on her right side.

"Where?" she manages, and he nods to the door beside the dresser. She dips her chin, hopping in that direction. They reach the opening, but they are too wide to both fit, so he scoops her up by the waist and lifts her through, setting her down on the edge of something cold. An instant later, the lights flash on, and Sylvia realizes she is in a huge bathroom, perched on the edge of a large bathtub. A shower stall occupies the corner beyond the tub, and a single sink sits across from where she rests. Another door that must lead to the toilet is next to the sink.

It takes Sylvia a moment to work out what is weird about the bathroom. The sink is simple but in that way that speaks of expensive taste. She rests on the edge of a luxurious soaking tub, small jets embedded in the sides showing it is also a jacuzzi. The glass wall of the shower is pristine. Sylvia has lived in apartments with glass shower doors, and she has never been able to keep them that clean. He must have regular housecleaning.

Or he never takes a shower here.

Her gaze strays back to the sink where the man has leaned down, retrieving items from the cabinet beneath. She looks up again, sure that she must look horrific after her evening, and her eyes pause on the blank wall.

He doesn't have a mirror. *What kind of guy has a bathroom without a mirror?*

A *vampire*, her mind replies.

But vampires aren't real.

You just flew here after being attacked by a monster. Don't start arguing about reality right now.

Oh crap. Sylvia looks down at her bloody legs, a few drops puddled on the floor beneath her right leg. *I'm bleeding in front of a freaking vampire.*

She looks at the man again. Jamie Fraser and time travel would have been easier.

"Hey, what's your name?" she asks. It's not what she means to say, but it's what comes out, and she decides that it works. She's tired of calling him Jamie Fraser anyway.

"Theodore," he replies, the name a melody on his lips. "Theodore Muldavian. Theo."

"Muldavian?" she echoes. "I thought it was Mulranian."

"That's for the show," he explains.

"Muldavian is definitely Germanic," she says thoughtfully. "But Theodore? That's super Greek."

Theo looks at her, an adorable smile on his face that crinkles his eyes, eyes that have lost that odd golden glow. "You are … surprising, Sylvia."

"Surprisingly clumsy," she replies, glancing down at her legs.

Theo frowns at the mess, then places the supplies he pulled from the cabinet on the floor at her feet: a stack of white cloths, a bottle of alcohol, a pair of plastic-handled tweezers, a roll of bandages, a smaller roll of white medical tape, and a small pair of scissors. "This will hurt," he says.

Sylvia inhales a slow, deep breath. "I know." She looks over his head at the empty wall above the sink. "Why not take me to the ER, Theo?"

He shrugs. "You don't need stitches."

"How do you know? Are you an EMT when you aren't playing a Viking?"

"I've bound my share of wounds, Sylvia," he tells her. "I know how to treat this."

"Hospitals have drugs," she says helpfully, thinking not of the splinter removal, which will hurt, but the steady throbbing from her ankle still encased in her boot. She should get the shoe off soon, or her swollen foot will get stuck in there.

"Drugs," he scoffs, giving her a long look. "I can help with the pain."

"How?"

"Let me help you," he counters.

"I am."

Something in his face shifts, the way he holds himself, and his skin does that weird subtle glow thing again. "No," he tells her, voice more forceful. "*Let* me help you."

Sylvia feels that pull, the need to disappear inside him, and she fights it. She doesn't want to lose herself in those eyes. She wants to get this over with. "Just do it," she orders. "Stop stalling."

He frowns again, then sighs, shaking his head as he reaches for her right foot. "May I?" he asks. At her brief nod, he takes hold of her boot, straightening her leg and slowly sliding it off her foot. Sylvia winces, and he jerks back suddenly, tugging her boot free. The pain bolts up her ankle, but he is already sliding off her blue paisley sock. Blood soaks the hem.

Her bare foot hits the cool tile floor, a wave of pain rolls up her leg, and she frowns, watching a trickle of blood rolling from her knee over her swollen ankle and pooling atop her foot. "I think it's broken," she whispers.

Theo doesn't look up at her, head cocked as he studies her foot without touching it. "It's not broken, or it won't be."

"What?" she asks.

"One thing at a time," he tells her. "First... let's look at those hands." He leans forward, arm reaching behind Sylvia to turn on the tap in the tub. His body is close to her, and Sylvia breathes him in, her heart rate finally settling down into a normal rhythm. He holds one of the cloths under the water, then sits back on his knees, reaching for her right hand to brush her knuckles, gently wiping the blood away. It stings, but the pain is bearable, and he leans forward again, shoulder brushing her other arm as he rinses the cloth. He flips the hand to study her palm, then pushes her sweater up a little bit to reveal her wrist.

"I think my arms are okay," she says, pushing the sweater up farther, but it catches about halfway up her forearms. The sweater is ruined, blood smearing the cuffs and the bottom. "I should just take this off," she decides, leaning back and sliding the sweater off her shoulders. He takes it from her, resting it on the sink behind him without looking. Sylvia bites her lip again, suddenly aware of how close she is to a virtual stranger while wearing only a tank top and a skirt. She hasn't been so near a man since breaking up with Adam, and even with him, she rarely showed so much skin. Her hand rubs absently against her lower belly, pulling the bottom of the tank down to make sure her stomach is covered.

Theo takes her right hand again, studying her forearm, then glancing up to her bicep. His eyes do not linger on her breasts, a kindness Sylvia appreciates. This is odd enough without bringing her sexual hang-ups into the picture, though it does make Theo seem even less human.

He releases her hand, resting it gently on her thigh, then moves to her other hand. The bright lights reveal what she suspected in the dark bedroom. Something has scraped her palm, and while the wound has clotted, the skin is a mass of blood and debris from the floor. Theo takes his time wiping it clean, using the tweezers to remove stray wooden splinters. His fingers are steady on the plastic coating of the tweezer tips, careful not to touch the silver of the actual instrument. When her hand is clean, he reaches for the bottle of alcohol.

"This will hurt," he says, "but I can help you."

Sylvia watches him pour the alcohol onto a new cloth, imagining the sting. "How?"

His body shifts subtly. "Let me in," he says, his eyes emitting that odd glow again. Sylvia wants to pull away, fight him as she has done in the past, but she thinks of the sting of that alcohol, and the pain to come, and instead, she allows herself to fall under his spell. His eyes never leave hers as he presses the alcohol-soaked cloth against her palm. It does hurt, her hand shrieking in sharp agony, but Sylvia doesn't care.

Morphine, she thinks, recalling the drug's effects from her time in the hospital. "It hurts," she says dreamily, "but I don't care."

"Good," Theo says, wrapping her palm in a bandage and taping it in place. "Let's see to those legs now." He reaches forward, and Sylvia looks down, the sight of his hands beneath her skirt sparking a thrill deep in her belly. As soon as she stops looking at him, her hand blazes, and she looks at it.

"I don't know how you do it," she tells him, "distance the pain like that, but I need you to do it again."

He nods, then reaches for her left foot, tugging the boot free gently so as not to jar her. Slowly, he peels off the sock, and Sylvia hopes her nervous sweat hasn't made her feet smell.

Way to make a great impression, she thinks, biting her lip. *A stinky, sweaty, bloody mess in his bathroom.*

He rescued you from some kind of monster, she reminds herself. *I doubt your feet matter very much right now.*

She rests both bare feet on the cool tile, and he looks up at her, hands reaching for the bottom of her skirt again. She nods at the question on his face, then he is lifting the black material, smeared with blood and dirt and house debris, folding her skirt over her knees. He pushes it above the gouge near her right knee, revealing her pale thighs to the bright light of the room, and pauses there for a long moment. His nose twitches, but he continues to stare at her face, meeting her gaze with his normal dark brown eyes. His tongue peeks out from between tight lips, a quick flash that reflects in his eyes, and he closes his eyes, takes a deep breath, and opens them again, mouth settling into a firm line as his eyes settle back down.

"Now," he says quietly, "you have to let me in again."

"I don't know what that means," Sylvia says, but she tastes the lie in her words. Even as she speaks, she can feel herself leaning toward him again, and the pain in her ankle fades.

"Yes," he whispers. "Like that." His hands move, probably grabbing the tweezers and another cloth, but Sylvia doesn't look, doesn't break away from his gaze. His eyes remain dark, none of that golden light peeking through, and though he still looks perfectly normal, Sylvia can feel the power rolling off him into her. She lets herself wallow in it, drowning in the magic he wields. "Close your eyes," he tells her in that same quiet voice.

Sylvia obeys, gritting her teeth and waiting for the pain as he digs out her splinters. Instead, she can feel pressure and movement on each of her legs as she drifts in warm darkness, but none of the sharp jabs she expects. His hands are warm when he touches her skin, and her mind runs through all the vampire movies and books she knows.

"You're warm," she whispers, eyes still closed.

"Should I not be?" he replies, voice quiet as his hands continue to move.

"Aren't vampires supposed to be cold? There's a whole thing in *Twilight* about that."

He chuckles, the sound warming more than her heart. "Am I a *Twilight* vampire then?"

She shakes her head slowly, somehow enjoying the simple pressure of his touch, her body completely immune to the pokes and prods of the tweezers. "No way," she tells him. "I don't think Edward could fly. He just moves really fast." She pauses, running through her favorite pop culture vampires. "You don't wear a Daylight Ring, like Damon and Stefan Salvatore in *Vampire Diaries*," she muses, recalling his bare fingers on both hands. "Though it is night, so maybe you already took it off." She frowns. "Maybe a Buffy vampire like Spike? Do you have a soul?"

Theo inhales, a sharp intake of breath.

Her words come out innocently enough, but she didn't consider the implications of the question. "I'm sorry," she blurts. "That was so rude."

There is a long pause, then Theo says, "It's too soon to be talking about souls, Sylvia."

"Right," she breathes. "Hmm, Dracula, then? Can you turn into a bat?"

He laughs. "Can't a man have his secrets?"

"Are you a man?" she blurts.

The touch of his hands leaves, and something shifts in the way she feels, still submerged in that soft comforting dark, but an edge of light limning the space behind her eyes. "I need to clean these now, Sylvia. I can't dull that completely."

Sylvia nods, biting her lip, and keeps her eyes closed as she grips the edge of the tub. "Do it." He doesn't make her wait, the sharp sting of alcohol running down her left leg. She winces, but the pain fades quickly. The feel of his hands changes, then he is wrapping a bandage around her left shin, securing it in place with tape. He moves to her right leg, softer now, wary of her ankle, and sighs. "This will be worse."

Sylvia takes a deep breath, preparing herself. "I know. Just do it." The pain in her calf is sharp and biting, but when he reaches the deeper wound above her knee, she jerks, the movement radiating agony down her entire leg. Her fingers dig into the side of the tub, but then he is holding both of her hands, urging her in that same hypnotic voice. "Look at me, Sylvia."

And she does. The room is bright after having her eyes shut for so long, but she barely notices, focusing all her attention on the golden light of his eyes. "So bright," she whispers, staring at the thin ring of honey surrounding his dilated pupils. He is careful of her left hand as he brings both of her hands to rest on his shoulders, then he reaches out, sliding his palms along her forearms and across her upper arms to rest on her shoulders. One hand continues to slide across her shoulder and rest against the base of her neck, pushing her hair out of the way so he can touch her skin.

Sylvia's heart speeds up, his touch igniting a warm glow in her lower belly. Her hands wrap around the back of his neck, unconsciously pulling his face closer to her. He tilts his head, eyes leaving hers to glance at the bare expanse of her neck, then he is gently pushing away from her, settling back on his haunches. Sylvia lets go of him reluctantly, a small frown on her lips as she narrows her eyes.

Why did he pull away? A quick glance down reminds her of all the blood he has cleaned up, and that golden hint to his eyes suddenly means something else.

"Oh crap," she blurts, leaning back on the edge of the tub. "I'm so sorry!"

He cocks his head, that predatory gaze still lingering. "Sorry?" he echoes.

"You're a freaking vampire, and I'm here bleeding all over everything like a snack." She moves to flip her skirt down, to cover her legs, but he moves forward to stop her. They pause there, his hands beneath her skirt, the sight of this stranger with his hands under her clothing causing heat to pool in her belly, and stare at one another. Theo breaks the silence.

"Wait," he suggests, gently lifting the skirt back on her thighs, watching her as she follows the line of his hands. "Let me wrap that first." He frowns, considering the bandage on her other leg. "Just that one, though," he says, nodding at the deep cut above her knee. "The others are fine open like that. Plus, we still need to deal with that ankle."

Sylvia nods, fear of the pain stealing the warmth from her limbs. "Can you do it again? That weird thing you just did?"

Theo wraps the bandage around her leg, and Sylvia realizes he is very careful not to touch her skin this time, only holding the cloth instead. When he finishes, he frowns. "That weird thing should have been enough to daze you completely."

"Oh," Sylvia says. "Was I dazed?"

He laughs, twisting to move the remains of the medical equipment to the sink. "With your running commentary on popular vampires? Hardly."

Sylvia looks away as he gets to his feet, turning to wash his hands in the sink. Her gaze sneaks up to watch his back, admiring the strength of his shoulders, the firm curve of his ass, the long lines of his legs. He really is beautifully shaped. She wants to touch him and curls her fingers around the edge of the tub, the bandage on her hand pressing into her skin. "Is there something wrong with me?" she asks when he turns around again. "Why didn't it work?"

He smirks. "That's a great question, Sylvia. A topic I will definitely explore at another time."

Another time? There will be another time? Sylvia tries to ignore the burst of joy at the idea. She wants to see him again.

He frowns at her ankle. "But right now, we have to fix that."

The joy evaporates at the reminder. "Did I mention the ER? I mean, I don't have insurance, but they can give me something, and I'll pay it off eventually..." She trails off, calculating finances in her head. *How much could a trip to the ER for a busted ankle really be?*

More than you can afford, she tells herself. She looks up at him. "Any ideas?"

"Maybe," he says, leaning back against the edge of the sink. "But I don't know if you'll want to try it."

Sylvia leans back, stretching her neck back as she looks up at him. "Let me guess—you have to bite me or something." She expects him to laugh, but his face is serious. "Oh fuck." She sits up straight, lifting a hand to her neck. The movement makes her ankle throb again, and she bites her lip. "Okay," she says, "tell me what you're thinking."

"Come sit on the bed with me," he suggests.

Sylvia narrows her eyes. "I didn't say yes."

"I know," he tells her. "But this isn't a conversation we should have with you perched on the edge of my tub."

"Oh," Sylvia nods. "Serious talk requires serious surroundings. I get it." She raises an eyebrow. "Do you always have serious conversations in your bed?"

He shakes his head, leaning down to help her to her feet. "We can sit on the couch if you prefer." Sylvia bounces on one foot, and he wraps an arm around her waist. "Or the kitchen table." He secures his hand on her hip, then tilts his head. "Hold my neck," he instructs, and when she does, he lifts her effortlessly out of the room, but through a different door than the one they came through. They move down a short hallway, and the apartment opens into a large space. A torchiere lamp casts a dim light from the corner of the living room, and Sylvia takes in the Ikea couch, the simple bar stools lined up along the kitchen counter, and the large glass dining table against the far wall of windows. Another rooftop patio is beyond the glass door behind the table.

"Wow," Sylvia breathes. She's never been in a place this big before, and definitely not a penthouse apartment. Her gaze catches on the couch, the piece basic in comparison to the rest of the furniture. "I almost bought that couch," she comments. "But then I got a futon." She looks around again. "I don't have this kind of space at my place."

"It serves its purpose," Theo says. "Where would you be comfortable?"

"I guess the couch," she says, and he carries her over to it, settling her gently on the stiff pale blue cushions. Her ankle throbs again. The pain is bearable if she doesn't move it, but her skin is purplish and puffy. Distracting herself from the sight, she notices that her bare feet rest on a fuzzy gray carpet that looks like it came right out of a catalog. She studies the sparse living room decorations: the simple light in the corner, a coffee table with a remote control on it, and a large flatscreen TV on the wall. The apartment doesn't have the knickknacks she expects of a place well lived in. It's more like a hotel room.

In fact, the only personal item is a small blue lava lamp sitting on the kitchen counter. The blue blobs rise slowly in a hypnotic wave. Sylvia looks away from it.

Above the couch, there is a large black and white photo of a beach. Sylvia is reminded of Clyde Butcher. *In this place*, she thinks, *it's probably an original print*. "I don't get it," she mutters, resting her hands on her lap, very aware of her dirty skirt again.

"What?" he asks, sitting down a foot away, giving her space on the sofa.

"This place," she gestures around. "You."

"We did just meet," he comments. "I don't expect you to get me right away."

"But this is weird," she says. "Clearly you have money—penthouse apartment, original artwork, huge TV—but then this Ikea couch."

He shrugs. "I'm not here very often."

"Oh." Sylvia looks down. "You sleep other places often?" Sylvia doesn't like the small twinge of jealousy that burns through her at the thought of Theo wrapping that body around a different woman each night.

"I'm a vampire, Sylvia. I sleep in a coffin." His words are light, and when she looks up at him, he is smiling.

"Seriously?" She looks around. "Where is it?"

"A vampire's sleeping place is his most guarded secret," he says, still smiling, but a bit more serious.

"You think someone will Van Helsing you during the day?" Sylvia scoffs.

Theo lifts a shoulder. "Wouldn't be the first time."

She narrows her eyes at him. "How old are you?"

"Old enough," he replies. "Now stop stalling. That ankle is only getting worse."

Sylvia glares at him. "Fine. What are you going to do?"

"Try," he corrects. "I'm going to *try* something ... if you agree." He takes a deep breath, steeling himself. "Normally, I can use my power to ... subdue people. Make them not care about what I'm doing. Or distract them with desire."

"Oh," Sylvia breathes. She planned to give him a Yoda speech after he said he would try, but this new admission chills her. "That's what it is." Suddenly, her need to touch him, the odd pull tugging her toward him, makes sense. *It's his vampire magic.*

"What *what* is?" he echoes, confused.

"Nothing," she says quickly. "Go on."

"You seem immune to it, though," he says. "To me."

Sylvia's stomach drops. *Maybe it's just me, then. Of course it's me*, she tells herself. *I'm always attracted to the wrong people. Why would a vampire be any different?*

"It only partially works on you, and only after you decide to let me in, like in the bathroom." He shakes his head.

"Why?" she asks.

He shrugs. "I have no idea. But we will figure that out later. For now, I have another idea." He pauses, then his words come out faster. "When I bite people, they tend to lose all sense of the world around them. They are dazed, unaware. If you were like that, I could fix your ankle, and you wouldn't feel it."

"Can't you just give me some vampire blood and heal me?" she asks, thinking of vampire pop culture.

He winces, letting out a low sound. "Not exactly."

"So, what then, *exactly*?"

"Vampire blood does heal," he explains. "You're right about that. But your ankle needs to be set. It's dislocated. Any blood right now would only heal it like that, and I assume you want to walk normally again. I need to distract you from the pain first."

"And biting me is a distraction. Got it. But what happens to me after you bite me?" She pauses. "Do I become a vampire?" She gives him a serious look. "I don't want to be a vampire, Theo. I like the sun way too much."

"You'll be fine after," he reassures her. "Just don't die tonight, and it will be like it never happened. Except your ankle will be healed."

"So, *Vampire Diaries* rules, then?" she asks. At his confused expression, she adds, "People who die with vampire blood in them become vampires—but they have to feed in the first day or they really die."

Theo nods thoughtfully. "Not quite how it works, but close enough for our needs. I will only give you a few drops. By tomorrow morning, you'll return to normal."

Sylvia considers him. She has already decided to let him bite her, but she's working through the logistics.

"So, if I'm dazed by your vampire powers," she begins, "what's to stop you from drinking all of my blood and killing me?"

"I won't kill you, Sylvia."

"Fine," she says, raising an eyebrow. "Let's say I believe you won't kill me. How do I know you won't take advantage of me? This is like agreeing to be roofied."

He holds his hand before his chest, fingers oddly spread, and says in a solemn voice, "I swear I will not harm thee."

She bites her lip at his archaic speech, then reaches for his hand with her good one. "What does this mean?"

"It's an oath," he explains, the fingers relaxing as her hand meets his. His skin is still warm, and small streaks of fiery pleasure slide across her palm as their hands press together.

"That is serious," she whispers. "Vikings take their oaths very seriously."

He nods, his other hand reaching for her, resting gently on her right arm as his body slides closer on the couch. "Blood sharing is serious business," he tells her. "It's ... personal. I understand if you want to say no."

"I don't mind personal," she tells him, still caught up in the delight that touching him brings. "I like it." Their hands move together, both gently pressing against the other as they bring them in front of their chests. "I like you," she says.

"And I you," he says, sliding even closer, his face inches away from her. "May I kiss you?" he whispers, breath soft against her skin.

"Please," she tells him, then he is closing the gap between them, his mouth warm against hers.

The kiss is chaste, the soft press of his lips against her, but a trail of fire snakes through Sylvia's body, pooling in her lower belly with liquid heat. Her left hand slides up his arm, relishing the hard muscles of his upper arms, and she leans into him, moving her mouth gently, enjoying the push and pull of his lips on hers. She waits for more, for him to slide his tongue between her lips, but he doesn't. Instead, he keeps the kiss sensual but innocent, running his hands up her bare arms to rest on her shoulders, one moving to caress the back of her neck. Sylvia thinks he will move to her neck to bite her, the thought causing her to stiffen, and Theo pulls away, breaking the kiss and sliding a hand back down her right arm to her hand. He lifts it gently, fingers sliding against her skin and leaving a trail of sparks, then he lifts it to his face, bringing her wrist to his mouth. Those soft lips press against the delicate skin of her inner wrist as his eyes meet hers, one final request for permission.

She nods, biting her lower lip as the sensations rush through her body, and he strikes. The pain is sharp, but it is gone quickly, replaced by a warm floating feeling that starts in her hand and rushes through her entire body. She is aware of Theo's eyes, the color shifting from a familiar brown to a light honey glow as he drinks from her. Her world shrinks to his face, then his eyes, and then there is nothing at all.

CHAPTER 6

THEO

THEO WATCHES HER FACE AS HE DRINKS, FORCING HIMSELF to focus, waiting for the moment when she drifts away, lost in the euphoria of his bite. It takes longer than it should, and by the time she starts to slump over into his arms, Theo is close to losing control. He pulls himself away with more force than he intends, jerking her body in a way that surely jolts her ankle. Sylvia doesn't respond to the movement, a sign that she is finally incapacitated by the bite, and he lowers her to the couch.

Her hair slips over her shoulder, revealing a swath of creamy neck, and the beast in Theo rises, urging him to strike. Her wrist was just a taste, the dark voice insists, but now he needs the real thing. He should drown himself in her blood, drink until he is surrounded by everything Sylvia, gorge himself until nothing matters anymore.

Sylvia matters, another voice whispers, and Theo slides away from her, backing up slowly while he regains control. It was risky to bite her, especially given how much he wants her, but besides subjecting her to human medicine, he didn't see another option.

Sure you didn't, that quiet voice continues. *It's not as if you could bring her to Samson or anything.* He frowns, the thought of bringing his Sylvia to the handsome shifter causing a small burn of possessive jealousy in his chest. Of course, Samson would be able to heal her ankle—he was the best (and only) healer for the supernatural community in the city.

But I would have had to move her again, and I don't want it to get any worse.

Sure, keep telling yourself that it was the trip there, and not the way you imagine her face would light up as Samson spoke to her, leaning down to touch her skin. A slow rage builds under Theo's skin at the image, and he dismisses it. Samson has to be charming; most supernatural creatures wouldn't let him touch them otherwise.

But Sylvia is human. Theo could hardly trouble the healer for such a small thing as a dislocated ankle. And the wily dragon's office is downtown.

You know he would have made a house call, the voice tries once more.

And now he doesn't have to, Theo tells himself. *Now I can heal her, and she will be fine.*

He moves close to Sylvia again, the bloodlust in him faded. He straightens her on the couch, lifting her legs onto the cushions so her body lays flat. Kneeling on the floor beside her, he reaches for the ankle, checking her face for signs of pain as he touches her. Seeing none, he holds her foot firmly, fingers sliding over her ankle, feeling the bones and finding the dislocation. He's not a healer, but he was raised among fighting men. Injuries were common, along with their remedies. Some of the methods have advanced for sure, but ankles are still ankles, and he knows what they feel like. Finding the injury, he uses his strength to pull the joint straight, then shifts it into place. The joints and muscles resist at first, swollen from being out of place for so long, but finally, they ease back into place.

Theo nods, moving to sit beside Sylvia's head. Her breathing has shifted, deeper now as she falls completely under the magic. He sighs in relief. For a moment there, he didn't know if it would work at all. Normally, the tiniest pulse of his power is enough to daze people. He hit Sylvia with enough energy to take out a bear, and now he thinks maybe he overdid it. She will sleep until sunrise, at least.

Theo pauses, recalling the look on her face, the sense of her still very present as she nodded that final time, fully in the sway of his power but still herself, not lost to desire like most of his victims. There is something different about her, something that shields her from him just enough to stay herself in his presence.

His assistant Grace has a similar reaction to him, but that's because she is completely in love with her husband Remi—and she has zero desire for anyone else. Theo hasn't come across it very often in his long life, but people in satisfied relationships rarely react to his power, walking past him on the street without a second glance. From the way she kissed him, Theo doesn't think Sylvia is contentedly in love with someone else, so it must be something else about her.

He takes the moment to study her face, memorizing the lines of her eyelashes, the shape of her lips. She is lovely to behold, her face relaxed in complete release. Theo doesn't think Sylvia lets go very often.

He has a quick flash of that face beneath him, cheeks flushed red in pleasure, but he looks away. She agreed to a kiss. He will not take more than she promised him.

Sighing, he brings a finger to his mouth. A quick bite pierces his skin, and a few red drops rise to the surface. He holds the finger over her mouth, dripping the blood between her slightly parted lips. He is tempted to put his finger in her mouth, if only to make sure she gets all the healing blood, but he knows such a thing will lead to poor choices, and he holds himself back.

A few drops should do it, he decides, watching the smallest wounds on her legs knit close. Her ankle changes from mottled purple to a faded pink. It will be sore for a few days, but no more than that. It is much better than she would fare if he did nothing.

Sitting back on his haunches, Theo studies her, trying to figure out why she interests him.

She is pretty, and he has always been a sucker for a pretty girl, but this is more than that. Their kiss was sweet, trembling, and unless he is incredibly mistaken, the nervous energy of a virgin. He's kissed his share of girls, and he hasn't had a kiss like that since he was a human teenager.

There is also the matter of the demon hunting her. He didn't know she was wanted when they met, but now that he knows, he cannot leave her unguarded until he finds out why.

Watching her drift into deep sleep on his couch, he decides to stay near her. He stands, heads to the bathroom for an ace bandage to roll around her ankle and stops by the bedroom to grab a shirt as well. He plans to bring her back to her home, the small apartment he glimpsed in her mind, and the air is chilly. Her sweater is ruined, but he covers her bare arms with a soft button-down shirt after wrapping her ankle and bandaging the small wound on her wrist.

He gathers her up again, tucking her close to his body, and heads back out into the night, stopping to collect her abandoned purse in the old building before heading to the address listed on her license. The downstairs door opens easily enough, only wedged shut but not locked, and he carries her up the flight of stairs without trouble, but when he reaches her front door, turning the keys in both locks is not enough, the door open but blocked by an invisible barrier.

"Syl," he whispers to the sleeping woman in his arms. When she doesn't respond, he says it louder, infusing the word with some power to jolt her back to consciousness.

"Theo," she moans, eyes flickering, then closing again.

"I need you to invite me in," he tells her, body pressing against the magic guarding her home, the old hospitality laws catching him off guard.

"Sure," she agrees, the word slurring into a snore.

He bounces her in his arms. "Say the words, Syl," he instructs. "Invite me in."

She giggles, the sound young and girlish as her eyes open wide but without seeing. "Of course, vampire," she laughs. "I invite you in, Theo. Come in, come on, come on in…"

The wall of force disappears, and Theo enters her living space. *She wasn't kidding when she said the studio was small.* Theo kicks the door shut behind them, depositing her purse on the floor beside the door, ignoring the hook near the front door since the strap is broken.

He steps forward, looking over the layout. A tiny kitchen lines the wall to his left, apartment-sized fridge and ancient gas stove jammed together next to a sink and a counter the size of his bathroom sink. A tiny two-seat table sits across from the sink. There is a small walkway directly across the apartment to a fire escape window, a small bookshelf crammed with paperbacks sits next to the window, the top littered with half-empty glasses of water. *Sylvia must sit out there often.* The right side of the room contains her futon, opened as a bed, a small chest pressed against the foot, an armoire jammed into the corner opposite a milk crate that serves as a nightstand. Next to where he stands near the front door, there is a rocking chair heaped with clothes. A door behind the chair leads to a small bathroom. The walls are covered with tapestries in various colors and designs, Sylvia's attempt to make the small space feel cozy rather than claustrophobic.

Theo lays her down on the bed, putting a small bag with her boots, socks, and bloody sweater on the floor. He pulls out the small cane he brought her and rests it against the milk crate nightstand, so she will be able to reach it in the morning when she wakes.

He stands up, surveying the apartment once more. He reaches for her blanket, about to tug it up over her, when he notices her dirty skirt, her bloodstained tank top.

If it were me, he thinks, *I wouldn't want to sleep in filthy clothes. Especially not if it means I would have to wash the sheets with a healing ankle the next day.* Frowning, he glances at the mound of clothes on the chair, spying another tank top and a pair of sleep shorts jammed into the side.

"Syl," he whispers, hoping he can wake her as he did at the door, but he is rewarded by a deep, long snore. She is out.

"I can do this," he tells himself and the room. "I'm a gentleman." Biting his lip, he kneels alongside the futon. He slides the shorts up over her legs, careful of the bandages, and secures them at her waist before slipping her skirt off. "See?" he says to the empty apartment. "Totally fine." He frowns at her tank top, wondering at the logistics. The bottom edge is stained dark with blood. Staring down at Sylvia, his eye catches on a silvery shadow at her waist, and he leans closer to identify it. Theo has seen his share of scars, but he does not expect to find the long winding line of silvery scar tissue across Sylvia's lower belly. The gasp leaves him in a burst as he is genuinely shocked by the viciousness of the wound. His own body is lined with scars, the marks of a human life spent fighting, but he doesn't expect to find such marks in this time, and not on fragile-looking young women.

Some things about her behavior slide into place, raising an entire new host of questions. For all that he may know about Sylvia—her blood, her lips, her face— there is so much more he does not know. He hears Oren's voice again, asking him about mates, but he dismisses the idea. Sylvia intrigues him—nothing more.

"Oh, Syl," he whispers, reaching out to touch her face. He pulls his shirt tighter around her body, closing the buttons and covering up her scars. At least his shirt is clean. She can change her tank top when she wakes.

He secures the blanket over her, then leans down to place a soft kiss on her forehead. For a moment, he worries about the demon, wonders if it will come hunting for her here, but he dismisses the concern. Demons cannot enter without invitations, just like vampires, and he doesn't think Sylvia will venture far from her apartment the next day, not with her ankle still healing. There is always the chance that something will happen to her during the day, but Theo has been a vampire for a long time, and he knows better than to worry about what he cannot control. He will return with the sunset, and they will figure out why the demon is after her together.

"Be well," he whispers in his native tongue, and his hand shifts into a gesture of good luck, a motion he has not made since his youth.

CHAPTER 7

PILKINGTON

T HE DEMON KNOWN AS MR. PILKINGTON IS HAVING A ROUGH
day. Though he drops the honorific in his own realm,
presenting as Pilkington to his fellow demons and
when in his demonic form, his true name is a closely
guarded secret, known only to two living humans and
a handful of deceased ones. His plans to end the first
human have snagged on the tiny problem of a powerful
artifact with the power to unmake his existence—and
he knows he will never harm the other human, unable
to protect himself in the most fundamental way from
her dangerous knowledge. But none of these issues
plague him at the moment as he stands in the middle
of his library, water dripping from the ceiling above.

The magic-resistant leak has returned to the bathtub
again, water seeping through the floor to drip on the
Persian rugs covering the library floor below. While
Pilkington was trying to re-seal the pipes upstairs, his
soul-servant Billy took it upon himself to rearrange the

library again, sorting the titles into cryptic haikus that he insists are "an artistic depiction of his bleak existence." As Pilkington stands in the center of the room, growling his displeasure at his supposed servant, the ghostly young man only hovers with his hands clasped demurely behind his back, face suitably somber.

"You will put them back in their proper order," Pilkington orders. "Today." He uses the ever-expanding library nearly every day, researching the magical dagger that nearly killed him, and now he can't tell which books he's already gone through. He glares at his would-be servant.

"Do you see it though?" Billy moans, gesturing to the first shelf of random books. He lifts a hand to his face, wiping away an imagined tear.

"I see your unpleasant evening if this is not fixed the next time I come in here," Pilkington snaps, studying the soft gloves that cover his middle finger and continue over his forearms. The dark lines of his markings creep out from beneath the material, covering his dark blue skin and continuing across his bare chest. The markings glow faintly as the annoyance surges, but then he calms himself, his magic subsiding beneath the surface again.

Billy sighs, drifting over to the first shelf. Instead of rearranging the books as instructed, however, he pulls out volumes from the lower shelves, slipping them between the ones on the top shelf and pausing to read his new creation.

"Angels and Demons," he mutters, reading one spine before turning to the next. "City of Heavenly Fire... Great Expectations..." He shakes his head.

"William!" Pilkington yells, his leathery wings jerking in frustration, and the servant's see-through shoulders slump. He turns to face his demon master with a frown.

"Don't call me that," he sulks. "You know I hate it when you call me that."

Pilkington nods. "Someday, I hope you finally understand the nature of the servitude you agreed to, *William*. This is supposed to be eternal torment." He remembers the human his servant had been, recalling his vow in exchange for a lifetime of knowledge and power. Too bad a lifetime back then was only five decades.

"But my name isn't William," Billy complains, pulling down all the books and making new stacks on the table in the center of the room.

A drip from the ceiling lands on Pilkington's nose, and he glances up, sighing at the widening circle of water from the tub above. He hasn't used the tub since the leak appeared, yet the water continues to spread. He runs a hand through his shaggy dark hair, fingers deftly avoiding the two small horns poking through above each temple. Magic can clean his hair, but he misses the feel of actual hair products to smooth his locks. One of the demigods must have cursed him again—no doubt bitter about losing at cards—and until Pilkington finds the cursed object, he will have to deal with the leak.

"Look," he says, pressing his fingers to the bridge of his nose, "just stop doing this to the library. If you want to write terrible poetry—"

"Haikus," Billy interrupts.

"Whatever," Pilkington says. "Just use pen and paper like everyone else."

"But no one will ever see them on paper," Billy whines. "No one else ever comes here." He gives Pilkington a pleading look as he continues to slowly sort the books. "A guest would be delightful, my lord."

"My lord, is it now?" Pilkington chuckles, shaking his head. "Trust me, Billiacus, we are better off alone. Guests only invite trouble." He heads out of the room, determined to locate the curse and stop the leak. "You should try reading the books instead of just the titles," he suggests over his shoulder.

"Speaking of books," Billy says casually, "the one on your nightstand has disappeared. Did you move it?"

Pilkington frowns, shaking his head. Yet another curse, no doubt. Maybe he should try losing at cards for a little while.

"Damn," he sighs. "That one was just getting interesting."

"You could always read your mail instead," Billy comments, emptying the last shelf and moving to the next bookcase.

"Mail?"

"A summons arrived for you earlier today. Did I not tell you?"

Pilkington stiffens, a leathery wing catching on the doorframe as he jerks awkwardly back inside the library. "No, you didn't tell me! What summons? Where is it?"

"Oh." Billy shrugs, piling even more books on the table. "Well, now I've told you. It's on your desk."

Pilkington hurries from the library, making his way through the ever-growing house to his office.

The summons rests on his desk, the pale pink paper starting to smoke a little around the edges. The sender must have expected a response hours ago. Pilkington flips it over with a sinking feeling, recognizing the seal at once.

Lord Forneus. Marquis of the Realm.

It looks like the leak will have to wait a little longer.

Pilkington's position as a minor lord allows him to ignore much of the politics that govern the demon realm, but when summoners abuse their powers in the human world, he is often the one they call to deal with the problem.

Part of it has to do with his mother. The Lady Asa is renowned for her control of the elements, a power she passed down to her only son. The rest is because Pilkington is known for his discretion using those powers among the humans.

No one speaks of his father, and Pilkington is glad of it. He knows his father's true name, whispered to him once when his mother thought him asleep, but no one else even suspects his true parentage.

Certainly, Forneus does not care about Pilkington's father.

The Marquis stands across his fancy dining room, leathery wings hidden beneath his favorite glamour, an old human in fine clothes holding a golden cup of wine as he addresses his underling. "That's the third one this week," Forneus tells him. "I know Balaam demons are always being summoned to the human realm, but this one was different."

"Different how?" Pilkington asks, accepting the goblet of fine wine Forneus slides across the table. He knows better than to refuse the lord's hospitality.

"He returned in a state of disarray," Forneus says formally.

"Speak plainly," Pilkington says, taking a sip and returning the goblet to the table with a nod of appreciation. "I need details, my lord."

"Details," the Marquis muses, running a hand through his long white hair. Pilkington knows the Marquis' demon form has large horns on both sides of his skull—and no hair at all on his black skinned scalp—but the glamour allows him to feel what appears to be there. Pilkington's glamours rarely work the same way in his world. Here, he always feels like himself—small horns, smooth skin, long thin tail, clawed fingers, large leathery wings—though his fellow demons see whatever form he wears. Pilkington is very careful not to let other demons touch him, guarding his weakness almost as carefully as he does his name. This deficiency doesn't make him weaker—he is one of the strongest demons he knows—but the lack of a common ability would be seen as a failure, an opening for another demon to take advantage of him. Pilkington does not let himself be vulnerable among his own kind.

The human world is another matter. In the human world, Pilkington is special—he can manifest what he looks like, then that form becomes truth. This is a blessing and a curse. He doesn't have to worry about bumping into humans with his large wings, but he also loses his strength, only having the physical abilities of the form he inhabits. He does retain his demonic powers, but he has learned to be subtle while hiding among the humans. It's another reason the Marquis appreciates his skills.

"This is why I like you, lad. No frivolities. No wandering about the issue." The demon lord chuckles. "Details." He studies the painting on the wall for a long moment, a rendition of the Marquess, his long-vanished daughter Fana, before finally turning to face Pilkington.

"This Balaam was killed," he explains quietly.

Pilkington shrugs, the motion moving his wings but only shifting the open jacket he appears to wear. His usual glamour among other demons is subtle, retaining his demonic skin and facial features but erasing his wings. Most demons conceal their wings so they can wear fashionable coats like the humans, so Pilkington follows the trend, not wanting to draw any more attention to himself than his mother already does. He's always wondered if Forneus can see through him, see his true self beneath the weak glamour, but the Marquis has never said anything. Pilkington does not want to give the lord a reason to investigate him.

He waits for more information. Most demons must be killed in order to return to their realm. It was the easiest way for summoners to get rid of their burden once the task was completed. Sure, they could use words, carefully articulated agreements that end with the acquisition of the prize, but some summoners aren't smart enough, sly enough, to barter with a demon, and resort to homicide instead.

"It was killed," Forneus adds, "by a vampire."

Pilkington's head jerks up at this. Vampires are many in the human realm, hiding among the humans along with the shapeshifters and the magicians, but he doesn't know of any who would fight a demon. He purses his lips. "You think this vampire is in league with a summoner?"

Forneus shrugs, the motion causing his luxurious robes to sway and settle as he moves. "Summoners will always have some level of control over us in the human realm," he says. "We accept this as the price of our power." He pauses, shaking his head. "We have no dealings with the vampires, but we cannot abide such an alliance." He looks up at Pilkington. "Go. Track this summoner and the vampire. Return when you know more."

Pilkington nods, accepting his task, feeling the geas settle upon his shoulders.

"Subtlety," Forneus adds. "Any hint of a disturbance, anything that would unsettle our truce with the Klaviger, and you will return immediately."

The additional restraints snap into place, and Pilkington nods. "Very well, my lord." He leaves before Forneus can speak again, knowing that the old demon loves nothing more than to lecture to a captive audience.

As soon as he stands on the steps of Forneus' mansion, Pilkington uses his magic to teleport back to his home, a power he can only use in this realm, arriving inside his office. Calling Billy, he instructs the soul-servant to finish re-sorting the library properly and to do his best about the leak. The ghost frowns but says nothing, drifting out of the room to complete his tasks.

Pilkington sighs and heads to his bedroom, making a mental list of what he will need for a trip into the human realm. Clothing isn't a concern since his human form arrives fully dressed, but he will bring a few trinkets, protection against the unexpected.

He visits the human realm regularly, disguised and quietly watching the humans, but he takes a moment to recall what he has learned since his last disastrous summoning so long ago. He has no plans to be summoned again, and certainly not by the one with the magical dagger, but despite years of research, he hasn't been able to find out much about the weapon that wounded him.

Sliding down the elegant cloth armguard he wears, a fashion statement that hides the long thin white line down his forearm, he studies the scar that appears no matter what form he takes now. It hadn't been there the first time he'd returned after killing himself with a fall in the ocean, but as soon as he completed the geas and returned home, ending the spell, the line had appeared on his arm, faint at first but glowing brighter until it showed up no matter what form he took. He sighs, walking to the small chest at the foot of his bed. Opening it, he removes the top layers of clothing designed to fit his natural demonic body, adjusting for his height and wings, setting them aside to reveal the false bottom.

He pauses, listening intently for signs of Billy, but he can feel the soul-servant below in the library. A quiet word releases the spell on the bottom of the chest, and he reaches through it to retrieve a small silver compass on a chain. He resets the spell and replaces the clothing, getting to his feet and examining the compass in the light.

He doesn't keep it hidden because it is magical. In fact, it has very little power beyond the tracking spell his holding it for so long has placed on it. No matter where the compass ends up in the human world, he will know where to find it.

Staring at it as it spins and twirls, Pilkington frowns.

You really think you'll give it to her this time? When you haven't all the other times you've seen her?

He pictures Sylvia's face, the girl she was grown into a woman now. She hasn't seen him since she was sixteen, the summer things got a little too familiar, and he dragged himself away before he did something really foolish, like steal an innocent's virtue. But he has seen her over the years, just making sure she is alright.

The humans call that stalking, he tells himself.

The humans are barbarians determined to kill one another, he replies. *It's called watching over my investment.* He still owes Sylvia an honest answer, a favor promised years ago in a moment of foolishness.

He wraps the compass up in the palm of his hand, glad for the silver that will repel a vampire. If vampires are in league with summoners, the humans may need more protection than usual from the supernaturals that walk among them.

If his Sylvia is ever in any danger from vampires, the compass will protect her at least a little bit. Maybe this time he will actually give it to her.

CHAPTER 8

SYLVIA

SYLVIA WAKES MUCH LATER THAN NORMAL, COMING BACK to her body in slow twinges of pain, thrumming aches from both legs, and a sharp zing from her hand when she uses it to sit up, confused and disoriented. When her familiar apartment swims into focus, she takes a deep breath, bringing her hand to her chest to ease her pounding heart, her body's delayed reaction to the bizarre events of the previous night.

Her pulse settles quickly when she sees no apparent threat, and she sits there for a long moment, slowly taking stock of her injuries as her memory fills in the gaps from the night before.

Theo, she recalls, picturing those golden eyes. *He ... saved me?* Her ankle is wrapped in a brown ace bandage, so she unrolls it to examine the damage. The muscles ache, but it's not a sharp pain, more like the dull reminder of a week-old injury. Her skin is mottled pink, not the purple she expects. The rest of her legs are covered in lines and scrapes, mostly healed, and even the worst cut above her knee has a thick scab. She removes the bandages from her hand, examining the layer of scab across her palm, deciding that she will have to be careful with that hand for another day or so if she doesn't want it to start bleeding again.

She unwraps the thin bandage from her wrist, biting her lip as the two small incisions on the inside of her wrist scream at her. Unwilling to think about it quite yet, she examines the shirt she wears instead, a soft flannel that feels luscious against her skin. It is definitely not hers—too expensive, too fancy, too white. Sylvia would never buy a white shirt; she's too clumsy, always spilling things on herself.

She unbuttons it slowly, aware that even the buttons are fancy, made of some smooth cool material that isn't plastic. She is partly relieved to find her filthy tank top underneath, knowing that Theo didn't undress her, but also feeling gross from having slept in a bloody shirt. The thought makes her look down at her legs, and the pair of shorts now covering her bottom. A glance finds her skirt resting atop the mound of clothes on her chair.

So, he wraps me in his shirt, brings me home, and puts shorts on me. Nodding, she notices the cane leaning against her nightstand. *And gives me something to help me walk.*

A slow smile crosses her face. Theo may be a vampire, a creature of the night who drank her blood, but he is the most considerate man she's met in a long time.

Maybe the most considerate ever, she wonders, but then another face crosses her memory, a boy with a secret smile on a Ferris wheel. *Let's see if this one sticks around.*

With a groan, Sylvia levers herself out of bed and makes her slow hopping way to the shower.

Late afternoon finds Sylvia sitting on her fire escape, ankle propped up on the bottom step of the stairs leading to the floor above. She likes sitting on the windowsill like this when she isn't working, spending her evenings perched above the street, watching the people walk by beneath her feet. People so rarely look up, though they are surrounded by tall buildings.

Even though she slept late, the day has been a long one. Her boss had not been pleased when she called in sick, suggesting that by the time she could carry trays again, there might not be a job waiting for her. She ordered groceries and supplies—bandages and tape— even splurging on a delivery of Chinese food, and after hobbling around the small space all afternoon, she is tired.

She rested on her bed for a bit on her phone, chatting with Miriam about her evening adventures, telling her old friend all about the stranger. She doesn't tell her everything, keeping the supernatural out of her texts, but Miriam focuses on the new guy vibe and doesn't let go.

[Miriam: So you literally found a Viking at Viking Times? You're welcome!]

[Sylvia: Shut up. And thank you.]

[Miriam: I need pics, girl.]

[Sylvia: <Jamie Fraser.gif>]

[Miriam: You wish! But seriously, I'm happy for you. You deserve this.]

[Sylvia: I hope so. He seems pretty interesting.]

[Miriam: More interesting than a certain boy who shall remain nameless?]

[Sylvia: Maybe?]

[Miriam: Wow. OK. I thought no one would ever compare to him. New Guy must be amazing.]

[Sylvia: That was a long time ago. He was a boy. And I'm a grown-ass woman now! New Guy (Theo) is a man. A perfect gentleman.]

[Miriam: Well, let's hope that perfect man doesn't break your heart—because then I'll have to kill him. Have fun! Stay safe.]

They text throughout the afternoon, and Sylvia pulls out her sketchpad, flipping past several sketches of Phil to a new page, tracing the curve of Theo's eyes and the curl of his hair in pencil and charcoal. When she finishes, she draws the demon as well, pulling as many details from her terrified memory as she can—the hulking form, the hairy body, the long claws. When her hand starts to ache, she puts the sketchpad away, closing the cover and tucking it between the back of the futon and the mattress where it usually lives.

Maybe none of it was real, she considers, hearing the voice of her therapist. *The mind has many ways of coping with extreme stress.*

Resting on the familiar stone windowsill, she sinks into her memories of the previous night. It has been easy to convince herself that everything that happened last night was a dream, a fantasy borne of too much wine. She knows she went to Viking Times, the plastic helmet jammed into her scuffed and broken purse is evidence of that, but what happened after she left...

Sylvia shakes her head, peering up to gauge the fading light. The sun will set soon, and while part of her hopes to see him again, her mysterious vampire, a small logical voice has taken hold during the day. She's not sure what happened the night before, but the idea of vampires is crazy.

Phil disappeared too, you know. And just when you were sure he was into you.

The voice has been diligently ignoring her quiet arguments—though it was silent for a time when she recalled what happened in the cemetery when she was younger. *Witches,* she reminds herself. Talk of demons. Swirling magic. And a tall dark stranger who carried her to the hospital.

She tries not to think of the rest, how she knows she saw Phil run right off the cliff, but she saw him the next summer. And the one after that. The next summer though, had been their last, her strange companion vanishing as if he had never truly existed. Sometimes,

Miriam will ask her if Phil was real, or if he was a creation of her teenage mind. He was never there when Miriam came home for school in the fall. He always arrived after Miriam and her family had left for the summer, the Bellers eager to avoid the throngs that packed the seaside town during the summer months.

Phil was real, she assures herself. *And so is Theo.* Sighing, she waits as the last of the daylight fades, pale purples of early evening pooling in the shadows beneath her.

The minutes pass, and the fire escape sinks into darkness, Sylvia's eyes adjusting as the light disappears. She is about to give up, give in to the sensible voice inside, and retreat into her apartment when she hears a soft rush of movement.

Theo lands on her fire escape, feet gently settling on the metal slats. Sylvia tilts her head, heart beginning to pound at the sight of him there, a huge red-headed Viking taking up the small space between the stairs and the railing.

"You're here," she whispers, unsure of her voice. "You came."

"Did you doubt me?" He stays where he is, giving her space even though she could touch him if she moves her foot from where it rests on the bottom step.

"No," she says quickly, then bites her lip. "Maybe." She laughs awkwardly. "I thought maybe I imagined everything."

"Do you often imagine yourself injured?" he asks. Glancing down at her legs, bare beneath a pair of sleep shorts, he adds, "How are you feeling?"

Sylvia shrugs. "Good, all things considered."

"And the ankle?" He nods at the foot messily rebound in the ace bandage.

"Fine," she replies. "Much better than I think it would have been. It hurts, but it's not bad. I won't be carrying a tray any time soon." She frowns. "Wait, shouldn't you be fighting at Viking Times right now?"

Theo shakes his head. "We're only open on the weekends," he explains. "I don't have to be back until Friday."

"Don't you have another job?" she asks, curious.

"Why would I?"

"Because that's only part-time," she says. "I work 60 hours, and I can barely afford this place. Your rent must be..." Her voice trails off as she realizes what she is saying. "I'm sorry. That was so nosy!" She looks around, embarrassed. "I do love this place though, even if I complain about it." She glances down at her ankle. "I did not love the stairs today though. Thank god for delivery services."

Theo nods. "I didn't think about that," he says. "Forgive me."

"For what?" she prompts. "You saved me."

"And then immediately abandoned you in a place with stairs that you cannot use," he says. "Some savior."

Sylvia snorts. "I'm a grown-ass woman," she tells him. "I have a phone. We live in the modern age where one button will give me whatever I want."

Theo takes a small step closer, a grin spreading across his face. "Whatever you want?" he echoes. "All on your phone? I must know what app you use for that, Syl."

A warm flush creeps up Sylvia's neck as he draws near, her body responding to his presence as much as his words. "You know what I mean," she snaps, withdrawing her foot from the step and sliding on the windowsill so her back is inside the apartment. "So," she begins, the question that she has avoided all day spinning in her mind, "will I be okay?"

Theo smiles. "You seem to be healing just fine."

"That's not what I mean," she says pointedly, lifting her hand so her wrist faces him, the small pinpricks white slashes against her skin. "What about this?"

Theo gives her a long appraising look, then shrugs. "It's nothing," he says. "It's already out of your system. I told you it was only a few drops."

"So, if it was more than that, would I be healed completely?"

Theo frowns but nods slowly. "Yes, but there are side effects of more blood."

"Like?"

"Like things we can discuss should you ever ingest more of my blood," he says, closing the topic for discussion.

"You think that's unlikely, then?" Sylvia presses. "You're not turning me into a vampire?"

Theo gasps, the sound surprising from the offended large redhead. "I would never!"

Sylvia narrows her eyes, indignant. "Why not? Am I not worthy of being a vampire?"

Theo's face chills. "You seem to be well-versed in vampire lore. Would you seriously want such a burden?"

Sylvia purses her lips, considering. She releases a sigh. "Not really," she admits. "I love the sun too much. Besides, I'm pretty squeamish around blood. And I don't really like enclosed spaces, so that coffin thing would be really hard."

"I'm glad you've thought this through so well," Theo observes.

"Look, I think I'm doing fairly well for someone who just found out that vampires are real," she says tartly. "Because if you're real, then that means witches..." She trails off, eyes drifting to the darkness behind him, wondering how many other supernatural creatures walk the streets of the city day and night. She's always known there were witches, and she thought there were demons, but years of therapy insisted otherwise, promised that what she had seen in that cemetery hadn't actually been what she thought, her mind making things up to deal with stress. But she always knew it was real. A shiver rakes up her spine, and she sags back into the window even more.

And here I am sitting out here like an All-you-can-eat-buffet.

"Are there others like you?" she asks.

Theo shrugs.

"Is that a yes, or a you-can't-tell-me?" Sylvia asks.

Theo leans down so his face is closer to her height. "It's a there-are-things-we-shouldn't-discuss-outside-like-this."

Sylvia nods. "Serious conversations require serious surroundings," she tells him, echoing his comment from the night before.

"Exactly."

"You want to come in then?" she offers, suddenly shy. She knows he has been in her apartment already. Any mystical protection she had is gone, but there is something incredibly personal in inviting him inside while she is awake. She has kissed him, and he drank her blood, but inviting him in seems like crossing a different threshold.

Theo seems to sense her anxiety because he shakes his head. "What if we could go somewhere else to talk?"

"Where? Your place?"

Theo shakes his head again. "Somewhere else." He glances down at her foot. "Somewhere that ankle will appreciate."

Sylvia glances down at herself, taking in the pale tank top, the light sweater, the small shorts. "Should I change?"

"No need."

Sylvia laughs, wiggling her bare toes. "Should I put on shoes? Or will you be carrying me everywhere as per usual?"

He returns her grin. "No need. You're fine as you are."

Sylvia narrows her eyes. "Fine for what? Seriously— no shoes? Where is this place?"

"It's better if I just show you," he says, standing up. He holds out a hand to her. "Do you trust me?"

"Apparently I'm a crazy person because yes, I do trust you." Shaking her head with a sigh, Sylvia takes his hand.

CHAPTER 9

THEO

FROM THE MOMENT HE WAKES, THEO'S THOUGHTS ARE OF Sylvia. Normally, his first few moments after sunset are spent with his eyes closed, adjusting to his vampiric body as if it hasn't been the same for a thousand years. Theo remembers his human body, the feel of it, as well as he does because he spends a few moments each night cataloguing the differences, an old delaying ritual that he never abandoned. Back in those first few years, Jolena teased him mercilessly for what she called laziness.

"Honestly, I thought Vikings were all passion and action," she would sneer, frowning at him when he did drag himself into her presence. "I blame the Romans for such inaccurate observations."

Theo had said nothing, knowing that to oppose Jolena meant a day of her foul temper. She was a woman, physically smaller, but she taught him right away not to be deceived by her size. Her vampiric strength was far stronger than his, a result of her age, and as his Maker, she could command him to do anything she wished. Though he couldn't always resist riling her up despite the consequences, Theo always took the first few moments of consciousness for himself.

Tonight, however, he nearly flies out of his coffin, heading to the apartment and dressing quickly while appreciating his shower the previous morning. He speeds through his evening routine, brushing his teeth and hair at the same time. Running wet fingers through his hair, he mourns the loss of a mirror, wondering if he can spare the time to stop by Oren's so the vampire can check his appearance. He decides against the idea, partly because he doesn't want to deal with the merciless teasing that would follow such a trip, but mostly because he doesn't want to delay seeing Sylvia any longer than absolutely necessary. He smooths his shirt one more time as he heads to the patio, then shrugs, hoping for the best as he launches into the sky. The desire for Sylvia burns until he finds himself standing on her fire escape, appreciating her ethereal beauty in the soft light from the streetlamps below. When she holds out her hand to him, his heart stutters in his chest, a feeling he hasn't experienced in centuries.

I just want to find out about the demon, he reminds himself as he gathers her close to his body. *It's curiosity and the desire to unravel a mystery. That is all.*

But as the scent of her skin invades his senses, Theo knows he is lying to himself. He flies above the buildings, moving swiftly to get away from any prying eyes. Theo is very aware of the bare skin of her legs pressed against his arms. He watches his height carefully, not wanting Sylvia to freeze in the colder air higher up, but not wanting anyone on the streets to notice them either. Not that anyone ever does see him when he flies. He thinks it's another feature of the magic that allows him to remain unseen when he wishes.

Magic and biology, he thinks, trying not to notice the way her body presses against his chest, the soft catch of her breath as he rises and falls a little as they travel. *If I were a scientific man, I would have explored the nuances centuries ago.*

Looking down at Sylvia, who grins at him when she sees him looking, Theo knows he's always been a different kind of man, focused on action and—he admits ruefully—women. Such lines of detailed inquiry are beyond him. Neither Oren nor Harald, his companions over the long years, had such a leaning either, and so they have all fumbled through their gifts—understanding some and guessing about others.

Jolena was never a very good teacher. Taskmaster and mistress, yes, but she never willingly told her pets anything useful. It had taken a long time, but the cruelty inside her eventually dimmed her beauty in Theo's eyes. He knows he would still jump if she beckoned, a feature of his existence as her creature, but he doesn't see her as a beautiful woman anymore.

Watching Sylvia's face as she scans the world beneath them, Theo is reminded of what he once would have called beautiful.

They pass beyond the city, the lights fading away into the moonlight as they rise into the mountains directly to the north. A journey that would take an hour in a car is over in ten minutes as Theo heads for a small clearing hidden behind a wall of rock. Impossible to reach by foot, the area is notable for the small pool of water within. Theo sets down on the black volcanic rock, gently putting Sylvia on her feet. Her eyes widen at the sight of the steaming pool.

"What is this?" she asks, reaching out a hand to lean against the rock wall a foot away. She settles herself against it, eyeing the water two dozen feet away, cheeks flushing in the steam wafting over them. "Hot springs? Are you kidding me?"

Theo chuckles, walking over to the edge of the pool and sinking to his haunches as he reaches in to test the water temperature. Nodding, he withdraws his hand and stands up, lifting an eyebrow in challenge.

"How hot is it?" she asks, returning the eyebrow quirk.

"It's nice," he tells her. "Like a warm bath." He glances down at her ankle and the messy bandage. "Your ankle would appreciate it," he suggests. He steps over to her, then looks down at her face. "Will you swim with me, Sylvia?"

Sylvia bites her lip, an adorable motion that makes him want to kiss her, but he stays where he is, waiting for her reply. She narrows her eyes up at him, glances at the water, then back at him. "Do you take everyone here for your serious conversations?"

Theo shakes his head. "No," he says. "I come here when I want to be alone."

"You don't bring other girls here?" Sylvia asks.

"And explain that I'm a vampire after I fly them through the night?" he asks, smiling. "No, I don't think that would be very successful."

Sylvia frowns. "Seriously? You don't tell people you're a vampire?"

Theo raises an eyebrow. "And get staked for my confession?" He shakes his head again. "No thank you."

"Times have changed," Sylvia says. "Vampires are sexy now."

Theo chuckles. "Sure, in movies and on TV. Not in your actual life."

Sylvia shrugs. "It doesn't bother me." She pauses, a hand on her hip. "So why did you tell me?"

"Well, the fight with the demon showed you I wasn't human, if my behavior before that didn't tell you something was different about me."

"True. But why not just whammy me with your vampire magic and send me home? You said you could make me forget about the whole thing."

Theo steps away from her, pausing before he answers the question he keeps asking himself. It's foolish to tell her. There are rules, however rarely enforced, that he should obey.

But he doesn't want to.

"I want to be able to talk to you truthfully," he says finally, satisfied with the answer. "I don't want to lie or skirt the issue. I want to … be myself."

Sylvia nods. "Okay, I can understand that." Theo marvels at her ability to simply accept him as he is. The relief is intoxicating. Her gaze strays to the water again. "Anything living in there?"

Theo laughs. "Not that I know of." He smiles. "The water dragons died out centuries ago if that's what you're worried about."

"Water dragons?" Sylvia's eyes widen. "Are you messing with me?"

Theo raises an eyebrow in challenge. "Am I? Why not swim and find out?"

Sylvia sticks her bandaged ankle out in his direction. "I don't want to get this wet."

"Allow me," Theo says, kneeling before her and slowly unwrapping the ankle. Her heart rate increases at his touch, her breath faster as his hands brush her skin, but when he looks at her, she is still Sylvia watching him, not a victim lost in desire. She still sees *him*. He rolls up the bandage and sets it on the ground. Looking up at her, he smiles.

"You didn't tell me I needed a bathing suit," Sylvia says.

Theo stands, shrugging. "I never need one." Before she can reply, he tugs the shirt over his head, revealing his bare chest and the stylized dragon tattoo that runs across his back and down both arms, the mark of his people and his position in a tribe long extinct. He hears Sylvia's quick gasp and turns to face her, enjoying her expression as her eyes slide over the lines of his skin, the ridges of his muscles, the marks of his scars.

"Dragons," she whispers. "Of course." She pauses, then asks, "Is that some kind of tribal symbol?"

Theo nods. "We were the People of the Dragon," he tells her. "Some say long ago our ancestors could turn into dragons."

Sylvia purses her lips. "Impressive. I see you went with the vampire upgrade instead, though."

"Not by choice," he says. His hands slide over the marks on his forearm, and his memory shifts from Jolena's mouth on his body to the day Ivan inked him, marking his passage into manhood in the eyes of the tribe. Theo still considers that day more important to his human life than his last one alive. The tattoo had ached for days, but he had been lucky and escaped any infection. And Ivan was an artist, the lines of dark ink still clear and precise on his skin as they had been when fresh. At least this part of the man's art still survived.

"You don't have to tell me about it," Sylvia says, somehow sensing the sadness in him. Her eyes flick to the water again. "Unless … you're related to water dragons?"

Theo laughs, the sound light, and he smiles at her. "I can swim very well, Syl, if that's what you mean." He gestures at his jeans, reaching down to his boots. He pulls them off one at a time, enjoying the feel of her gaze on his skin. "I cannot swim in jeans, though," he says, sliding them down his hips and revealing black boxer briefs. He doesn't always wear underwear, but he had hoped to swim with Sylvia tonight. He may swim naked without any qualms, but she is a product of her time, and he knows she's not ready for that yet. "This is much better." Sylvia stares at him, and he knows that part of her wants him to continue, to watch him get completely naked. "Unless you'd prefer the full package?" he offers, hooking his hands in the sides of his shorts.

Sylvia turns pink, then red, as she looks down at her own clothes, no doubt wondering if he expects her to return the favor. "I…" she says, then takes a breath and stands up straight. "I think you're fine as you are."

"Am I?" He winks at her. "I find you lovely as well, Syl."

"Flirt!" she says, removing her sweater and setting it atop the rolled-up ace bandage. She frowns, then hooks her fingers in the waistband of her shorts and slides them down, revealing a pair of black panties. Her shorts join the sweater on the ground, then she stands straight, injured foot raised so she stands on the toes only, keeping the weight on her other leg. Her fingers hover around the bottom of her tank top, but then her nerve breaks. Instead of lifting it over her head, she runs past him in an awkward jogging hop, sits on the edge of the pool in one motion to get her feet wet, then slips gently into the water, elbows resting on the edge of the rock as she leans her head back. Theo wishes he could see her face, but he can only see the back of her head.

He knows the pool is deep, so he takes a riskier jump, leaping over her head and landing in the water before her. He surfaces a few feet away, powerful legs keeping his head and shoulders out of the water as he kicks, and he smooths his hair out.

Sylvia watches him for a moment, then her body shifts forward, sliding away from the edge and letting herself dip beneath the water. Her arms paddle, and she surfaces, blonde hair a wave around her face, and Theo's chest tightens at the sight, every part of him yearning to touch her. A small voice inside echoes with warnings of water sprites and dangerous women, but he ignores it, as he has for most of his life. *Just one more kiss*, he thinks. *One more taste*.

Not yet, he tells himself. *Not now.*

For now, Theo decides, he will be satisfied with this—a beautiful girl, a perfect night, and a quiet conversation.

CHAPTER 10

SYLVIA

SYLVIA TREADS WATER SLOWLY, WAITING TO SEE WHAT HER vampire companion will do. The water is warm, soothing her aching ankle and heating her skin. She enjoys the sultry slide of her wet clothing as she moves, water dripping down her face as she stares at Theo. She has gone swimming in her clothes only once before, a moonlit summer night in the ocean with an old friend, and for a moment, she sees his face instead, dark wet hair around his face and his eyes staring hard into hers. She shakes her head, freeing herself from the vision, and Theo comes into focus. His beauty pricks her heart, his face replacing the other in her mind.

The vampire swims a few feet away from her, red hair curling into ringlets around his face with the heat of the steamy water. Theo's hair has a slight wave when dry; Sylvia didn't imagine it would be quite so curly when wet. She wants to touch it, to wrap a tendril around her finger as she wraps herself around him.

"Your hair," she breathes. "It's so curly."

Theo nods, reaching up to brush it back into a smoother wave. "A gift from my mother," he tells her.

"Tell me about her?" she asks, kicking back to lean against the edge.

"Is that really what you want to talk about?" he asks, following her. He hovers a foot away, arms reaching around on both sides of her body to hold the rock wall.

"You said this was a good place for serious conversations," Sylvia says, unable to look away from his mouth.

Theo nods, eyes tracing her gaze. His tongue slips out and slowly licks his lips. Sylvia's face gets even hotter, if that's possible with the warm water already heating her skin. "And you think I brought you all the way out here to talk about my mother?"

Sylvia smirks, daring him to come closer. "Why did you bring me out here?"

Theo smiles, slipping closer to her, hands slowly moving from the wall to her shoulders. "Perhaps I thought I might take advantage of you," he whispers, face close to hers.

"It does look like I'm at your mercy," Sylvia agrees. "Or am I?" She slips beneath the water, out of his grasp, and swims across the spring, surfacing several feet away. Theo turns to face her but stays on his side of the pool, smile widening as he takes her in. "I grew up on the beach," Sylvia tells him. "I'm an excellent swimmer."

Theo nods. "I should have known. You're clearly a water nymph of some kind."

"Don't nymphs lure men to their deaths?"

Theo nods. "Some of them. But I'm willing to take my chances." He lets himself sink beneath the surface, red hair disappearing into the dark water. Sylvia scans the water but sees nothing. She lets out a squeal when Theo surfaces behind her, wrapping his arms around her and tugging her under. A moment later, he brings them both to the surface, and Sylvia spins in his embrace, body wrapping around him the way she has wanted since she met him. She hooks her legs around his back, very aware of the softer parts of her body pressing against the harder ones of his. Her hands link behind his neck, and she leans forward, kissing him while hidden under the hood of her hair. Theo returns the kiss, one hand settling on the small of her back but venturing no farther. They sink beneath the water again, mouths pressed together, and there is only the dark and silence and Theo's body pressing against hers.

They break the surface of the water together, Sylvia tearing her mouth away to gasp for air, and Theo chuckles. "Now I know you aren't a nymph," he observes.

"I can't breathe underwater," Sylvia says, coughing a little. "Wait, can you?"

Theo shrugs, moving them to the edge again and settling himself beneath her. "I can breathe, and I do, but I can go a really long time between breaths."

Sylvia nods, thinking about the ways he could use such a gift and trying not to let her thoughts show on her face, but she must be turning even more red because Theo grins at her.

"I'll show you some time," he says, winking.

Sylvia blushes even more, but her skin is pink everywhere from the warm water. She leans back, giving herself space to think, recalling the situation anew. "So," she begins, her serious voice signaling the time has come for some answers, "I have some questions." She glances around, confirming that they are alone. Theo does the same, and for a moment, he stares long and hard at the rocks to their right. Sylvia follows the line of his gaze, squinting hard to see what has caught his attention. "Now that we're alone?" she prompts. She doesn't see anything, but for a second, there is a tiny prickle of *something*. It fades immediately, and she wonders if it was even there at all.

Another moment of intense scrutiny passes, Theo still watching the wall, then he turns his attention back to her. "Now we are alone."

Sylvia nods, unwilling to explore even more weirdness than she is already preparing for. "Cool. So..."

Theo waits, face expectant. "You have questions," he says, gesturing for her to continue. "Go on."

"Well, I guess I'll start with the obvious," she says. "How did you become a vampire?"

"I was bitten by another vampire," Theo replies.

"But you bit me," she says, "and I'm not a vampire. So, what else happened?"

Theo frowns, clearly debating whether he should tell her. Sylvia feels for him, not wanting to put him in an awkward position. "Never mind," she says, waving her hand to dismiss the topic. "Can you tell me who bit you?"

Theo's frown turns into a scowl. "Her name is Jolena."

The country song echoes through Sylvia's mind despite the extra syllable: *Please don't take my man.* "Is?" she repeats. "She's still alive?"

Theo nods, sighing. "Unfortunately."

"Wait," Sylvia says, recalling her vampire lore, "so she's your … Maker? Can she command you if she wants to?"

"Unfortunately," Theo repeats.

"Where is she?"

"Far from here," Theo assures her.

"She just lets you run around as you wish?" Theo's face darkens, and Sylvia reaches out to touch his shoulder. "I'm sorry. First I start talking about your mother and now another woman. Totally uncouth." She pauses, thinking. "What do you want to tell me?"

Theo smiles, hand reaching back to cover hers on his shoulder, relief in the lines of his body. "I want to tell you everything," he says, spearing her with those eyes. "But there are some things…"

Sylvia nods, knowing that she has her own secrets she'd rather not discuss. She pauses, thinking of questions with less baggage. "How about Viking Times?" she asks. "How did that start?"

"As a joke," Theo admits with a laugh. "Harald and Oren complained of getting soft since we had stopped working out with our weapons. This was an excuse to get in some regular practice."

"So, they are also…?" Sylvia asks, recalling the two men who had moved so smoothly. "And Astrid?"

"Not Astrid," Theo tells her. "Grace, actually. She's my assistant."

"Your assistant?" Sylvia's hand slides out from under his hand. "What does she assist with?" The lovely, long-legged blonde in that fur bikini fills Sylvia's mind.

Theo chuckles, clearly reading her face. "She organizes my life during the day, schedules any meetings for after sunset."

"So… what is she? Your Renfield?" Sylvia frowns, not liking the comparison.

Theo scoffs. "Hardly." He gives Sylvia a serious look. "That's not actually a thing, you know."

"So, you don't have people serving you, hoping for a chance to be turned?" she asks, ignoring the specifics of the character for broader strokes.

Theo raises an eyebrow. "Well, when you put it like that, I suppose there are Renfields… or there have been." He smirks. "But not Grace. She is perfectly content to stay as she is."

"Well of course she would be … now. She's still young and beautiful. But give her a decade or so."

Theo shakes his head. "Grace knows what we are, and she sees the price of our existence. She wants no part of it, I assure you. And I expect her husband would have something to say about it." He narrows his eyes at her. "Do you want to be a vampire, Syl? You keep bringing this up."

Sylvia opens her mouth to speak, to tell him of course not, but then she pauses, giving the question the consideration it deserves.

Eternity, she thinks. *Immortality. Strength. No one could hurt me again.* She looks at Theo's face, the smooth skin of his cheeks distracting from the small worry lines in his forehead, no doubt forged from centuries of distress. She glances down to his neck and shoulders, suddenly distracted by all that honey skin.

She traces a finger up his arm, slipping over the deep line of scar tissue across the top of his left shoulder. He says nothing, and her finger continues its journey, hovering on the set of five raised circles on the right side of his chest, just above his nipple. Another scar runs down to disappear beneath his armpit.

"So many scars," she whispers. "So much pain." She pauses her inspection. "You were a warrior?"

Theo nods. "I was." He reaches up to grab her hand, retracing the line her finger just finished. He starts on his shoulder. "This sword nearly took my arm off." He slides to the five circles. "These are from the bolts on a shield that nearly crushed my chest." He raises an eyebrow wickedly, then slides her hand down beneath the water, pausing just above the line of his shorts. "And I have more scars in other places, should you want to feel them."

"What happened?" Sylvia breathes.

He gently moves her hand from his stomach to his thigh, her fingers facing the bottom of his shorts. "A spear," he admits, "and in such a place as to make a man thank his lucky stars he didn't move differently in the moment."

"Wow," Sylvia says with a sigh, "you took a spear to the groin and lived to talk about it?" Her hand rests on his thigh but does not move to explore farther.

Something shifts in his face, the teasing fading for an instant. "I wouldn't say I lived."

Sylvia frowns. "I'm sorry. I didn't mean to..."

"It's fine," Theo says, reassuring, and Sylvia believes him. "There are things you should know." He sniffs, then runs a hand through his damp hair, tucking it behind an ear in an endearing motion that makes Sylvia's heart speed up. "I was wounded, terribly wounded, during an ambush. Several of us were taken as prisoners." His face darkens at the memory, but he quickly continues, "We were all in a bad way. Only Oren and Harald survived the journey to the desert."

"Wait, you were taken prisoner in what ... Germany? Scandinavia?" He nods at her first guess. "I'm from Scandinavia, but we were campaigning far from home."

Sylvia nods, trying to recall her history. "I've heard of some Viking tribes," she says, "but not the Muldavians."

Theo frowns. "Yeah. Our people didn't last long after we were taken. Some were brought into other tribes, but most were killed."

"I'm sorry to hear that," Syl says, aware of how odd it is to apologize for the death of a tribe from centuries ago. "Can I ask how long ago this was?"

Theo narrows his eyes. "You certainly are persistent," he tells her with a grin. "I was born in what I think was 917 in a place near modern day Stockholm in Sweden."

"You think?" Sylvia echoes.

Theo shrugs. "My people weren't particular about years," he explains, "but looking back through history, it was likely that winter." He frowns, calculating. "My father stole my mother during the spring raids of 916, which were documented by the Byzantines."

Sylvia holds up her hand. "Wait, hold up. Did you say your father stole your mother?"

Theo grins. "Oh yes. He loved telling the story. She was on her way to be married off to some neighboring prince, and they raided the caravan and stole her away." At Sylvia's horrified expression, he adds, "She didn't love that guy. She was happy to be taken."

"If you say so," Sylvia says, grimacing. "Though it explains the Greek name." She frowns. "So, your dad must have been a big deal then, to get the girl as the prize?"

Theo narrows his eyes. "I'm sensing a lot of judgement here, Sylvia. This was a thousand years ago. The world was a different place back then."

"I believe it," Sylvia says, "but it's still crazy to think that they were your parents—not some people from ancient history."

"Ancient history is BC," Theo corrects. "I was born in the 10th century AD."

"Oh," Sylvia says mockingly, "forgive me—you're *only* a thousand freaking years old." Sticking her tongue out at him, she gestures, "Go on. Who was your dad?"

"The thane," Theo replies.

Sylvia sighs. "Of course he was. So, what—you're some Viking prince?"

"Thane," Theo says, "or I would have been, if we'd made it back."

"Why were you in Germany? Just the usual raping and pillaging?"

"I'm not a rapist, Syl," Theo snaps.

Sylvia stills. *Idiot,* she scolds herself. *A judgement of history is also a judgement of Theo's life.* "I'm sorry," she says. "I shouldn't have said that." She sighs. "I guess I'm still reeling from the kidnapped mother thing."

"You did want to talk about my mother," he reminds her. "I think she would have liked you though. She appreciated directness."

"Tell me when I cross the line from direct into rude," Sylvia says. "Apparently, I can't tell tonight." She waves her hands in the water. "Maybe it's because I'm warm."

"Do you want to get out?"

Sylvia shakes her head, hands still touching his body. She's not ready to let him go, not yet. "Tell me more about Germany."

"It was for silver, actually," Theo says, a hand reaching up to touch the leather choker around his neck. "Ironic."

Sylvia raises an eyebrow. "Why ironic?"

"I can't touch silver now," Theo admits. "It burns a vampire's skin."

Sylvia nods, filing the information for future use. *Just in case,* she tells herself. *Not for Theo, but for other vampires who may want to hurt me.*

"So, you were wounded and captured ... and taken all the way to ... where? The Middle East?" She contemplates the timing. "Constantinople? Persia?"

"Gur," he replies, "though it's in Iran now. I don't remember much of the journey there."

"But you lived?"

Theo nods. "Barely. By the time they brought me to Jolena, I was a lost cause." He looks away, sighing. "She saved me, in a way. She definitely saved my leg."

"And your friends?" Sylvia asks, remembering that he said several of them were captured.

"Harald and Oren were weak from their own wounds and the journey, but they could have lived. She changed them because she could." He pauses, exhaling hard. "Out of spite, no doubt." He looks up at Sylvia. "She'd never had three savage northmen as slaves before. She decided to keep us."

There is a long moment of silence as they both contemplate the other. "I'm sorry that happened to you," Sylvia says quietly, "but then again, I'm not."

"You're not?"

Sylvia lifts her shoulders, eyes wide. "If she hadn't changed you, we never would have met, and that would have been a loss ... for me." She bites her lip, staring into the eyes of this strange man she finds so appealing. "I'm glad to know you, Theo," she says formally.

"And I you," he replies. "I never have much cause to thank Jolena," he admits, "but I am glad to be here, now, with you."

Slowly, he leans forward, giving Sylvia time to pull away if she wants to, but instead, she moves forward into the circle of his arms, meeting his tender kiss. His mouth moves gently with hers, tongue slowly exploring new sensations as they drift in the warm water. Theo's hands slide down to hold her waist, careful not to sneak beneath her shorts and touch more sensitive skin. Sylvia twines her fingers in the hair at Theo's neck, playfully tugging the curls so they bounce back into shape when she releases them. When they part, Sylvia leans back in his embrace, wanting more but still nervous at this new connection.

"I will not trespass, Syl," Theo promises, his hands firmly on her waist and nowhere else.

Sylvia nods, appreciating his restraint while a small part of her wishes he would pounce and devour her the way she knows he wants to. But the promise means something, and she is grateful for his patience, his consideration of her feelings.

"I know," she tells him, feeling the trust growing between them. "But I need to get out of this water," she says, paddling slowly back to the wall and hopping on to the edge. She leaves her feet in the water, watching the slow curls of steam waft off her wet skin in the night air. Theo follows, sinking down next to her. He takes her hand as he sits, and they sit in companionable silence for a few moments, water dripping from their clothes.

"So, are there rules about telling people what you are?" Sylvia asks finally.

Theo grimaces. "It is ... not encouraged."

"What happens to those people who know?" Her mind fills with every vampire story she's encountered—most of them end with the human mercilessly hunted.

"Nothing will happen to you, Syl," Theo promises. "We can keep this quiet."

She nods slowly, accepting his word. "You could make me forget, though," she says. "Then you wouldn't have to bother with keeping me safe."

"Do you want to forget?" Theo doesn't look at her as he speaks, allowing her time to think it over.

Sylvia looks down at where her hand rests inside his grip. She doesn't want him to let go, doesn't want to go back to the world she knew before. The world without him in it.

Is it him, a small voice whispers, *or is it the magic?* She answers herself immediately: *Does it matter? His presence confirms that you aren't crazy, that what happened to you in that graveyard was real.*

She lifts his hand to her lips, kissing the back of his hand gently. "No," she says. "I don't want to forget."

He tugs her closer to him, kissing her hand at first, then leaning down to kiss her mouth. His skin is warm, but his clothes are starting to cool in the night air, and Sylvia shivers.

"I should bring you home," Theo says, pulling back.

Sylvia nods. "In a few," she tells him. "Before we go, I do have a random question, though."

Theo rubs his hand over her back, her shoulders, warming her with the friction. "Yes?"

"Do you eat, like, regular food?"

Theo raises an eyebrow. "I can, yes. Why?"

"Would you like to have dinner tomorrow?"

Theo smiles at her. "I would love to."

CHAPTER 11

PILKINGTON

T HE DEMON KNOWN AS MR. PILKINGTON IN THE HUMAN realm steps through the shattered remains of a wooden door, examining the room where the Balaam demon was killed. There is no body, nor evidence of the creature, but he can sense the residue of the fight that occurred here.

He steps carefully, nose twitching. He's in his human form, a nondescript male in his mid-thirties, dark hair, brown eyes, tanned skin beneath the jeans and green Henley, and while it's not his actual nose that picks up the magic in the room, his body has decided that is how it will show his search. Mr. Pilkington doesn't mind. A man casually sniffing is much less notable than a man with glowing hands or red eyes. His human form may be physically weaker than his true self, but it has its perks.

Maybe if this goes well, I can see her, he tells himself. *She's been lonely since breaking up with Adam.* Mr.

Pilkington can't help the smirk that crosses his face. His arusha finally came to the senses he credited her with.

She's not my arusha. She's my...

Frowning, Mr. Pilkington recreates the scene: the demon at the foot of the stairs, a minor scuffle, then dispatched by the vampire.

But what were they after? Was the vampire after the demon, or was the demon after something else?

Mr. Pilkington slowly ascends the stairs, an odd familiar sensation creeping up the back of his neck. He thinks of Sylvia again, the girl never far from his thoughts when he visits the human realm, but he is surprised to think of her now that he is investigating the scene. He reaches the top, then kneels, a hand brushing along the floor. He leans closer, eye spying a single strand of long blonde hair. Mr. Pilkington picks it up reluctantly, not wanting to admit what it means.

How is this possible?

The scent of blood captures his attention next, and he moves down the hall and examines the hole in the floor, the edges smeared in dark blood.

Human blood.

Familiar blood.

Blood he had smelled years before as it spilled over his hands, escaping a nearly mortal wound in the stomach of his arusha.

She's not my arusha, he reminds himself. *She's my... Sylvia.*

Mr. Pilkington scans the floor below but knows he will find no evidence down there. The vampire must have snatched Sylvia back before she fell through the floor.

So he wasn't pursuing her to kill her, then, or if he was, he wanted to drag it out. Mr. Pilkington glances around but finds no other traces of his human woman. *A vampire wouldn't take the victim back outside for all to see if he just wanted to feed*, he assures himself. *He certainly didn't feed on her here, though this is the perfect place.*

He took her somewhere.

Mr. Pilkington stands up, ignoring the racing pulse in his neck at the thought that something happened to his arusha.

She's alive, he assures himself. *If something permanent had happened, you would know. You would feel it.*

Would I? The question is quiet, and he ignores it as he backtracks down the hall, focusing on the scent of the vampire.

Of course you would. She's your arusha.

She's not... But he lets the thought trail off, satisfied that whatever happened here the night before, his Sylvia is in no danger now.

He knows that because the very first thing he did when he arrived was to check on her. He spied her through the window, sprawled on her bed eating Chinese food. He hadn't stayed long, just a few moments to see her smile as she took a bite of her rice. He tries to remember the details—she had been sitting in bed under a blanket, so he wouldn't have seen any cuts on her legs from this fall.

And if a vampire did take her away last night, clearly it wasn't for any ill intent, or she wouldn't have been home at all.

Mr. Pilkington frowns, focusing on the vampire again. He pushes a little bit harder than he normally would during an investigation, isolating the creature's path and highlighting it with his magic. The trail heads down the stairs and outside, but then doubles, as if he returned at some point, came up the stairs, then left again. Mr. Pilkington studies the landing again, making out an impression in the dust, a clean smooch that could be the mark of a bag on the ground.

So, Sylvia runs here, probably running from the demon, hides up here, leaves her bag when she runs again, nearly falls through the floor, then is taken away.

Mr. Pilkington heads down the stairs, following the vampire trail, but his mind is already racing.

What would a Balaam demon want with my Sylvia?

Mr. Pilkington leans casually against the building, waiting for the vampire to emerge from the basement where he keeps his coffin. It's easy to blend in. He keeps his phone out, appearing to scroll aimlessly so no one passing by gives him a second glance. One of his demonic powers allows him to blend into the background, but even with that, occasionally someone will see him, sensing his power. If it's a supernatural creature, they often hurry away, knowing better than to tangle with an unknown demon, but every now and then a human gives him a double take, a hidden gift alerting them to danger. Mr. Pilkington always scowls at these, not wanting them to get any ideas about approaching him. He is no mentor, no trainer, no master in need of lackeys.

He works alone.

It's easier. He doesn't have to hide if there is no one there to hide from. In his younger years, he would seek out the occasional human companion, but it has been a long time since anyone even remotely caught his interest.

Except her, a small voice whispers. Mr. Pilkington ignores it, deliberately blanking his mind of the blonde-haired woman who appears there.

The thought fades as Mr. Pilkington spots the redheaded vampire emerging from the building. Mr. Pilkington has learned it's not the same one in which he keeps his apartment. It has been a long day of investigation, starting at the building where the Balaam demon was slaughtered, tracking the scent of the vampire back to his apartment. He followed the trail to Sylvia's apartment, peering through the window once more to assure himself that she was well, but he left quickly.

Does Sylvia realize her rescuer is a vampire? She wouldn't have anything to do with him if she did, Mr. Pilkington assures himself. *Not after what happened in that grave-yard. She wouldn't have anything to do with any creatures— and certainly not any demons.*

She deserves more.

The mantra is familiar, almost habit after all this time. *You let her go,* he reminds himself, *so she could live a normal life.*

I didn't let her go so she could get involved with vampires.

And not just any vampire, Mr. Pilkington has learned. The Muldavian—a vampire with a long and bloody history of violence, though largely a result of the bidding of his mistress, the Lady Jolena.

Mr. Pilkington avoids vampire politics as eagerly as he avoids demonic intrigue, but this Balaam demon has him right in the middle of both. He recalls his purpose—find out what happened to the demon, track the vampire.

And finding out about the demon includes finding out why it is here at all. Mr. Pilkington hasn't made much headway in that direction—only discovering that it had been summoned two days prior in an old circle in an abandoned train station on the edge of town. The summoner hid the trail too well for him to follow, not uncommon practice for those who dealt in demons. There aren't many unbound demons roaming the city, but summoners learned to be careful just in case. And Mr. Pilkington isn't exactly unbound—the geas has grown tighter all day long, the spell demanding answers.

Tracking the Muldavian back to his coffin had been easy enough. The faintest scent of blood lingered about the vampire, Sylvia's blood, and Pilkington settled down for a long afternoon, waiting for sunset when the vampire would emerge.

Be subtle, he reminds himself. *Blend in. Follow him and find out what's going on. Do not engage with him.*

I can't imagine the Muldavian having any dealings with summoners. But the world changes, and I have seen stranger things.

Mr. Pilkington joins the throng of milling walkers, staying far behind the vampire but tracking him all the same. The Muldavian doesn't linger, walking fast through the crowd a few blocks and walking through the entrance of an upscale apartment building. Mr.

Pilkington doesn't follow, knowing that the vampire's apartment is on the top floor.

"Damn," Pilkington curses quietly, settling back to wait on the street, scanning the sky for the vampire's appearance.

So, he left his coffin and headed here to—what? Take a shower and get dressed? Make himself more presentable for Sylvia, he realizes. Mr. Pilkington is no stranger to desire, his own included, and he knows what this means. The vampire is courting his human. Mr. Pilkington understands jealousy, has seen his share of it in humans, but his own demonic nature doesn't quite allow for the emotion. He can comprehend the desire to be with someone who is with another, though, and he can only hope that the Muldavian's intentions are honorable. Nothing he has heard about the vampire suggests he is deceptive or duplicitous—only deadly. So long as he means Sylvia no harm, his arusha will be well protected.

A few moments later, Mr. Pilkington watches the vampire shoot skyward. He follows reluctantly, hating to fly—mostly because he can't actually fly without his wings.

He can levitate, so he does that immediately, rising directly above the street in time to see the vampire fly over the next few buildings, heading somewhere in a hurry.

Mr. Pilkington conjures a small breeze, just enough to push him in the same direction, though his body moves awkwardly. Slowly, he follows the vampire, not wanting to admit that he knows exactly where he is going.

Mr. Pilkington lowers himself onto a nearby building, looking down to where Sylvia sits on her fire escape. The Muldavian looms before her, speaking quietly. Mr. Pilkington focuses, picking up the words. His gaze traces Sylvia's body as he listens, noting the bandage on her foot, the healed cuts on her legs. When he hears the Muldavian speak of sharing his blood, a harsh buzzing starts in the back of Mr. Pilkington's head, but he stays where he is, the restraints of the geas combining with centuries of patience. He knows Sylvia isn't afraid—she wants to be near the vampire.

When the Muldavian steps forward, Mr. Pilkington moves despite himself, forcing past the restrictions on him, but he pauses on the fire escape of the neighboring building when he sees that the vampire hasn't moved beyond the one step.

He is giving Sylvia space, and his words seem genuine. His body language is hopeful, curious, but Mr. Pilkington can sense the desire pouring off him. He wants Sylvia, and seeing the way she responds to the vampire, Mr. Pilkington knows what his arusha wants.

The demon doesn't move when the vampire reaches out to her, and when Sylvia takes his hand, Mr. Pilkington watches them fly away.

He tells himself that he doesn't need to follow them, that he understands what has happened. Clearly, the vampire was protecting Sylvia. Mr. Pilkington has spent the afternoon thinking about it, and there is only one man who would send a demon after his arusha. Mr. Pilkington can begin hunting him right away.

But Sylvia has just been taken to a private place with a vampire, the Muldavian—*of all vampires to focus on his arusha!* He just has to be sure she's alright.

He follows at a distance, lingering long enough to see them get in the water, for Sylvia to lose herself in her desire for the vampire. Mr. Pilkington stays until she asks if they are alone. The Muldavian's gaze cuts to the rocks the demon hides behind, and he knows it is time to leave. Satisfied that she will be safe, though her virtue is certainly in peril, Mr. Pilkington backs away.

He isn't jealous. He knows that emotion well. Sylvia may be his arusha, but she is a woman now, free to make her own choices, and Mr. Pilkington can think of few others he would find worthy of her affections. He walked away from her years ago, freeing her to learn about the world on her own. He can sense that still she is virginal, but judging by the display in the water, he can't imagine that will last much longer.

The Muldavian is a fierce warrior, a fine protector, and Mr. Pilkington knows the man desires her.

Now, if he breaks her heart, we may have words. Until then, I trust her.

Deciding to start searching carefully for Charlie Wagner, the old summoner who escaped so many years ago, Mr. Pilkington slips back to the city.

Before he begins his search in earnest, he stops at Sylvia's apartment. Standing on her fire escape, he pulls the compass from his pocket. *I wonder what it would have felt like to put this around her neck.* Sighing, he sets it on the windowsill where she will see it.

I hope she puts it on, he thinks, *this small token of my affection. But it's her choice.*

Mr. Pilkington trusts his arusha to find the right direction.

CHAPTER 12

SYLVIA

THE NEXT EVENING FINDS SYLVIA IN HER APARTMENT, standing in front of the full-length mirror on the bathroom door, turning her body this way and that. Her ankle has mostly recovered, Theo's blood working wonders on her healing speed, and she stands easily enough, holding up first one sweater, then another as she contemplates her options. Sighing in disgust, she throws both choices down on the bed, picking up another instead. Most of her wardrobe is laid out on the bed, and Sylvia is painfully aware of just how few items of clothing she owns.

Her job at the diner had a uniform, a small dress that she reminds herself to return one of these days, now that she no longer has a job there, and she wore that most of the time. Her indoor wardrobe is mostly sleep shorts and tank tops, and she has five long flowy skirts. Looking at them now, she can recall the moment she bought each one—the beach with Miriam the summer she returned home for a visit, the trip to Vegas when she graduated high school, the small thrift shop around the corner that supplies most of her sweater needs, the store with her mother so many years ago that she really should retire the skirt, and that one time Phil had taken her shopping in the small shops along the boardwalk. She stares at the last one for a long moment, recalling the wind in her hair, the way he looked at her that summer, and she bites her lip, Phil's handsome youthful face slowly replaced by the daredevil gleam in Theo's eye when he leans down to kiss her. She pushes the skirts aside, knowing that none of them are suited for dinner with Theo.

What was I thinking to invite a clearly wealthy vampire out to eat? I should have just offered to order Chinese food for us to eat on my bed.

The image conjures another, and she imagines the small containers piled on the milk crate that serves as her nightstand, food forgotten as they kiss even longer, sliding down into her bed.

You know you just want to make out with him again, she tells herself. *Dinner is absolutely a ruse.*

She frowns. *Well, no one will want to make out with me if I wear any of my normal clothes.*

This is Theo, she reminds herself. *It needs to be something special.*

She turns back to her wardrobe, staring at the few hangers that remain inside. She slides her winter coat aside, along with her raincoat, peering behind them to see what may be hidden in the back. She spies a plastic bag over a dress, and she yanks it out, heart fluttering in excitement.

Yes! The dress for Amanda's wedding! She pulls the plastic off the hanger, revealing a dark blue sleeveless dress with small embroidery on the bodice. She'd never worn the thing, not after Amanda decided to call off the whole wedding and run off with that guy from medical school. Poor Jeremy had been devastated, and Sylvia held onto the dress, a small part of her sure that Amanda would change her mind as soon as she realized what a huge mistake she had made.

The dress has hung in the back of her wardrobe for nearly a year now, and while Sylvia still talks to Jeremy occasionally, Amanda has completely ghosted her. Sometimes she will joke that she got Jeremy in the divorce—and the useless dress.

She slips it over her head, glad that Amanda, for all her flaws and poor choices, had some sense in her choice of bridesmaid dresses. The dress falls perfectly around her slim form, the tight bodice accentuating her small breasts while the sheer layers of the bottom flare slightly around her hips to the floor. It's a nice dress—elegant even—without screaming wedding dress.

Sylvia nods, twisting her hair this way and that as she stands in front of the mirror.

Yes.

Her fingers caress the small compass hanging from her neck. She's fairly certain that Theo left it for her, the small circle resting on her the windowsill, the silver glimmering in the morning sun. It doesn't quite fit with the dress, but she doesn't want to take it off.

Now I just have to figure out what shoes to wear. The thought is ridiculous—she only owns a pair of simple black sandals, a pair of sneakers, and her comfortable boots. The sandals will have to suffice.

Sylvia glances out the window at the darkening sky, considering the temperature. She turns back to the wardrobe, remembering that the dress had a shawl that matched it, but it's not on the hanger. A quick search on the wardrobe's floor and surrounding clothes finds the shawl half hanging on another summer dress, and she tugs it free, shaking it out. Luckily, the material hasn't wrinkled, and she wraps it around her shoulders, loving the combination of fabrics against her skin. With a smile, she begins gathering up the rest of her clothes and jamming them back in the wardrobe. After wedging the door shut, she clears the bed, smoothing the blanket and straightening the pillow, wanting it to look inviting if they decide to come back here after the meal. Her chair still has some clothes on it, but she tosses a throw pillow on top of the small pile, unwilling to put those away. That chair's purpose in her apartment is to hold clothes she can still wear—a messy habit even Theo couldn't force her to change so easily. She turns back to the mirror, lifting her hair up into a bun, when there is a sound at her apartment door.

"Theo?" she asks, surprised to find her vampire approaching the traditional way. She expects him on the fire escape as he has met her the night before, but she smiles, letting her hair fall back to her shoulders.

She glances at the clock: 7:52. *Theo is early.*

She moves to the door, running her hands down her sides to make sure the dress is in place. She is standing in front of it, hand reaching out to the doorknob, when she hears a key scratching in the lock, and the door pops open, pushing in and nearly smacking her in the face. She steps back quickly, not quite understanding what is happening, but when she looks up to see her ex-boyfriend Adam standing on the doormat, a small bronze key in his fingers and that awful grin on his lips, it all makes sense. Sylvia moves forward, blocking his entrance into the apartment.

Adam moves faster, darting inside before she can close the gap, and Sylvia whirls to face him.

"Adam!" she cries, taking in the warning signs: the unbuttoned top of his shirt, the wrinkles in his pants from a long day of abuse, the soft haze clouding his vision. "What the fuck?"

"Yes, Sylvie," Adam drawls, her name stretching out on his lips, "exactly." He holds both of his hands out, gesturing around at her apartment before pointing at her. "What the fuck?"

"You need to leave," she says firmly, not wanting to fight with a drunk Adam. Their breakup hadn't been particularly ugly, but Sylvia knows how he can get when he drinks (part of the reason for the breakup—though not the only one). She did not know he still had a key to her apartment. She'd given him one back when they were together, when he would drop by her place on his lunch breaks on her days off, since his office was only around the corner from her, but he'd returned it when she'd told him they were through.

He hadn't even been angry about it. That Adam had been calm and understanding, agreeing with her when she explained just how they were too different and wanted different things. He'd accepted her words and left quietly enough.

Staring at him now, she remembers what he always wanted—and what she'd never been willing to give him.

"Leave?" he echoes incredulously. Then, he gives a sharp nod, as if remembering something. "Yes," he says. "Leave—and you're coming with me."

"No," Sylvia tells him, voice firm but quiet, not wanting to encourage his behavior, not wanting to anger him. She glances at the clock: 7:53. Theo will be here soon enough. Sylvia wants Adam long gone before her vampire arrives.

She knows Theo will not react well to having her drunk ex-boyfriend in her apartment shouting nonsense at her.

"I'm not leaving with you," she tells Adam, stepping aside so the doorway is clear. "You need to go." When Adam makes no attempt to obey, she adds, "Now."

Her ex stands there for a moment, weaving drunkenly, but then something shifts in his face, his seemingly vacant expression darkening into something sinister. Sylvia takes an involuntary step back, biting her lip as her heart begins to pound. "No," he whispers, echoing her word back to her in a hiss. "No?" He glances around at the apartment, noticing the made bed, the semi-tidy floor, then looks back at her, gaze sliding up the dress she wears. "Who you waiting for, Sylvie?" he slurs, eyes narrowing. "Who you dressed up for?"

"You need to leave," Sylvia repeats, but her voice is small as the warning in her mind turns into panic. She's been cornered before, and while logically, she knows that she has options—the open window is right behind her—her body has frozen.

"I don't think so," Adam murmurs, moving toward her. Sylvia stands petrified, watching as her ex casually closes the door and leans against it, fingers spinning the lock behind him. "I think we need a moment here, give us some time just for ourselves."

"What do you want?" The question comes out without her permission, her voice a tiny, frightened thing, and she knows immediately that it is the wrong thing to say to him.

He smiles, and though she remembers finding him attractive once, cute and even endearing, the look only freezes her blood, panic skittering up her back. "You know what I want, Sylvie," he says quietly, "what I've always wanted." He steps toward her, and though she wants to move back, she doesn't, letting him close the distance between them. "You never dressed up like this for me, Sylvie." He looks away, gaze searching the window for a moment before returning to her. *What is he looking for out there?* "I'm supposed to bring you back as is," he whispers. "Intact." He steps closer again, and now she can feel his breath on her face, the sharp tang of liquor potent. Her brain scrambles to understand his words. *Who wants him to bring me back to them—as is? What does that even mean?*

Her heart speeds up even more as a possibility creeps into her mind, and for a moment, she is back in that cemetery, tied to the altar she'd thought would be her deathbed. She knows Adam isn't a witch or anything like whatever Charlie Wagner had been, but he's talking like one of them.

"So lovely," Adam whispers, raising a hand to stroke her cheek. The touch breaks Sylvia's paralysis, and she bolts away, careening farther into the apartment and sliding to a halt in front of the kitchen sink. She spins, facing Adam across the small kitchen table. Her apartment isn't big enough for this game. There is nowhere to run. He blocks the front door to the hallway. Her only other option is the fire escape, but she doesn't have enough time to lower the ladder and escape. She could run up the stairs there, but every movie she's ever seen tells her that's a terrible idea.

Not much choice, she tells herself, watching Adam for the moment he decides to move. She decides she won't wait, hoping that her dive for the window will be unexpected enough to give her enough time. She leaps sideways, throwing her body at the opening.

Her hands reach the frame, and she begins pulling herself up, but then something grabs her hair and jerks her back into the room. Her neck makes an awful sound that echoes inside her head, and she lands hard on her back. When she regains herself enough to see, Adam is standing over her, the window shut behind him.

"Don't run from me, Sylvie. There's nowhere to go," he says, kneeling down between her splayed legs. Sylvia's body is slow to respond, the jerk to her neck and the hard landing on the floor dazzling her wits, so she lays there as he comes closer, wedging his knees between her legs. She manages to struggle when his hands run along her thighs, pushing up the dress as he goes. Her hands fly uselessly against his chest, her limbs still not quite obeying her commands. Sylvia becomes aware of small whining sounds, and she only realizes they are coming from her when Adam shushes her. His hands continue their slow progress up, the dress piling near her waist.

"No one will save you, Sylvie," he says. "No one will ever want you but me." He pauses, then meets her eyes, some of the alcohol haze fading as he stares at her. "Not after what he did to you."

Sylvia's mouth falls open, trying to figure out what Adam means.

How does he know what Charlie did to me?

"I need to see it."

Her hands go to her waist, pushing the dress back down, frantically trying to cover the skin of her stomach before Adam sees the scar. For all the time they had been together, she was always very careful to never let him see her scar, not wanting to answer the questions that came with it. She never imagined he would say such things to her about it.

A small distracted part of her is very happy that she never gave in to Adam, never gave him what he wanted from her. *He doesn't deserve any part of me,* she tells herself, *not then and certainly not now.*

"Let me see," he croons, hands pushing the dress back up again. "I'll tear this dress right off you," he snarls as she begins fighting back in earnest, her body recovering from the blow to her head.

"You will not!" she screams, suddenly putting all her weight and energy into getting away from him. Adam seems surprised by her renewed vigor and presses himself down harder on top of her. Sylvia manages to catch a foot against his knee and slides herself out from beneath him, closer to the kitchen table. She grabs the leg, but Adam yanks her back, and the table jerks hard behind her, the movement knocking one of the chairs over. Sylvia uses the distraction to roll over onto her stomach, determined not to let him see her belly. She begins crawling away from him again, but Adam uses the new angle to grab her hair again, jerking her back and up, her body pressed against his chest. His free hand continues sliding her skirt up around her waist.

It occurs to Sylvia that Adam may want more than just to see her scar, and the idea of him forcing himself on her adds new strength to her fight. She pushes forward again, ignoring the scream of her scalp as Adam's grip pulls out several hairs. She makes it a few feet away, but then Adam is snatching at her feet. She is pulled back under him again, her skin making an awful sound as she slides across the floor. The burning follows a moment later, but Sylvia ignores it, rolling onto her back again, determined to claw his eyes if he doesn't get off her.

She is fighting him, determined, but a small part of her knows that it's pointless. Her struggles feel just like that day in the cemetery when all the fighting in the world didn't matter, and she was just as helpless then as she is now. He's bigger and stronger and eventually, he will win.

Fuck that, another voice, a stronger voice says, and instead of randomly flailing, Sylvia decides to take a more specific approach. She glances around quickly, taking stock of anything she can use as a weapon, eyes settling on the table leg as the only thing available. She latches onto it and yanks hard, tugging it closer to her body. She's not sure what she plans to do with the table itself, but she's pretty sure there is at least one half-empty glass of water sitting on it—her habit of leaving glasses everywhere finally useful. She yanks again, pulling Adam closer with her other hand. He allows himself to be pulled, not understanding her plan, and Sylvia's timing is perfect, the glass beer stein sliding off the edge to slam on the back of his head with a dull thump. She watches his eyes widen at the blow, jaw sagging in confusion, and she releases the table leg just in time to snatch the heavy mug before it rolls over and into her face. Her hands are sweaty, panic driving her movement, but she manages to swing the glass at the side of his face, the solid mug connecting with a satisfying crunch. Blood sprays from the corner of his mouth and nose, spattering Sylvia's cheek, and she scoots up and away from him, body underneath the table now. She kicks him again for good measure as she gets clear before scooting to the other side of the table, sitting up to defend herself again.

A loud crash distracts her, and a blur of motion streaks from her now open door to where Adam lays on her floor. When Sylvia can focus again, six feet of furious vampire has Adam pinned to the wall next to her window, her ex's feet drumming frantically as he tries to escape Theo's grip.

"The lady said no," Theo snarls, smacking Adam's head against the wall with each word.

"Theo!" Sylvia exclaims, finding her feet and staggering across the room. "Put him down!" The vampire ignores her, continuing to bang Adam's head against the wall. A halo of blood circles the spot around Adam's hair, and Sylvia grabs Theo's arm, fingers wrapping around muscles like iron. "Let him go!"

Theo turns to her slowly, but his face is distant, more monster than human. His body glows, his eyes a thin ring of honey. "He must die," he says, voice thickly accented.

"No," she insists. "You cannot kill a man in my living room!" She bites her lip, frantically trying to think of how to reach him. "I said no," she implores, "and it is no different when I tell him the same."

Theo's face clears at her words, and he blinks at her, some of the man she knows resurfacing in those dangerous eyes. "But..." The word trails off as he stares at her in confusion.

"Put him down, Theo," Sylvia whispers. "Let him go." Adam's feet are barely twitching when Theo obeys, and the man sways dangerously as he draws a ragged breath. Sylvia glances at the wall, seeing that some of the blood there is a result of her hitting him with the mug, relieved that Adam's skull is still in one piece. Her ex staggers a few steps before propping himself up by holding the table. Theo takes Sylvia's arm and gently moves her behind him, putting his body between her and the threat. The vampire is eerily still, no doubt still watching Adam for any sign of aggression.

When Adam can stand on his own again, he glares at them both through bloodshot eyes and a bloody face. His blond hair is stained red, but he seems like he will live.

"Get out," Sylvia says, stepping out from behind Theo. She doesn't bother demanding his key. A quick glance across the room shows the door hanging askew in the frame. New locks are the least of her worries.

Adam looks as if he's about to speak, to say something that will get himself killed, but Theo cuts him off. "If I see you again," the vampire says in a quiet voice like death, "I will kill you. Make no mistake." He looks at Sylvia, then back at Adam, who has started to slink toward the open doorway. "You are only alive now because she wills it."

Adam makes a noise in the back of his throat, something that probably wanted to be a scoffing jeer, but all that comes out is a small wheeze. Theo's eyes darken dangerously, then Adam is running awkwardly out of the room. His body weaves as he moves, but Sylvia can hear his uneven tread on the stairs in the hallway, then he is gone.

She stands for a moment, just breathing, then her heart begins pounding frantically and she slides to her knees. Theo catches her as she collapses, sinking to the floor with her in his arms, and they sit there for a long moment as Sylvia falls to pieces in the safe circle of his arms.

CHAPTER 13

THEO

THEO WAKES EARLY THAT EVENING, COUNTING THE MIN-
utes until sunset releases him from his coffin. He
tries to make the time pass faster with a few games
on his phone but killing zombies doesn't bring him the
usual joy and the minutes drag on. When he feels the
last of the sun set in his bones, he flings the lid of his
coffin wide, hurrying to the apartment for his evening
routine. He debates a few moments over what to wear,
knowing that Sylvia mentioned dinner, but he isn't
sure what she has in mind.

He frowns at the three options laid across the bed in
the apartment's bedroom, deciding that the suit is too
formal, and the collared shirt is too casual. He settles
for the black pants and light blue button-down shirt,
tugging on a belt just in case they go somewhere nicer—
he can tuck in his shirt. He ties his hair back with a
simple hairband, tucking his necklaces beneath the
shirt collar, transforming from barely tamed savage

to a moderately respectable upper middle class modern man. He looks down at himself, wishing again that he could see his reflection, to check his appearance before going to see her. Sliding his hands down his sides to smooth the shirt, he heads for the door, deciding to take the traditional way down to the lobby, letting himself be seen leaving just in case they decide to come back here after dinner.

He doesn't spend a lot of time at the apartment beyond dressing each day, but he's not ready to show Sylvia where he keeps his coffin. *Will I ever be ready to trust her that much?*

It's about more than trust, he thinks, walking swiftly down the streets to her apartment, checking his watch to make sure he won't arrive too early and surprise her. Others would use Sylvia to get to him, if they could. Sharing his daytime resting place could get her tortured for the information, should certain people find out about his relationship with her.

Relationship, he thinks, toying with the word in his mind. *Is that what this is? A few kisses in a hot spring and now suddenly I'm in a relationship?*

He frowns, but the idea doesn't displease him the way he thought it would with anyone else. *It's just dinner*, he reminds himself. *Yes, dinner with Sylvia. No pressure.*

Maybe a few kisses tonight. Maybe more.

Maybe she'll let you bite her again, a small voice whispers, and Theo ignores it. *No, this all started because of the demon attack.* He reminds himself to find out more about why demons would be hunting her.

You will ask her tonight, he tells himself, *before getting distracted by her mouth.* He buys a bouquet of roses from

a vendor on the corner, just a small bundle of flowers—
nothing too extravagant—but he is imagining her face
as she brings the buds to her nose, the way her skin will
flush as she breathes in the scent.

He enters the door of her building a few minutes
later, senses expanding to take in the surroundings as
he pauses on the bottom step. The street door has a
lock with a buzzer, but it is broken, the door resting
against the hinges. Theo checks his watch: 7:53. He
is early.

Maybe I should walk around the block once, he thinks.
I don't want to intrude—

A muffled thud interrupts his thought, the sound
coming from Sylvia's apartment, then Theo is flying
up the stairs, barreling through the door, and snatching
an intruder by the neck.

Death, he thinks, lifting the man up and pressing
him against the wall. "The lady said no," he snarls,
smacking the man's head against the wall for emphasis.
He doesn't press hard enough to kill, though it would
be easy enough. By the blood spatter, Sylvia must
have already hit him on the head and face with something heavy. *Control yourself,* he thinks. *Don't let him die
too quickly.*

"No!" Sylvia shrieks. "Put him down!" Theo isn't
sure he heard her correctly, sure she must have said
something else. Then her small hand is touching his
arm. "Let him go," she says, voice quiet but determined.

Theo turns to look down at her, not releasing the
man but trying to understand what she means. "He
must die," he says, his accent clear as his control
threatens to break. The blood in the room has his
senses on high alert—the dead man's blood combined

145

with the pounding of Sylvia's heart is enough to make him lose himself completely.

"No," Sylvia says, "You cannot kill a man in my living room!" and this time her voice is indignant, her pulse slowing. She bites her lip, and he stares at it, transfixed, remembering the taste of her mouth, the touch of her lips on his, the man in his grip nearly forgotten. "I said no," she whispers, "and it is no different when I tell him the same."

Her words hit hard, and his grip on the neck loosens. *Does she really think I am like this man?* "But..." He lets the word trail off, focusing on regaining control of himself. It would be so easy to let go, to kill this intruder and take his Sylvia for his own.

Take her?

Theo stops, the thought enough to break him free from the rage coloring his vision.

"Put him down, Theo. Let him go." Theo obeys, letting the man slide down the wall to regain shaky feet. The intruder takes a hacking breath before he staggers across the room. He pauses at the table, using it to keep himself upright as he catches his breath, then he glares at them both. Theo grabs Sylvia, sliding her behind him with the grace of a warrior protecting his family, determined to defend her should the man attack again.

"Get out," Sylvia says, stepping out from behind Theo, and he lets her go, trusting her to judge the situation. The man moves as if to speak, but Theo cuts him off, knowing that the man will be unable to do more than croak for a day or so. "If I see you again, I will kill you. Make no mistake. You are only alive now because she wills it." The man hesitates for a moment, then he darts out of the room, footsteps echoing down the stairs. Theo knows he can follow the man's scent, track him to wherever he tries to hide. He contemplates killing him later on—there was a time when there would not have been the slightest hesitation—but Sylvia's words echo in his mind.

He turns to her, waiting for her reaction. Her heart has picked up again, delayed adrenaline to the attack, and her hands have started to tremble. The heavy glass beer stein she holds in her hand falls free, thudding on the floor and rolling over to rest against the handle, and her knees give out a moment later. Theo catches her easily, sinking to the floor and gathering her close in his arms. She is silent for a moment, heart rate increasing to an erratic pace, then she begins shuddering, small hiccupping sounds leading to quiet sobs, and she buries her face in his shoulder.

Theo is silent, unmoving, allowing her to come apart in his arms, offering comfort but not requiring anything more of her. After a long moment, her sobs quiet, and her heart slows, her breathing returning to normal. She turns in his arms, her head on his shoulder, her mouth close to his neck. He can feel the warm brush of her breath against his skin.

His hands resist the urge to hold her tighter, to pull her closer, letting her come to him on her own terms. The soft fabric of her dress is nice against his hands, the warmth of her skin emanating through the dress. She moves, and his hands caress bare skin for a moment. Sylvia looks down, noticing that the dress has been torn up the side. She sighs but doesn't reach to close the gap or remove his hand.

"I'm sorry," she says finally.

Theo chuckles, the sound escaping before he can contain it. "Whatever for, Syl?"

"I just freaked out on you there. Sorry." She sits up, looking at him.

"You were just attacked. You should freak out. That is the appropriate response to the situation."

"I just can't believe he would..." Her voice trails off as she stares at the broken door, still leaning on its hinges. The hallway beyond is empty, but anyone walking up the stairs would see right inside her apartment.

"Who was he?" Theo asks softly, not letting any of his simmering rage show in his voice.

"Adam," she replies. "My ex. I didn't think he still had a key."

Theo nods, not wanting to think about another man having a key to Sylvia's apartment. "I see. And he came here because?"

Sylvia shakes her head. "I'm not sure." She shivers, eyebrows furrowing. "He said he wanted me to go with him." She frowns. "As is," she repeats slowly. "Intact." She shakes her head again. "I have no idea what he was talking about."

Theo cocks his head. "As is?" he echoes. "He said that?"

"He also seemed to know about my—" Sylvia breaks off abruptly, glancing down at her belly, hands smoothing the wrinkled dress over her stomach as she sits up straighter. Theo notes how she seems unconcerned about his hand on the bare skin of her thigh but very focused on keeping her middle covered. He remembers the scar he spied on that first night and assumes she is hiding that. But what else went with the scar? *Who hurt her?* He can hear her heart speeding up again, nerves spiraling out of control.

"Sylvia," Theo whispers, gently, raising a hand to her chin. "Take a moment to settle yourself." He surveys the apartment, eyes settling on the bathroom door. "Take a bath," he suggests. "You'll feel better once you've had some privacy."

"A bath," she repeats. "That would be nice."

Theo moves slowly, lifting her to her feet and standing with her. "Go," he murmurs. "I will take care of everything."

"Are you sure?" she asks, eyes scanning the mess in the apartment—the fallen chair, the abandoned mug, the shattered door. Several roses litter the floor in front of the door, evidence of Theo's manners.

He nods. "I'm sure. Take your time. I will make dinner and sort this out."

"Thank you," she says, taking a step toward the bathroom. "Seriously, Theo. Thank you."

Theo nods, mind whirling at the next steps. He watches her walk across the apartment to the bathroom door. "Syl?"

She turns to face him, hands on the bathroom doorknob behind her. "Yeah?"

"I have some questions for you. When you're ready."

Sylvia nods. "Okay." She takes a breath, releasing it slowly. "And you'll be here when I get out?"

"Of course," he assures her. "I'm not going anywhere."

CHAPTER 14

SYLVIA

SYLVIA TAKES HER TIME, ENJOYING THE FEEL OF THE WARM water soaking into her bones soothing her frayed nerves. Her thighs burned when she first got in, the skin raw from where she was dragged across the floor, but it has calmed now. She washes her hair slowly, standing up and using the shower to rinse herself before stepping out of the bathtub onto the small blue bathmat. She drips for a long moment, realizing that while her ruined dress is hooked over the bathroom doorknob, she didn't bring any clothes inside the bathroom to wear. She dries off slowly, contemplating her options: she can wear the towel into her room to retrieve clothing, or she can slip on her satin robe, the one abandoned on the hook behind the door, and walk out to face Theo's questions. She saw his expression when she mentioned Adam's key, and she knows that an awkward conversation is coming, but maybe it won't be so bad if she is wearing a silky robe.

I can distract him by opening my legs a little bit, she thinks with a smirk, *if the questions get too weird.*

But he might see your scar, a small voice whispers, and the smile fades. She glances at her reflection in the mirror, the jagged edges of the scar running across her stomach and around her side. She is lucky to still have all her major organs fully functional. The doctors said her survival was miraculous, with the nurses joking about magic before she was released from the hospital.

"You have someone looking out for you," the doctor told her when she left that day.

She traces a finger along the skin, marveling as always at the way sensation disappeared on top of the red scar tissue, only pressure remaining. *What would Theo say if he saw it? Would I mind if he did?*

I want him to see me, she admits. *All of me.*

I want him.

The thought is shocking in its simplicity, and she quickly finishes drying off and brushing her hair. She brushes her teeth again, just because she can, then slides on the robe, tying the belt at her waist. She takes a breath before opening the door, very aware of how much of her legs are exposed. The robe ends at mid-thigh. *Then again,* she tells herself, *it's not shorter than what I went swimming in last night.*

Steeling herself, she opens the door into her apartment. A waft of cheesy goodness hits her nose, and she turns to find Theo standing at her kitchen sink, his back to her as he washes a few dishes. The light inside her oven is on, so the smell must be coming from whatever he is cooking. She turns to her left, noting that in addition to making dinner, Theo has fixed her door. New hinges and a different lock are screwed into both sides. *How did he manage to find the super and get every-thing fixed so quickly?* The last time she'd needed repairs, it had taken the super three days to come fix the leak. *How long was I in there?* Then again, she isn't a vampire who can mojo people into doing her bidding.

There are definitely perks, she decides.

She moves toward the kitchen, standing behind where Theo works at the sink. He finishes washing the cutting board, then turns off the water, moving to dry off the board and slide it back on top of the refrigerator. He turns around to face her, leaning against the fridge door but says nothing as his eyes travel from her face down the silky robe and over her bare legs.

"Good bath?" he asks finally, and his voice is husky, his eyes slightly tinged gold.

Sylvia has a sudden urge to move over to him, press her body against his, and kiss him wildly. He would spin her around, pressing her against the refrigerator, and they would savage one another like animals, eventu-ally ending up naked on the kitchen floor while what-ever he had cooking burned in the oven. Something of her thoughts must show on her face because Theo takes a step closer, but then Sylvia's stomach growls loudly, and they both look at it and laugh nervously.

"Hungry?" he asks.

"Apparently?" she replies, glancing at the clock on the stove. 9:25. *Yeah, I would be hungry.* They should have been at dinner over an hour ago. "What is that?" she nods at the oven.

"Lasagna," Theo says, answering all her wishes.

Sylvia recounts what she had in her kitchen, won-dering how he had managed to conjure lasagna, but then she relents. Cooking has never been her strong suit. "I had the stuff to make lasagna?"

Theo shrugs. "Mostly." He smiles at her. "Remember? You live with a phone that can order anything you need."

Sylvia nods. "Right." She looks at the door, then back at him. "Thank you for doing this. I really appreciate it."

Theo smiles, accepting her thanks. "I figured I owed you a new door since I'm the one who broke it." He gestures to the table, where the heavy beer stein is now filled with water and holds five red roses. "Have a seat."

Sylvia sits, crossing her legs so the robe covers her thighs, and leans in to smell the roses. They are lovely, and she smiles at him. Theo reaches into a cabinet to retrieve two glasses, then turns to her. "What would you like to drink? I ordered wine, but there's water and tea in the fridge if you prefer that."

Sylvia contemplates, knowing that the wine will loosen her tongue and free her senses, but she wants more focus. "Tea, please," she says. "It's unsweet," she adds. "I don't like sweet tea."

Theo nods, pouring two glasses and bringing them both to the table. "So," he says, sitting down across from her, "shall we talk?"

Sylvia takes a sip, then settles back in her chair, watching his face over the roses. "Okay," she says carefully. "What do you want to know?"

"Tell me about him," Theo says without preamble. "Adam."

Sylvia frowns, then sighs. "There's not much to tell. We dated for a few months, then broke up. He didn't seem too upset about it. I never thought he would come back—and not like that."

"He had a key?"

"I thought he gave it back, but he must have made a copy," she explains. "I don't know why, though. It seems very random."

"How long has it been since you've seen him?"

Sylvia considers. "Maybe three weeks?" she guesses. "Miriam got me those tickets for Viking Times to go with him, but we broke up. He hasn't come around at all."

Theo nods. "And that night, when we met, the demon who was following you?"

"Demon following me?" Sylvia echoes, horrified. "What do you mean?"

"The creature that was hunting you," Theo says, "the demon that chased you into the building."

"What do you mean it was hunting me?" Sylvia asks. "I thought it was somehow connected with you!"

Theo shakes his head. "I was following you—and so was it." He pauses, takes a sip of his tea, then gives her a serious look. "You are being hunted, Syl. Why?"

Sylvia shakes her head. "I have no idea."

"Are you sure?" Theo doesn't look at her. Instead, he stands up and pulls the tray of bubbling lasagna from the oven, setting it on top to cool. He takes the flowers from the table and sets them on the counter, freeing the surface, then takes his seat across from her again. "Think, Syl. Who would be after you?"

Sylvia shakes her head, ignoring the small frisson of fear that snakes up her back.

You know who.

"I..." she begins, meaning to say she doesn't know, but it would be a lie, and she knows it.

Sensing her struggle, Theo reaches across the table to take her hand. His grip is firm and reassuring, and he looks at her expectantly.

"I think … maybe someone from my past might be back," she says in a small voice.

"Adam?" Theo asks.

Sylvia shakes her head. "No, I don't know what he has to do with it." She bites her lip, then swallows hard, steeling herself for the words. "When I was younger, I was attacked. The man who … hurt me … was in prison." She pauses, then adds, "He got out about a month ago."

"Have you seen him?"

Sylvia shakes her head, not knowing what she would do if she ever saw Charlie Wagner again. "No," she insists.

"But the demon," Theo prompts.

"I don't know anything about any demons," Sylvia says, but Theo gives her a hard look, and she sighs. "Maybe… maybe it's Charlie again. He did…" She swallows again, her hand gripping his tightly on the table. "He did … hurt me." She looks up at the ceiling, then back at Theo. "I think he meant to use me to summon something," she blurts. "Like a ceremony. There was a witch."

"A witch?" Theo echoes. "And what happened to them?"

"She died," Sylvia whispers. "My fr—another man killed her." Sylvia closes her eyes, memories of that night rolling over her. She hasn't thought about it, not really, in a very long time, her therapy training allowing her to refocus on other things. She hasn't deliberately faced any of this in years, mind skipping away whenever she got close to the memory. "There was a witch with a dagger, and Charlie Wagner, in the cemetery. They wanted to summon a creature, and they almost succeeded, but then another man showed up and saved me." She thinks of another person, the boy she had known, the boy she had convinced herself died that night by running right off the edge of the cliff, but then Phil had returned the following year, and she knows that she must have just imagined his death, imagined his presence entirely that horrible night.

There was something about the man who saved her though, something familiar. She knows there is something important to recall there, if only she will allow herself to do it, but she doesn't want to.

"Someone saved you?" Theo pushes. "A man?"

Sylvia nods. "He killed the witch, and Charlie ran away, but he hurt me as he left, so the man took me to the hospital."

Theo nods. "And Charlie Wagner?"

"He ran, but they caught him a few weeks later." She laughs, but the sound is hollow. "He was actually trying to come back to the house."

"For you?" Theo asks.

Sylvia shakes her head. "I don't think so. I think he was looking for something or maybe leaving something." She thinks of the dagger, the way the three creatures above her seemed fascinated by it. "My mother called the police, and they arrested him." She pauses, frowning. "He received ten years for attempted murder, but I guess he was good, so they let him out after eight instead."

"You think he might be finishing what he started?" Theo asks.

Sylvia shrugs. "Maybe?" She frowns. "But the demon... How can Charlie Wagner summon a demon?"

Theo sits back, keeping his hand with hers. "Eight years is plenty of time for a summoner to learn spells, especially a summoner in prison with nothing to do but read and study. Did you know this man was a summoner?"

Sylvia snorts. "I didn't even know that was a thing. I still don't really know what it means. I only know there was a witch because that's what he called her. A Tallardy witch." She looks over at Theo, a small smile on her lips as she looks him over. "I didn't know there were vampires in the world either."

"There are many things in the world," Theo tells her. "Vampires, witches, demons, and summoners. Even shifters." At Sylvia's raised eyebrow, he adds, "Creatures who can change shape, often taking on animal forms."

"What, like werewolves?" Sylvia shakes her head. "This is crazy."

"No crazier than vampires or magicians who can summon demons," Theo says.

"True. So how does it work? Can anyone summon a demon?"

Theo half nods and half shakes his head. "Sort of. There has to be some natural ability, but in the end, it comes down to having the right tools and a sense of timing."

"What does one need?"

"To summon a demon? The demon's name, really. A salt circle. A strong will. A facility with words. Demons are clever, you see, and they sometimes kill their summoners—if the deal allows it. Otherwise, summoners will kill them when they are done with them, sending them back to their realm."

"Demons have a realm? Like, another world?"

Theo nods. "I've never seen it, but I've seen the portals to get there. Demons come in and out of this world that way."

"But why summon a demon at all?"

"Many reasons, but mostly for power. Sometimes it's to get something that the summoner can't get on their own. Sometimes it's to get rid of an enemy." He looks at Sylvia. "Sometimes it's to find someone."

"You think Charlie Wagner summoned that demon to find me," Sylvia says. "Are there different kinds of demons?"

Theo nods. "The one you saw was a Balaam demon, pretty basic. Stupid. Strong. Stubborn. They're mostly used to retrieve things... and people."

Sylvia wants to ask about other kinds of demons, but she doesn't, focusing on the real question instead. "But why would he want me?"

"Why did he want you the first time?"

Sylvia shakes her head. "I don't really know. I think they were trying to summon something out in the ocean, something huge. They wanted to use me as a sacrifice to make a circle," she says suddenly, recalling more of the strange conversation from that night. *But Phil did something,* she thinks, *something to stop them ... by running off that cliff.*

She remembers the blood running down his arm from the dagger's cut, the warm liquid spraying her ankles, then the look on his face as he ran. He hadn't been running away. His expression had been too full of intent, of specific purpose.

When she'd seen him the following summer, she had wanted to ask him about that night, but every time the words came close, something happened to distract her. In the three years of their friendship after that night, she had never asked him, not even on that last night they spent together. The night when she had been sure he would kiss her.

He had been looking at her the same way Theo was watching her now, face intent on hers as she worked her way through her memories.

"Well," Theo says, standing up to make their plates, "no one is using you for a sacrifice while I'm around."

"I'm glad to hear it," Sylvia says, smiling. On a whim, she stands up, takes a sip of her tea, then walks up to stand behind him, pressing her body against his back. She wraps her arms around him, and he reaches up to cup her hands, abandoning the spatula on the counter. They stand that way for a moment, Sylvia breathing him in, pressing herself against him, then he spins in the circle of her arms, his hands wrapping around her back. He leans down immediately, then she is kissing him, losing herself in the feel of his mouth against hers. She slides her hands up his back, reveling in the strength of his muscles, the surprising heat of him in her arms. His hand moves up and cups the back of her head, fingers slipping beneath her hair to caress her neck, then he breaks the kiss with a hiss, jerking his hand away from her.

"What?" she asks, looking up at him.

Theo raises an eyebrow, then reaches down to touch the collar of her robe, tugging it away from her skin to reveal the silver compass on the necklace around her neck. Sylvia follows his gaze with a frown.

Theo looks at the necklace for a moment, then his gaze shifts to consider her face.

"The necklace?" Sylvia asks, reaching up to lift it out from beneath her robe. "I thought..." Her words trail off. Theo is still holding her with one hand, but the other hovers a few inches away from the necklace. "Wait," she says, "did my necklace just hurt you?"

Theo bites his lip, suddenly embarrassed. "It's silver," he says, as if that explains everything.

"Yeah," Sylvia nods. "Is that a problem?" A moment later, she gasps, recalling their conversation at the spring. "Oh no!" she says, stepping back and lifting the chain over her head. "Silver burns vampires." Sylvia thinks of the necklace resting on her windowsill, a gift from a suddenly unknown admirer. Clearly, Theo didn't give it to her. The tiny compass swirls, then reorients to a specific direction, pointing at the wall of her kitchen. Sylvia knows that north is the direction of the fire escape, but she ignores the thought, leaving the mystery of the necklace for another day. She coils it in her hand, then steps away from Theo to deposit it on her nightstand. Theo follows her a step behind, but he waits for her to put the necklace down before reaching for her again. Sylvia takes his hand, cradling it gently and lifting it up so she can see his fingers. A pink line of irritated skin shows where he touched the necklace, and Sylvia kisses the spot. Theo moves to sit on the edge of the bed, then tugs her gently to stand between his knees, hands neutral on her hips through the fabric of her robe. She leans down to kiss him, enjoying the height standing affords her. With him sitting, she can reach his lips easily. His hands slide along her back, the robe shifting as he moves, then his hands are on her shoulders, and he breaks the kiss to look at her as one hand starts to slide the robe off one shoulder, eyes asking permission as he moves slowly. Sylvia nods, biting her lip, and Theo leans forward to kiss the newly exposed skin of her shoulder. She moans, pressing herself closer to him. His hand moves to her other shoulder, trying to tug the robe down on that side, then his hands caress the bare skin of her back, his mouth planting butterfly kisses along her collarbone.

The robe falls open even more, revealing the top of her breasts, and Theo watches her again as his hands slide down to cup her, waiting for her subtle permission. At her nod, he leans forward, sliding the material down and taking her nipple in his mouth. Sylvia moans at the wave of pleasure, running her hands through his hair.

Her robe is below her breasts now, held in place by the belt still tied around her waist. Sylvia knows what's coming, but instead of dreading the moment, she reaches down and unties the belt, letting the robe fall to both sides, revealing the scarred skin of her stomach to his gaze. Theo stares at it for a moment, then places a slow line of kisses across her belly, both above and below the jagged line. He looks up at her face, eyes slowly moving down her body before meeting her gaze again.

"You are beautiful," he whispers, and Sylvia leans down to kiss him. His hands close on her waist beneath the robe, then he is pushing her down on the bed beside him, and he moves to kneel on the floor, tugging her body closer to him, pressing himself against her sensitive skin. He teases her stomach gently, tracing the skin above and below, clearly mapping where sensation turns into pressure atop the mottled skin. When Sylvia squirms under his touch, fire burning beneath her skin, he turns his attention lower. Sylvia dissolves in waves of pleasure beneath the pressure of his mouth and hands, and soon she is crying out his name in a tone she hasn't used before.

She regains her senses slowly, knowing that this is something routine in the bedroom, but still reeling from the new sensations. Theo's face rests on her thigh, watching her as she catches her breath, and she looks down the hills and valleys of her body to his face.

"Wow," she breathes. "That was ... amazing."

"I'm glad I can bring you pleasure," Theo says, fingers trailing back up her thigh in silent promise. She watches his hand, considering, but then she sighs, deciding she wants something else.

"Come up here," she says, patting the bed beside her. Theo obeys, sliding on to the bed to lay next to her. He is still fully clothed, but his hair has come loose from the tie, red waves hanging free around his face. Sylvia sits up, aware of her nudity despite the robe still lingering at her elbows and looks at him. "You are beautiful," she tells him, running a finger down one cheek. "Can I see you?"

At Theo's raised eyebrow, she reaches for his shirt, undoing the top button to reveal the hollow of his throat. He grins, resting his arms at his sides, and lets her unbutton the rest of his shirt.

She pauses at the necklaces, lifting each one. "What's this?" she asks, fingers trailing beneath the thin leather choker close to his skin.

"Oren and Harald," he says, reaching out to touch it and her. "We swore a blood oath, when we were young, never to leave the others behind."

"This was before?" Sylvia asks, leaving the rest of the question unspoken. Theo nods. "But it's leather," Sylvia says. "I know it can last a long time, but if you've been wearing it all the time... for hundreds of years..."

"A thousand years," Theo says helpfully, then smiles. "It's not the original. We replace them every now and then. It's a good reminder of our bond."

"They mean a great deal to you," Sylvia says. "Your friends."

"Oh yes," Theo says, "and so do you." He tugs her down for a lingering kiss, and Sylvia's hands explore the smooth planes of his chest, lingering on the lines of his tattoos, the dragon on his back spreading down both arms.

Pausing, she lifts the other necklace, another leather thong, but this one smooth and hard in her fingers, a series of small beads woven into it. "And this?"

"This," he says, taking it from her, "was my father's." He holds a red bead between his two fingers. "Sven," he says, "son of Jurgen." His fingers move to the blue bead at the new name. "Son of Harald," he announces at the yellow bead, then lastly, "Son of Bane," on the black bead. Sylvia reaches out to touch the clear bead. "And this one?" she asks. "Theo, son of Sven?" Theo nods. "This is leather too, but it feels ... different."

Theo nods again, lifting the beads to study them. "It's magic," he explains. "These are the thane's beads, the mark of my family."

"So, you had magic even before ... everything?"

Theo shrugs, letting the beads fall. "Not really. But back then, there was more magic in the world, more miracles in the mundane. These beads would have survived anything whether or not a vampire wore them."

Sylvia senses his sadness, a sorrow for a world lost so long ago, and she traces her fingers along the lines of the scars on his chest, finding the swirl of his tattoo and following it up to his shoulder. "And this?" she asks. "More markings of the thane?"

He chuckles, reaching out to touch her hair as it drags along the naked skin of his chest. "No, just the usual marking of the warrior." He moves so the shirt slides down to his elbow, and Sylvia helps him take it off the rest of the way. Sylvia stares at his chest for a long moment, taking in the gorgeous lines of this man who is somehow, miraculously, half-naked in her bed.

She remembers the demon from that first night, recalls the blood on Theo's shirt. She traces her fingers along his skin, finding no evidence of any recent wounds. "Did you heal already from the demon?" she asks. "How quickly do you heal?"

Theo smiles at her, his hand covering hers and bringing it to his lips for a quick kiss. "I heal very fast," he says.

"And faster with blood?" Sylvia prompts.

Theo kisses the skin of her wrist, where two small white marks show where he bit her. "Yes," he tells her.

"And do you have to ... drink blood often?" she asks, watching as Theo takes one of her fingers and slips it slowly into his mouth. His eyes sparkle at the question, and for a moment, she leans back, enjoying the feel of his tongue on her skin. "That's a serious question,

Theo," she says finally, tugging her finger free and leaning over him. "How often?"

Theo frowns, hand sliding up her arm to her shoulder, fingers tracing her neck. "Do you really want to know?" he whispers. "Do you want to talk about this now?"

Sylvia bites her lip, skin shivering under his touch, and she looks at his body again, desire pooling in her belly. *No, I don't want to talk about how you feed on other people.* Eventually, she will have to know, but for now, she lets it go. Her eyes focus on the line of his pants, the belt around his waist. Her hand traces a line down his chest, settling just above the buckle.

"What if I talk about your scars?" she asks instead. "I heard there was a wound in a particular area that's worth seeing." She grins at Theo.

"Indeed," he says, "a wound that makes a man thank the stars he moved left instead of right."

Sylvia's hand moves to his belt, tugging the buckle free and sliding his zipper down. She pauses, biting her lip, savoring the moment as she slides her hands over Theo's hips, pulling his pants down to reveal black boxers and thick, muscular thighs. She lets the pants fall to the floor, her hands skimming Theo's calves, noting the small scars there before moving back up his legs. A jagged edge of silver skin peeks out from the leg of his boxers, and she touches it, marveling at the skin's texture there, so like her own scar, yet different.

She glances at Theo for permission, and when he grins at her, tucking his hands up beneath his head as he settles in to watch, her fingers follow the scar upward, piling up the leg of his boxers as she goes.

The wound is longer than she expects, and she frowns at it. "How big was this spear, Theo?" she asks, taking in the full eight inches of the scar, very aware of the bulge of him near her hands, but she wants to draw out the moment.

"Normal spear," he says, "but they tried to drain the wound when it turned. They had to scrape it and fill it with cloth, too."

Sylvia winces, thinking of the medical treatments available a thousand years ago. "That must have been terrible!"

Theo frowns. "I don't remember most of it. I was pretty far gone."

Sylvia traces the scar again, letting her fingers drift more. Theo bites his lip, skin glowing the faintest bit, and a small smile crosses her lips. "Can I ... take these off?" she asks tentatively, hands reaching up to touch the waistband of his boxers. "Just to get a better look, of course."

Theo smiles at her, eyes glinting gold, as he dips his head and lifts his hips. "Of course."

CHAPTER 15

THEO

WATCHING SYLVIA SLIDE HIS SHORTS ASIDE AS SHE traces his scar is one of the sexiest moments in Theo's life. Seeing her expression when she asks to undress him completely is even better. The feel of her eyes on his body is intoxicating, and he rises to the occasion. Sylvia may be inexperienced, but she touches him with some skill, her hands sending waves of pleasure through his body. When she bends down to take him in her mouth, Theo closes his eyes, losing himself to pure sensation.

It hasn't been that long since he was with a woman, but those encounters seem mechanical now, an exchange of sensation without depth, everything undercut by the knowledge that the connection was a one-time meeting. The magic that allows him to attract victims makes it easy for people to obsess over him, so sometimes he makes the woman forget all about him afterward to save them both the agony.

But Sylvia knows who he is, what he is, and his powers seem to have little effect on her at all. He knows she wants him, but it's just attraction, human desire, and he sinks into the moment with her, letting himself go to experience the feel of her warm mouth on his skin, her fingers tracing lines on his skin.

For all that she is a virgin, this is definitely not her first time giving a man pleasure, and Theo puts a hand on her head, surrendering to the wave that crashes over him. His mouth opens with a loud moan of release, then Sylvia's hand is sliding up his chest, over his neck and across his chin, a finger sliding into his mouth. In his excitement and arousal, his fangs have lengthened, and her finger brushes against the tip.

The warm blood drips onto his tongue, a tiny drop, and Theo, already on the edge from her mouth, feels the iron control he has over his bloodlust shatter completely.

Before he can stop himself, he is sitting up, Sylvia pressed close to him, reaching for her hand and holding it tight against his mouth, teeth slicing down her finger to get more of her sweet blood.

Sylvia makes a surprised noise at the intrusion, tugging her hand back, trying to free herself, but he only pulls tighter, shoving two more fingers into his mouth and biting down.

"Theo!" Sylvia exclaims, and the fear in her voice shocks him, brings him back to himself, and he yanks her fingers out of his mouth, shoving her hand away and scooting his body out from under her. He lands on the floor between the bed and the armoire, one foot braced to move and his knee pressed hard into the wooden floor. He wipes a hand across his mouth, shame filling him, washing away the euphoria of a moment before.

"Gods, Syl," he says, wondering how to explain, what he could say. "I..."

"It's okay," she assures him, hand pressed against her robe, small lines of blood from her fingers staining the blue material. She pulls it free to examine the wounds, frowning when more blood wells up along the holes in her skin, then presses it harder into the robe, using her other hand to apply pressure. "I'm fine," she says. "That was silly of me. I shouldn't have done that. I'm so sorry, Theo."

"You're sorry? You have nothing to be sorry about! I'm the one who just attacked you like an animal."

"I'm fine," she repeats, "and maybe I like this animal side of you." She grins wickedly. "I definitely enjoyed the growling, especially at the end there." When he opens his mouth, though he doesn't know what he plans to say, she stops him. "I like that I can bring you pleasure, Theo." She checks her hand again, nodding to see the bleeding has slowed, and she turns to the rocking chair behind her. She shucks off the robe, wrapping it up so the bloodstains are inside. It's a nice gesture, but Theo can still smell her blood. He watches as she grabs a dark shirt and wraps her hand again, then tugs a purple t-shirt over her head. She scoots back onto the bed, holding out her unwounded hand to him.

"Come here, Theo. It's fine now."

"It's not fine," he mutters. "I hurt you." *I lost control like some teenage boy!*

"It's no big deal," she says with a shrug, hand still held out to him. "I shouldn't have tempted you like that." She leans back to kneel, her hand falling to her thigh. "I'm still learning the rules for making out with a vampire." She laughs.

Theo shakes his head, standing up to sit on the edge of the bed. She reaches out her hand again, and after a moment of hesitation, he takes it, careful not to get too close. "That was dangerous, Syl. I am so sorry."

CHAPTER 16

SYLVIA

SYLVIA STARES AT THE HORRIFIED NAKED VAMPIRE SIT-
ting on the edge of her bed. "You have nothing to
be sorry about," she insists. "This isn't like you beat
me or anything. You're a vampire, and I just basically
teased you with my blood. I don't know what happened,
really. I just wanted to touch you." She pauses. "I like
touching you." Her fingers twist in his hand, caressing
him, soothing.

"I like when you touch me," he says. "But we need to
be way more careful when we do things like this."

"You mean in the future?" she asks. "Next time?"

"Definitely," he says, leaning closer to take her hand
in both of his. He keeps the rest of his body away from
her though.

"So, there will be a next time?" Sylvia hates the
wheedling note in her voice, but she can't help it. She
wants to see him again, hopes that her mistake tonight
doesn't make him decide to leave and never return.

171

"Gods, I hope so, Syl," he breathes, raising her hand to his lips and kissing it gently. "But next time, I will be more careful." Theo releases her hand, nodding to himself, then slides off the bed to retrieve his clothes.

"More careful?" Sylvia echoes, watching him as he slowly dresses, those long legs disappearing into his pants. "What does that mean?"

Theo shrugs his shirt over his arms and buttons it quickly, shaking his hair free and reaching a hand down to where she still sits on the bed. Sylvia accepts, allowing him to pull her to her feet and into the circle of his arms.

"Come," Theo says, leading her across the small apartment, "let's eat."

"Don't change the subject," Sylvia says, pulling out the kitchen chair as Theo puts a hand over the lasagna. Frowning, he opens the oven, grabs the pan with a kitchen towel as a potholder, and puts it back inside, planning to reheat it for a few minutes. "What do you mean by 'more careful'? What are you going to do?"

Theo turns, leaning back against the counter and flipping the towel over his shoulder. Sylvia smirks at him. "I do have potholders," she tells him. "You don't have to use the towel."

"It works," Theo says, watching her from where he stands. "This could work, Syl, if you want."

"What could work?" she asks, suspicious now.

He gestures back and forth between them with the towel. "This. Us. You and me."

"I thought it was working just fine," Sylvia whispers.

"I could have killed you just now, Syl," Theo says, his voice deadly quiet. "I can't lose control like that."

"What could happen?" Sylvia sputters before she can stop herself.

"You could die," Theo repeats.

"But you wouldn't let me die, would you?" she prompts. "So, let's worst case scenario this thing: you bite me, and I bleed."

"You bleed *to death*, Syl," Theo tells her.

"Fine, I bleed to death," she repeats. "Would you let me die?"

Theo pauses, biting his lip, then he shakes his head. "No. Not if I have the power to save you."

"Well, that's reassuring," she snaps. "So, what would you do? Is this like a Dracula thing—you feed me your blood or something? Or more *Vampire Diaries* where I'd die if I didn't kill a human by the next day?"

"Neither," Theo says. He stares at her for a long time, clearly debating with himself, then he releases a long, low sigh. "I'd feed you my blood," he says finally. "You wouldn't die because my blood can heal you."

"And then?" Sylvia prompts when he falls silent again. "Would I become a vampire?"

"Only if you died after exchanging blood with a vampire," Theo murmurs. "It's not enough to just have my blood in your system—it needs to be an even exchange."

"So, if I don't die after that, then what? It just goes away? How long?"

Theo cocks his head. "Depends on how much blood—a few days are likely. You'd be stronger, faster, from my blood in you. But you'd also have some of the penalties of vampiric abilities—sunlight aversion, silver allergy. I mean, a stake in the heart will kill anyone anyway, but it would kill you more easily." He pauses. "Certain types of wood can be ... problematic."

"Like?"

Theo smirks. "Just don't ever lead me near a banyan tree," he says, "and we should be fine."

"Anything else?" she asks.

"What do you mean? What else do you think there is?"

Sylvia shrugs, finishing her glass of iced tea from earlier, the contents tepid now but still refreshing. She swallows, then frowns. "I'm not sure. I mean, there has to be some magic about the whole thing, right? Like how you can whammy people? Would I be able to do that?"

"If you died and became a vampire, you would have some abilities," Theo says. "It's different for everyone. I have the ability to, as you say, whammy people. Others can compel mortals or simply make them forget." He shrugs. "We all have something that helps us survive."

"And how do you survive, Theo?" Sylvia asks, her throat suddenly dry despite the tea.

Theo turns his attention to the oven, peeking in at the lasagna and pulling it free. He busies himself at the counter for a moment, his back to Sylvia, serving the warmed lasagna onto two plates. When he turns and places both plates on the table, Sylvia picks up a fork to take a bite, her stomach growling. She tries the food, pausing to blow on it first, but Theo pulled it at the perfect moment. The food is warm but not scalding, the combination of pasta, cheese, and sauce heaven in her mouth. They eat in companionable silence for a time, both lost in the flavor of a meal long delayed. Sylvia gets up to refill their tea glasses, then sits back down to finish her plate.

"That was freaking amazing," she says, belly full as she leans back in the chair. "Where did you learn to cook like this?"

Theo swallows his last bite, wiping his mouth with his napkin before speaking. For a Viking, he has impeccable table manners, and Sylvia is reminded that she is eating this meal wearing only a t-shirt. A low thrill of desire builds at the thought, but it is quickly doused by the satisfying food in her belly, and she contents herself with looking at him across the table.

"I like to cook," Theo tells her. "I don't have to eat, but I can if I want to, so cooking is always a treat for me. A perk."

Sylvia nods. "I get it. I'd probably enjoy cooking too if I didn't have to do it every day." She smiles at him. "I eat a lot of cereal."

"Nothing wrong with cereal," Theo says. "Sometimes, it's just what you want."

"What do you want?" Sylvia blurts, the words out before she can stop them. She bites her lip, suddenly nervous and cursing herself for blowing the mood.

"I want to see you again," Theo replies. "Do you want that?"

Sylvia nods. "Yes. I want this." She gestures between them, mimicking his motion from earlier. "Us. I want to try this."

Theo leans back in his chair, finishing his tea and setting his glass down on the table. "Well, then," he says, "I think I owe you a dinner. Will you go out to dinner with me, Syl?"

"If at first you don't succeed," Sylvia quotes.

"Try, try again," Theo finishes, speaking with her. "Will you go on a date with me, Sylvia Copland? Will you do this vampire the honor of your company for an evening?"

Sylvia smiles, nodding. "Of course. Every evening," she says.

CHAPTER 17

THEO

OVER THE NEXT TWO WEEKS, THEO SPENDS MOST OF EACH evening with Sylvia, out at restaurants, in his dressing room at Viking Times, lounging in her bed at her apartment. She even shows him her sketchpad, and Theo marvels over the image of his face, something lost to him for centuries. Theo assumes his lack of image is magical—since mirrors aren't made with silver anymore and even cellphones don't register his presence. He has seen himself in the minds of others, but never so clearly as her clean lines on the page.

There have been many kisses, and even more familiar pleasures, but the arrival of her monthly courses postponed deeper relations. Sylvia remains a virgin, and Theo is happy to pause in their physical explorations, wanting her to be comfortable with him for her first time. He certainly has no qualms about blood—in fact, he could sate himself easily enough, but sitting near her on that first night had been an exercise in agony, and he decided that if he was going to retain his control, he needed to hunt before seeing her, sate the bloodlust completely before arriving at her side.

He still remembers the taste of her blood in his mouth, the sound of her gasp as she tried to pull away, and the wave of shame that flooded his chest when he had not released her immediately. It has been a very long time since he pursued any kind of relationship with a mortal, and he has been slowly regaining his feet in the process.

Talking to Oren had helped. His friend had been the one to suggest feeding before seeing her. "That's what I always did with Morena," he explained, unconsciously fingering the silver necklace he wore, seemingly oblivious to the small pink lines forming on his skin at the contact with the metal. "Especially when she was bleeding. Dude," he had shaken his head, "it's almost impossible to keep your head around them then." He had smirked, giving his old friend a friendly shove on the shoulder. "Though you could turn it into some very sexy fun times, if you wanted."

Theo returned the grin, thinking similar things, but he had shaken his head, dismissing the idea. Sylvia is young and inexperienced. Such things may appeal to her in time, but Theo isn't about to suggest them yet.

Sitting across from her now in the restaurant, her skin radiant, cheeks a little pink from the wine, Theo is very glad that he fed before seeing her tonight. Sylvia is no longer bleeding, no longer the beacon of temptation, but he still wants her, wants more of her, and the bloodlust would only complicate his desire.

"This is really nice," Sylvia says, taking in the dining room, eyes skimming over the fabric on the walls, the fine tablecloths, the fancy dress of the other diners. "I've always wanted to come to Mis En Place." She says the word with a French accent, a sigh almost, as she takes another sip of her wine. "Even the chairs in this place are expensive."

"They have great food here," Theo says, taking a sip of his own wine. They are between courses, having arrived after the cocktail hour ended, though the waiter still brought them a small plate with samples of the hors d'oeuvres and amuse-bouche. Sylvia had taken a bite of each one, nodding at the zucchini fritters but frowning at the bite of the sweet potato chips with goat cheese and vinegar. Theo smirked at her, commenting about how her mouth did not seem amused by the combination.

"Do they always feed you before they feed you?" Sylvia asks, nodding at the empty plate between them. "How much food is on this chef's menu?"

Theo leans back with a smile, happy he can indulge her taste buds. "It's a twelve-course meal," he says, "so it's a lot of food but spread out over a long time."

"Planning to keep me here all night, are you?" Sylvia raises a brow, teasing him.

"Not all night," he replies, moving his foot beneath the table so it rests next to hers on the floor. "I hoped we might explore other appetites after dinner."

"I like where your head's at," Sylvia says with a nod. "Note to self—do not eat so much I end up in a food coma."

Theo laughs. "Eat what you like, Syl. The food here is always exquisite."

Something in Sylvia's expression changes at his words, and she frowns at him, putting down her glass.

"So, you come here often then?" She doesn't say it, but Theo can hear the implied question: *And with whom?*

He shrugs, putting his glass down and watching her for a moment. He knows there will be moments like this, times when his history will clash with her expectations. He talked to Oren about that as well, though with little practical advice in the end. Other than "don't piss her off by being an idiot," Oren hadn't offered much. Harald hadn't said anything—simply sat there with a thoughtful expression. "I know the chef," Theo says neutrally. "I knew his father."

Sylvia's face is carefully blank as she asks, "And his mother?"

Theo shrugs. "Lenore was a lovely lady, but I didn't know her well. I spent more time with Gerald and Lucas."

She bites her lip, regret on her face. "Was lovely?" she echoes. "I'm sorry."

Pursing his lips, Theo leans forward. "Lucas is a fine chef," he says, changing the subject. "His menu offers a nice variety, so I hope you like the next course."

Sylvia narrows her eyes, returning to their previous point of discussion. "And do they always bring you a plate of something after they're done serving it?"

He is saved from answering as the waiter arrives and sets two bowls of soup before them. Sylvia delicately dips her spoon, lifting it gently to her lips. She closes her eyes, savoring the taste, and Theo watches her enjoyment. He wants the moment to linger, to lose himself in the obvious pleasure on her face, but he knows the peace won't last. Sylvia's eyes are filled with questions, with doubts, more each night he sees her.

Eventually, they will have to talk about it. Theo hoped for more time but staring at her as she finishes the small bowl of soup, he knows his time is up. "What is it, Syl?" he asks, watching as she licks the spoon once more before returning it to the table. "Talk to me. What is this about?"

Sylvia looks away at first, studying the room as she bites her lip, but he sees the moment she finds her courage, straightening her back and looking directly at him.

"Have you been feeding on other people before you come see me?"

"Yes," Theo says.

She nods and releases a heavy sigh, swallowing. "Why?"

Theo tilts his head, a matching sigh leaving him. "You know why." He pauses, then says, "I don't want to hurt you—"

"You won't!" she interrupts, a fierce whisper.

"You don't know that," he says. "I don't know that." He shakes his head. "I'm not willing to risk you," he says bluntly.

"Don't you want me?" she asks. Her voice is so tiny, his heart aches.

"Gods yes!" he says, the words bursting out of him. "That's why I have to do it. I can't lose control like that ever again, Syl. I won't."

"Why can't you use me?" she asks, eyes shining with unshed tears. "You don't kill the people you feed on every night. You could do the same with me."

Theo shakes his head. The waiter slips past the table, scooping up both bowls without breaking pace, clearly seeing they are in the middle of a serious conversation.

Another reason Theo loves this place—that and the fact there is not a single mirror in the entire building, not a reflective surface in sight. He reaches across the table to take Syl's hands, and she returns his reassuring squeeze. "No, Syl," he tries to explain. "I can feed from them because I *don't* want them. There's no risk there. It's just... mechanical... biological." He searches her face. "But when I'm with you..." His voice trails off. "I just don't want to lose myself and hurt you. You have to understand that."

Sylvia scoffs, looking away bitterly. "I understand," she says finally. "I just hate it."

"Do... do you not want to see me anymore?" Theo asks, releasing her hand and leaning back, giving her time and space to consider her reply. He doesn't want to pressure her, but he also knows it will hurt if she says yes. He doesn't love her, not yet, but he's definitely on the path there, and leaving her behind will gut him.

But he will if it will keep her safe.

The waiter returns with another course, placing small plates of mushrooms stuffed with cheese before them. Sylvia considers the appetizer, cutting the mushroom in half with her fork, then spearing it and holding it out to him. "I want to see you, Theo," she admits softly. "Share a mushroom with me?"

Theo accepts the bite, then uses the fork to cut his own mushroom in half, offering her the same bite, watching as she chews.

"This isn't fair," she says after she swallows. "You know I'm a sucker for cheese."

"You know I'm a sucker for you," he replies, and she smiles at him. The argument hasn't gone away, but at least it's out in the open now. She still wants to be with him, still chooses him, and for now, it is enough.

They are through their salad and fish course when his phone rings. Theo silences it immediately, embarrassed. "I thought I turned it off," he tells Syl. Before he can pocket it, the screen lights up, ringing again. Theo can't help but see the caller: Grace. He frowns at it but puts it away. It's not that strange for Grace to call him, though he is fairly certain she knows he is out with Sylvia. She hadn't participated in his talk with Oren and Harald, but she is smart enough to see what's in front of her. He looks up to Sylvia's curious expression.

"Grace," he explains.

"Oh," she says. "Do you need to take that?"

He shakes his head. "No. I'm sure it's fine."

"Theo, can I ask you what Grace is to you?" Theo furrows his brow, but there is no malice in the question, no suggestive undertone. She genuinely is curious.

"She's my assistant," he says.

"With Viking Times?"

He nods. "Well, that, and other things."

"What do you actually do for a living, Theo? Do you really afford that fancy apartment by fighting on the weekends?"

Theo chuckles, wondering when he will tell her about the buildings he owns in the city. Sylvia does not strike him as the type of woman who would want to be taken care of like that, though he will offer at some point. "Not entirely, though Viking Times does well enough." He sniffs, wondering how to explain it so he doesn't seem like a stereotype. "I ... help people explore their ideas."

"That sounds super shady, Theo. What do you mean?"

Theo considers his words. "I mean, if Grace hears about someone with a good idea, she tells me about it, and if I think the idea has merit, I fund them to get started."

"So, you finance business ideas? Like an investor?"

Theo nods. "You could describe it like that. I like to think I help people see their dreams through."

"You must be pretty good at it," Sylvia says.

"I do alright," he says, leaning back to allow the waiter to set two plates of the first course—roast duck—before them.

Sylvia laughs. "I do alright, Theo. You thrive."

"I've had a long time to understand how people work," Theo says. "And Grace has an amazing sense for a great possibility. We helped four women get a small publisher off the ground a few years ago," he shares. "Now it's a Fortune 500 company."

"So, was that your genius or Grace's keen eye for business?" Sylvia asks, taking a bite of her duck and closing her eyes in pleasure. "This is insanely tasty," she adds.

"Both," Theo admits. "I like the idea of books. Grace saw the potential in them." As he speaks, his phone rings again, the light glowing against his shirt.

"You should really answer that," Sylvia says. "It seems important."

Theo frowns, lifting the phone from his jacket to peer at it. He glances around, his sense of propriety about talking on a cell phone at dinner warring with a slight nervous feeling in his gut, like something is wrong. He's too old to ignore that twinge, and he apologizes to Sylvia before dialing Grace's number. It rings several times before going to her voicemail. Theo leaves a tense message, then hangs up and scrolls through his missed calls. Grace has called eight times over the last half hour. The feeling in his gut tightens. He sends a quick text.

[Theo: Hey, everything ok?]

He waits a beat, but the message remains unread. The feeling in his gut tightens.

This is bad.

"Everything okay?" Sylvia asks, no doubt sensing the shift in his mood. His Sylvia has a sensitive soul.

"Maybe Emma has her phone," Theo muses, thinking of Grace's daughter as he frowns at the phone. Even if she has her mom's phone, Emma would click on the message.

"Maybe," Sylvia agrees. She narrows her eyes. "But you think something is wrong, don't you?"

Theo sighs. "I don't know," he admits.

"Then you should go," Sylvia says. "Go check on your friend."

Theo glances at her, raising an eyebrow. "And leave you here?"

Sylvia looks around the restaurant, still filled with people eating their meals. "I'm a grown-up," she says, spearing another bite of her food. "I can get myself home." She pauses, grimacing at him and scrunching her adorable nose. "Though you should probably pay for dinner first?"

"No worries," Theo assures her, knowing he can settle up later. He frowns, dialing Grace again. More ringing, then her voicemail. That awful feeling intensifies. "Do you mind if I do leave?"

Sylvia gestures with her fork. "Go! I'll be fine. Come by my apartment when you find her and let me know everything is okay."

"You are ... amazing," he breathes, getting to his feet. He catches the waiter's eye, tilting his head toward the exit. The man nods in understanding. Theo leans down to kiss Sylvia, a brief brush of her lips against his. "I will see you soon," he promises, then heads out to check on his assistant.

CHAPTER 18

Pilkington

Pilkington is sitting in his library, books spread all around him, when the summons comes. He looks up, the call resonating in his bones, setting the book down on the small table beside his armchair as he gets to his feet. He knew it was coming, knew it as soon as Charlie's trail went cold, but it doesn't make the summons any easier.

He doesn't have time for many emotions before he must obey, but the red rage that sweeps through him at the summoning is enough to send a wave of power through the house. It has been many years since he was last summoned like this, and Pilkington vows to slay the magician slowly, painfully, for his arrogance.

He considers the possibility that another could know his name but dismisses the thought. He killed everyone in the mortal realm who knew his name centuries ago.

If those bastard brothers are giving my name as theirs again...

In the moment before his body is pulled through the ether into the circle, Pilkington shifts out of his gray sweatpants and soft blue robe, allowing his wings and horns to manifest entirely as he covers his lower body in leather pants and boots, schooling his face into a scowl.

If the summoner wants a demon, he shall get a demon.

It may have been centuries since he was last summoned into a circle, but Pilkington remembers the sensation. He is still powerful, retaining all his abilities, but he is at the whim of his summoner. Pilkington plants the most terrifying sneer on his mouth as he appears inside the magic, feet settling on the concrete floor beneath him, wings brushing up against the smooth walls of the circle, a barrier that begins at the line of salt and blood arranged on the ground and rises in an ever-shrinking column overhead. Pilkington knows there is no escape that way, though he did try when he was young and foolish—only to find himself wedged before sliding back down to the ground with an awkward crash.

Pilkington surveys his surroundings instantly. He recognizes the mortal realm by the feel of the place against his skin, even inside the circle. He is underground somewhere, likely an old subway station. The walls are constructed, not caves, so he must be near or in a city. A few moments will allow him to orient himself to which one.

She is nearby, he realizes, trying to ignore the fact that it is habit now to find himself in the world according to where he is in relation to his arusha.

She is not my... He doesn't finish the thought, knowing there are more important matters to focus on.

Looking out of the circle, he recognizes the face of his summoner, though time has not been kind to Charlie Wagner. Pilkington isn't even surprised to see the ancient magical dagger in the old man's hand—a hand that trembles with the effort of holding the spell in place. *Can I distract him long enough for his power to fade before he can tell me what he wants?*

But Charlie Wagner isn't alone. Standing next to him, eyes wide with shock and awe, is a young man with blond hair and fading bruises on his face. *Someone beat him within an inch of his life,* Pilkington thinks. No doubt that explains part of his reason for being party to this ceremony. He can sense the rage inside the man, the desire for revenge, for the strength to defeat his enemies. That's nothing new, nothing surprising. Humans have always lusted for power.

Charlie Wagner's desire is a bit more complicated, laced with nuance and patience, but at its core, it's the same impulse that drives him—though he would gladly sacrifice his assistant if it meant more power for himself. Pilkington waits, biding his time and gathering more information, unable to do much else.

"Demon," Charlie Wagner says in a voice gone thin with age and fatigue, "you will obey me in all things."

Pilkington frowns, allowing his fangs to show. The blond takes a step back, but Charlie only stands there, holding the dagger out like the threat he knows it is. *Not all things,* he wants to say, but he holds the words back, a captured demon awaiting his orders.

Does he know that I am the same demon? Pilkington knows Charlie must have learned his name from his last summoning in the cemetery, but that had been different. He'd been summoned mid-geas, something that had never happened before or since. Pilkington knows he must get that magical artifact away from the summoner if he plans to survive this encounter.

He stands in the circle, posture angry but subdued, waiting to see what the man will demand.

Not her, he chants quietly, *not her, not her, not her.* As Charlie opens his mouth to speak, Pilkington hopes frantically that her vampire is with her, and that at least half of the rumors about the Muldavian are true. A tiny voice whispers that it doesn't matter what the summoner demands—he will not be able to harm his arusha in any way. Their bond will protect her.

He waits for the denial that always comes on the heels of the thought—and finds nothing.

"I order you to bring me the blood of Sylvia Copland," Charlie says, and Pilkington feels the order zing through him, the command binding his being. "You will not tell anyone more than this request. You will say nothing of me or my plans for her. You will do this tonight. Right now."

Pilkington nods. "Very well, my lord." He adds the honorific to distract Charlie, hoping the man won't add anything else to his demand. He seems to consider it for a moment, then glances at the blond standing next to him and closes his mouth.

He'll ask me for more later, Pilkington knows. *After I return with her blood.*

Charlie gestures with the dagger, releasing the circle and freeing Pilkington. The demon pauses, waiting for additional orders. This is usually the part where the summoner starts adding rules—*don't be seen, don't kill anyone I don't specify, return immediately*—that sort of thing. But Charlie, the fool, just nods at him to go.

Pilkington wastes no time, huge wings flapping and sending him up into the darkness overhead. It is not hard to find a way out of the underground station, and Pilkington emerges into the night air. He cloaks himself, even though he has not been ordered to, not wanting to alarm anyone who may see him.

He didn't give me any specifications, Pilkington muses, heading skyward to contemplate his situation. *Just retrieve her blood. I can do that easily enough without hurting her... if her vampire doesn't object.* Pilkington frowns, knowing that the Muldavian will probably not be cordial in his response, especially if he's still courting her.

You know he's still with her.

Pilkington circles for a few moments, thinking. He can sense his arusha, knows that she is on the move, and he heads slowly in that direction.

You will have to actually speak to her.

But like this?

Pilkington isn't afraid that she will recognize her old friend Phil inside the demon; he doesn't think Sylvia would ever think his natural form and that boy could be connected.

But she will run from me like this. He tries to shift his appearance, though he knows it is useless. Summoned demons can act on their own, so long as it does not contradict their command, but they are trapped in the form they are summoned in. That's why Pilkington chose to appear as his demonic self—this form was strong and fast, hard to defeat and harder to kill. If Charlie didn't have the dagger that could unmake him,

Pilkington might have risked an attack in the seconds before Charlie gave his command.

He glances down at the leather armguards on his forearms, picturing the thin white line up one arm beneath, the mark of the dagger. He had come perilously close to dying that night in the cemetery. He chuckles at the thought. He actually had died—his human form, that is—but that artifact could unmake his existence with a serious injury. Even now, he is aware of the part of himself he lost that night, the power that never returned, magic stolen by that dagger.

Think of what you gained that night, he reminds himself. *Your arusha.*

Shut up.

Pilkington picks up speed, heading closer to where he knows Sylvia is, deciding to form his plan when he sees the circumstances.

He really hopes he finds her alone.

CHAPTER 19

SYLVIA

SYLVIA LINGERS OVER THE ROAST DUCK, ENJOYING THE taste even as she considers her conversation with Theo. She knew it was coming, knew they had to talk about his feeding habits and the dark jealousy burning in her gut whenever his cheeks flushed in amusement.

What is there to say, though? She takes another bite and puts down her fork, stomach full despite the small size of the portions. *Theo was right about one thing,* she muses. *The food here really is amazing.* She lingers for a moment, and the attentive waiter returns, whisking away her plate and returning a moment later with a small dish containing what looks like sherbet.

Sylvia frowns at the tiny scoop, knowing that it fits the pattern of everything else she's eaten tonight, but it really is a small portion. She takes a little scoop with the provided spoon, expecting mint by the smell. The taste explodes on her tongue, erasing everything from her mouth but the cleansing mint. Sylvia takes one more tiny bite, understanding why the sample is so small. Eating too much of this would scour her mouth of everything.

She pushes the dish away, deciding that she's not a huge fan of the chef's idea of dessert, but still counting the meal as a win. She wipes her mouth, takes one more sip of her wine, and gets to her feet, heading out of the restaurant. On her way to the door, she passes by her waiter. He holds another plate in his hand, a small cut of steak, and he looks at her curiously as she leaves.

Oh, she realizes, *that wasn't dessert! It was one of those...* She pauses, searching for the phrase she knows she's heard in movies somewhere. *Palate cleanser! No wonder it tasted so strong.*

She frowns but continues walking. Theo did say it was a twelve-course meal, and they were only at number eight. She is sorry to miss what she's sure would be a fabulous dessert, but the meal has lost its appeal without Theo.

Sylvia heads out into the street, contemplating a cab but deciding to walk instead. The night is cool and refreshing, and though she knows that demons and vampires and other creatures occupy the city with her, she decided from the start that she would not live her life in fear of them. She's not planning to stumble down any dark alleys—or even near their entrances. She can stick to well-lit streets and make it home just fine. The night air will give her some time to think.

She is worried about Grace, hoping Theo finds his assistant home and well and with a phone hijacked by a toddler, but her mind spins away from there to more pressing matters.

What do I want? She considers the question, knowing that's what she really needs to decide. *And do I really need to know right now?*

She frowns, eyes scanning the street for any threats as she walks, debating but not so deeply that she loses track of her surroundings. It's one thing to be brave; it's another to be foolish.

He's a vampire, she reminds herself. *He's got all of eternity to wait. And is that what I want—for him to wait for me? No,* she answers immediately. *And I don't want to be like him, frozen eternally and dependent on blood to survive.*

So, what then? Is this a dalliance, a nice way to lose my virginity with a great guy, have some fun, and move on? Is this just "fun" or is it something more?

Do you want it to be something more?

I don't know.

Her recent relationship with Adam has her pursing her lips, recalling the rage in his face when he attacked her, so different from the way he had once looked at her when they first started dating. She had never imagined that Adam would look at her like that. *Could* look at her like that.

In the end, will Theo do the same? She hates the question, hates herself for asking, but her history forces her to face the possibility. She knows that some people can be awful, can shift into monstrous creatures, but now she also knows that some people are creatures from the start. *What terrible transformation is Theo capable of?*

She glimpsed it that night in her apartment, the snarling rage that would have killed a man right in her living room without a thought. Something inside assures her that Theo would never, could never turn that on her, but she can't ignore the part of her that questions him.

Anyone can hurt you. Anyone can turn on you. Charlie Wagner's face appears in her memory, and she pushes it aside, replacing it with another face, a younger man.

She tries not to think about Phil too often, knowing that it will only bring her sadness. They had spent two glorious summers together, talking, laughing, swimming in the ocean. He was the only person she had ever met who seemed to understand her entirely, never judging her weird opinions (like how mustard is the absolute worst condiment ever invented and only serves to make food edible for birds) or doubting her resolve (to get out of that town and see the rest of the world). That last night they had been together, though, things had shifted between them. Sylvia had known their relationship was changing, growing, and when she was certain he would turn and kiss her, he had stood and backed away, hands out as if to ward her off.

"I can't do this," he had whispered, dark hair blowing wild around his face in the ocean breeze. "I won't do this to you."

"Do what?" she had asked, but he wouldn't answer, taking a few more steps away from her.

"Go," he had said finally. "Live, arusha." Then, he was gone. Sylvia had waited for him to return, teenage heart imagining him climbing into her window at night, standing outside with a radio overhead, appearing to take her to prom—all manner of ridiculous romantic notions.

But what did he mean? The thought isn't new. *Live arusha? What is arusha?* Sylvia had looked it up but found nothing referencing the term. She wonders if it's a name or a place or a specific thing—but whatever he meant, she plans to follow the first part and live.

And if setting aside her jealousy in the face of reason is the cost of being with Theo, she will pay it. She knows her anger is illogical, that she can't judge someone for doing the very thing that keeps him—and her—alive, and she knows that her desire for Theo is stronger than her jealousy.

She wants Theo, wants to know him in every possible way. She reaches her apartment with a small smile on her lips, changing out of the nice dress Theo bought her to replace the one Adam ruined. She settles down on the window ledge in her tank top and sleep shorts, a light sweater covering her arms against the night air, a glass of water in one hand as she fingers the small silver compass from her secret admirer with the other.

She doesn't wear it around Theo, knowing how it burns him, but when she's alone, she likes to watch the compass spin as she holds it out, always homing in on a random direction. It doesn't seem to point north like a traditional compass, though the cardinal points are carved into the edges—sometimes it points down to the south, other times to the southwest or southeast, but tonight the compass continues to spin until she points it skyward. Sylvia squints in the general direction, wondering what the compass senses that she cannot. After a few moments, she tilts her head, blinking hard to clear her eyes.

There is something above the building next to hers, and it isn't Theo. The large creature moves closer, not threatening in its posture, but terrifying in its appearance. When it gets close enough for Sylvia to be sure it's heading for her, she breaks free of the odd frozen panic trapping her on the ledge, jerking herself back into the safety of her apartment. She smacks her head on the bottom of the window on the way in, hard enough to see a starburst of white light behind her eyes, and her hand drops the glass of water onto the floor beside her. The glass shatters with a spray of cold water and tinkling shards, and white heat lances up Sylvia's forearm.

She returns to find herself sitting on the floor in a puddle of water and glass, compass in a silver pile near the refrigerator, head pounding. Reaching out to explore the damage, she can feel the beginnings of a lump on top of her head, and a dull thrumming headache begins low in her neck. She opens her eyes again, blinking fast at the feel of warm wetness on her thigh. Looking up, she sees the cut on her arm, blood running down to drip on her bare legs beneath the shorts. She covers the wound with her other hand, taking in the damage. She doesn't think it will need stitches, but Theo will surely notice it when he arrives later.

If she is still here when he does come back.

Sylvia gets to her feet slowly, staying away from the open window. The creature hovers on her fire escape, and she can see its chest through the opening. It must be at least seven feet tall, broad-chested with huge leathery wings that flap lazily in the night before curling back. Its skin is deep blue, lined with black markings that disappear into the line of leather pants. As she watches, the creature settles to stand on the metal floor, the structure creaking a little as it takes the weight. Sylvia can see two arms with leather bracers hanging casually at its side. The creature ducks down, its face coming into view, and Sylvia stares at the smooth skin, the two horns that jut through the dark tangle of hair on top of its head, the gleaming red eyes that stare at her with intelligence.

But not malice.

They stare at one another for a long moment before the creature speaks. "You should take care of that." The voice is pleasant and deep, not the sound she expects from that mouth. *Definitely male then,* she thinks, though that sculpted chest should have been her first clue.

"Huh?" Sylvia manages. Her mind hammers at her that she should be terrified, screaming, anything but standing there bleeding in front of this monster. But something else, something deep inside whispers that this monster will not harm her.

This is your *monster,* a quiet voice whispers.

"Your arm," the monster says, gesturing with one long black nail at her wound. "You're bleeding."

Sylvia nods, looking down at her arm, then scanning the glass spread across the floor. Taking a careful step to her left, she swipes the kitchen towel from the stove and presses it against her arm. She faces the creature standing just outside her window, head tilting to one side as she takes it in. "What," she begins, then steels her spine, gathering her nerve. "*Who* are you?"

The creature executes a bow far more extravagant than should be possible on her fire escape, wings furling in to hug his back as he bends at the waist, dark curtain of hair falling forward around his horns as his arm sweeps out. "I am known as Pilkington, my lady," he says, his formal manners both at odds and totally in keeping with his appearance.

"Well, Pilkington, what are you doing on my fire escape in the middle of the night?"

The creature frowns, revealing the tips of fangs, and Sylvia takes a deep breath, maintaining her calm in the face of the seeming cordiality of the encounter. "This is a matter of some delicacy," he says. "Perhaps you should clean up the mess before we speak of it. I'd hate for you to cut your feet."

Sylvia nods slowly, lifting the towel to check the bleeding. Seeing that it has slowed but not stopped, she wraps the towel around her forearm and tucks the edge underneath. Her arms now free, she reaches for the broom tucked between the refrigerator and the wall, not taking her eyes off the mannered monster outside her window. She knows that Theo could not enter without an invitation; she hopes this creature is subject to the same rules, though it is clearly not a vampire. The notion of shapeshifting flits across her mind, but she dismisses it. If Theo could change into *that*, it probably would have come up by now.

She begins sweeping the glass into a small pile, pushing it onto a dustpan that she dumps in the garbage can. A few paper towels clean up the remaining water and any stray shards. Pilkington does not speak as she works, merely standing on her fire escape with both hands held at his waist.

Non-threatening. Polite.

Sylvia finishes clearing up the mess, gets herself a bottle of water from the fridge, gathers up her fallen necklace, and steps over to stand in front of the window. "Okay," she says, "what's this all about?" She wraps the silver chain around her hand, knowing that certain creatures cannot abide silver. It's a small weapon, but at least it's something. The creature's eyes dart to her hand then up to her face, a flash of realization there and gone. Sylvia moves her hand to her side, non-threatening but ready to act.

The monster—*demon,* Sylvia realizes, putting together the horns, wings, and tail—hunkers down, lips pursing as he seems to consider his words. Sylvia begins cataloguing the differences between this demon and the one that attacked her in the alley. Her demon is larger, winged, and seems generally smarter than the Balaam from weeks before. His eyes seem to notice everything. "I find myself in a rather awkward position," he finally begins.

"What position is that?" Sylvia leans back on her good ankle. Her other ankle is totally healed, but she still favors it in stressful moments like these—when she might have to run.

"I find myself under—" Whatever word he tries to say refuses to come out, and he scowls, the expression terrifying. Sylvia gasps, and his face immediately rearranges in that neutral, non-threatening mask. "It seems I cannot..." He looks away, then his eyes flick to the towel wrapped around her arm. "I find myself in need of something that you possess," he manages to say, each word carefully chosen.

"What do you need from me?" Sylvia asks, still on guard, but finding herself warming to the strange visitor. An idea strikes her, a memory of a conversation with Theo about demons. "Wait," she says, "are you under a compulsion?"

The demon jerks his head once, chin dipping to his chest in a nod, before returning upright. He winces, as if the movement cost him effort. *Is he resisting the compulsion not to share his mission with me?*

"What do you need of me?" Sylvia asks, aware that her words are open, inviting, but not promising to fulfill that need.

"I require some of your blood," the demon says, expression unhappy at his words.

Sylvia steps back automatically, wariness snaking up her spine. A quick scan reveals the broom to be her closest weapon—not the best situation—but Sylvia is honest with herself. She is no match for this creature if he decides to attack her. Theo is strong enough to burst through her locked door; she can only imagine the strength in this demon's muscles. He has so many of them.

"How much blood?" she asks, each word pronounced carefully. Part of her insists she should be running from the room, screaming for help, calling Theo to her aid, but that tiny voice inside whispers words of calm again. She is safe. This demon will not harm her. *Cannot* harm her.

"Not much," Pilkington replies, eyes flicking to the towel again. "Just a few drops."

"*Why* do you need my blood?" Sylvia presses.

Pilkington looks like he wants to speak, but he shrugs instead, the motion curling his wings up and back. Sylvia finds the move oddly hypnotic, brain skittering around the logistics of life with a wingspan.

"Did your…" she searches for the word Theo used, "summoner bind you to this task?"

Pilkington nods again, that same jerky motion that seems to defy some magical compulsion.

"Can you tell me who summoned you?" Sylvia asks, but she isn't surprised when Pilkington shakes his head in negation. "Will you be free after you receive my blood?"

The demon pauses, biting his lip to reveal another fang tip, considering how to reply, and Sylvia is about to ask another question when another voice in the darkness growls, "No one is taking your blood, Syl."

Theo appears behind the demon, the vampire's face a mask of fury, his entire body glowing with power. There is a brisk whooshing sound, a loud thump, and her fire escape is suddenly empty of all supernatural creatures. She climbs out the window, leaning over the railing to look down at the street. Theo looms over the body of the crouching demon, Pilkington making no move to attack, but also ready to defend himself.

"Wait!" Sylvia shouts down at them, trying to stop the imminent violence. "He's not here to hurt me! He wasn't doing anything!"

"He's after your blood," Theo says, not abandoning his threatening stance, taking a step toward the crouching demon.

"He's compelled!" Sylvia explains. "It's not his fault!"

"She speaks the truth, Muldavian," Pilkington says quickly, holding himself steady exactly where he landed.

The vampire's nostrils flare, and he flicks his gaze up to Sylvia, taking in her towel-wrapped arm. "You are bleeding, Syl," he says quietly, his voice terrifying.

"I knocked over a glass," she says, "and cut myself. It's fine."

Theo levels his gaze at the demon before him. "No doubt startled by the arrival of such a creature. Who sent you?" he demands.

"He can't tell you," Sylvia says. "He's compelled. Don't kill the messenger!" Sylvia can see that her words are having an effect, so she continues speaking to soothe him. "I was trying to find out who sent him, but he can't say a lot."

"I have no doubt of that," Theo scowls. He hasn't moved, but he is still looming over Pilkington. "Demons rarely say what they mean."

"He has been a perfect gentleman," Sylvia argues. "For fuck's sake, Theo. *Look* at him! Does he seem like a normal demon to you?"

"Demons are tricksters," Theo says, but something in his body relaxes as he studies the demon's expression, the way the demon hasn't made a threatening move since they landed on the street. Theo straightens, a decision made as he addresses Pilkington. "Go back to your Master. Tell him there will be no blood tonight."

Pilkington bristles a little, getting to his feet. "I have no Master," he snaps. At Theo's look, he adds, "I have ... a temporary arrangement involving compulsion." He looks up at Sylvia standing on the fire escape above. "Farewell, lady," he says with a graceful bow. Straightening up, he pins Theo with his gaze. "I will leave, but more will come. They will not stop at one failure."

"Is that a threat?" Theo growls, stalking a step closer.

"I am not your enemy, Muldavian," Pilkington tells him, and a noise down the street catches Sylvia's attention. She, Theo, and Pilkington turn to gape at a circle opening in the air above the street, a panel of darkness that grows from a small line in the air, stretching to a large circle before a shape pushes through it, a large creature with huge claws and bristling fur. The Balaam demon shrieks as it appears, lunging in Theo's direction. Pilkington gestures at the newcomer streaking toward them, stepping back to stand against the wall of the building. "I am not so certain about him, though."

Theo turns to face the creature, arms out to defend himself. The demon hits him at a run, and they both go hurtling backward, bodies tumbling on the empty street. Sylvia moves on her fire escape to see what is happening, voice caught in her throat. She thinks that Theo is strong enough—she saw him defeat a demon the night they met, but she also remembers the blood on his shirt. Sylvia holds her breath as the vampire rolls over with the monster. The demon swipes its claws at the vampire, but Theo grabs both of its arms and shoves it back, though not before a claw scrapes down one of his arms, leaving a trail of blood behind. The demon lunges again, and this time Theo kicks it in the center of its massive chest, sending it hurtling a few feet down the street to land in a crumpled heap. He turns back to Pilkington, who stands with his wings pressed against the building below, hands held carefully at his sides, face impassive.

"Not so certain?" Theo snarls. "Is this where you attack me as well?"

Pilkington shakes his head. "I assure you, Muldavian, I am no part of this rabble." There is another tearing sound, and another hole opens in the center of the street, a second demon clawing out of the empty space. This is not a creature Sylvia has seen before, all long sinewy limbs and red skin, long black claws and what look like two whipping tails tipped with barbs. Pilkington looks at Theo. "That one is definitely here to kill you."

CHAPTER 20

THEO

THEO'S REPLY IS INTERRUPTED AS THE SECOND DEMON runs into him, spinning him to the side with a slash of its tail and knocking him to the ground. Pilkington stands aside, watching as the vampire wrestles the newcomer, but when the first demon gets to its feet, the demon mutters, "At your back, Muldavian."

Theo swings himself around, placing the second demon between himself and the first. This one is much faster, ducking and weaving as it swipes at Theo with claws and tails. The vampire manages to fling the new demon away and scrambles to his feet, body ready as both demons advance on him. He is aware of Sylvia on the fire escape above, safe for the moment, and is relieved, though he can feel her frantic heart-beat. Adopting a defensive stance, Theo considers his enemies, knowing this will not be an easy fight. The fast demon requires one method of attack while the stronger takes another. Theo will have to keep shoving them back and adjusting his style as they approach—not the best strategy, but the only one he can see as he makes his stand, wishing for a moment that he had his sword with him. It's not the first time he's fought barehanded, but weapons make things much easier. He has fought demons before, knows the gist of their fighting style, but these demons both seem stronger, faster than he expects.

There is strange magic in this.

The fast demon's first barrage is clumsy, a flurry of hands and those sharp tails just as the stronger demon lumbers close. Theo manages to shove both creatures back, but a burning on his chest tells him that not all those claws missed their mark. His shirt is wet, blood flowing freely. He readjusts, using the wall of the building at his back to secure his position, propelling himself from it to push the demons back. His fists are steady, his punches perfectly placed to do the most damage, but the demons keep getting up, keep coming back, and each time, their claws do more damage. After a particularly close encounter that leaves blood streaming from his cheek, Theo reconsiders his tactic, using the slower demon's clumsy but brutal attacks against the other as often as possible, ducking out of the way to allow the large demon to hit the smaller one instead. The quick demon grabs hold of the remains of Theo's shirt, but the vampire sinks to the ground, slipping out of the bloody rag and landing an uppercut to the chest that sends it tumbling end over end. When the creature gets up again, it moves slowly, awkwardly slipping back into the fray.

Theo knows that he is strong, but he also knows when a battle is lost, and each barrage is taking a toll on his endurance, his strength leaking from every wound on his torso. He weaves, unsteady on his feet, but still moving, vision blurring with white spots.

As he falls to one knee, stopping himself from complete collapse, he has enough time to hope against hope that Pilkington will somehow protect Sylvia. Fear for her safety is enough to propel him to his feet for another blow.

CHAPTER 21

SYLVIA

"**D**O SOMETHING!" SYLVIA SCREAMS AT PILKINGTON, HANDS gripping the railing of the fire escape, the blood-soaked towel forgotten in her hand.

The demon stands in place below her, hands in his pockets. "I cannot."

"Please!" she shrieks, glancing frantically around for the release on the fire escape so she can get down to the street. She doesn't know what she can do to help, but she will not stay up here and watch Theo bleed to death. She hits the lever and the ladder slides down, nearly landing on Pilkington's head. She climbs down awkwardly, then grabs the demon's arm, pleading. "Help him! You can help him!"

Pilkington shakes his head again, a jerking motion, and Sylvia can feel the tension in his body, a form that seems to be leaning toward the fray but is frozen in place. "You're still compelled," she realizes, and a crazy idea runs through her mind. "Here!" She grabs the blood-soaked kitchen towel from where it has fallen to the street and tosses it at him, grasping at the chance. "Take my blood. Your obligation is fulfilled."

Pilkington stares at the towel, then tucks it neatly into his pants. He seems to shudder for a moment, then he steps away from her with a nod.

Theo has managed to fend off both demons, and now he punches one in the face with devastating force, the demon's head jerking backward at an awkward angle. The large creature wavers, then drops slowly to the ground in a heap. As Sylvia watches, the body fades away into nothing. The remaining demon seems not to notice the absence of its companion, continuing to swipe at Theo. The claws gouge into Theo's chest as the vampire reaches out to throttle his enemy, tails swishing as they seek more flesh. Theo is weak, strength fading as his hands raise to push them aside.

At the moment when it seems like the demon just may be able to deal a deadly blow, Pilkington steps up behind the creature and neatly decapitates it with a crisp swipe of his claws. He steps away to avoid the blood spray but still brushes at his chest and the few stray drops that hit him before the second body dematerializes. Theo wavers on his feet for a few seconds, unseeing eyes scanning for Sylvia, then drops to the ground senseless.

Sylvia runs to Theo's side, lifting his head and looking for signs of life. The vampire isn't breathing, but she knows that he doesn't normally. She looks up at Pilkington. "Is he dead?" she whispers, heart pounding in her ears.

The demon considers the prone vampire. "No. Not yet."

"What can I do?" Her voice is small, so quiet compared to the roaring in her head.

Pilkington raises a dark eyebrow, tucking hair back to reveal a pointed blue ear with silver hoops through the top. "You know what he needs."

Sylvia stares at him for a long moment, then her brain starts working again, panic receding as she takes charge.

Of course. That roaring subsides, replaced by cool certainty. *Theo needs blood.*

She looks around the street, still miraculously empty, but certainly not staying that way for long after the noisy fight. Sylvia is surprised no one else is outside already.

"Yes," she says, mostly to herself, then tries to move the vampire, shifting his shoulders, but his dead weight doesn't budge. Grabbing both arms to try to drag him, she looks at the ladder to the fire escape, then up to her apartment window. Impossibly far away. She considers the entrance to the building, but that would mean dragging the unconscious vampire around the corner and up the flight of stairs to her front door. "I have to get him inside," she says, looking at the demon. Her voice is steady as she speaks. "Will you help me?"

The demon nods, then moves to Theo's side, lifting the vampire with ease. A flap of those wings has him off the ground, and another has both creatures on her fire escape overhead. Sylvia climbs up the ladder with shaking hands and shoves the lever to pull the stairs back up behind her, not pausing to make sure they lock into place. The demon waits outside the window holding Theo in his arms, and Sylvia has to maneuver around them both to climb inside. She turns around, gesturing at the demon. "Put him on the bed."

But Pilkington still stands outside, Theo's limp bloody form in his arms. "I may not," the demon says.

"Fuck," Sylvia curses, thoughts crashing in her mind. She has to invite him in. She stares at the demon on her fire escape, considering and discarding alternatives. She can't get Theo inside on her own—she has to trust the demon. *He did just save Theo's life*. "Fine," she says, clearly speaking the words, "I invite you in to put the vampire on the bed."

He looks at her carefully, the invitation taking hold, then nods. "Well said." The demon steps over the windowsill, contorting his massive frame with what looks like magic to get inside with Theo in his arms, careful to keep the vampire from jostling too much. He lays Theo on the bed, then steps back to the window, eyes swiftly scanning the apartment. His gaze settles on the silver necklace, abandoned on the floor when she climbed onto the fire escape. He reaches down to pick it up, settling it gently on the inside of the ledge.

"Thank you," Sylvia says, barely aware of the demon in her apartment as she snatches a towel from the bathroom door and sits beside Theo on the bed, pressing it to the biggest wound on his chest.

Pilkington executes a cordial bow that Sylvia catches in the corner of her eye. "I wish you well." He turns to leave, stepping gracefully through the window again, wings warping in her vision, but he turns back to face her once more from the fire escape, calm words breaking through her focus on Theo. "More will come, no doubt." He gestures at the window frame when she looks up at him. "I would shut this."

At Sylvia's nod, Pilkington reaches up to shut the window, sliding it down with a gentleness that belies the raw strength in his arms. His body shifts, turning around and bending down, and Sylvia realizes he is locking the ladder back into place. Standing up, he faces her window again, nods formally, then lifts with a powerful thrust of wings and disappears into the night.

Sylvia stares at the empty window for a moment, marveling at the idea of flight, then turns her attention to the vampire on her bed, cataloguing the damage. His chest is a mess, the lines of his tattoos hidden by the smeared gore. His arms are lined with weeping cuts, but the puncture wounds just over his heart are the worst, a steady stream of blood running down to cover her hands. She presses the towel against them again, taking off her sweater and using it to first wipe down his arms, judging the cuts there before moving back to press harder on his chest. He has some wounds on his legs too, but nothing like the chest. Sylvia ignores them for the moment, focusing on his chest, pressing harder, watching his face for any signs of life. She wipes the slice down his cheek, dismayed to see the line open wide, a sluggish drop running down to drip off his chin.

Theo isn't healing.

She tries to rouse him, calling his name, pushing against him and prodding his wounds in a way that should have jarred him awake, but nothing seems to work. The blood flow slows, and though Sylvia wants this to be a good sign, she knows that it is not.

Theo is dying.

She remembers the demon's words. *You know what he needs.*

But how?

She glances around the apartment. *Should I use a knife?* She abandons the soaked towel on his chest, shoving her wet sweater aside as she climbs off the bed to raid the kitchen. Choosing a steak knife, she returns to her bed with the blade in hand. She looks at her hands, thinks of what she knows of vampires and Theo's needs, considers the seriousness of the situation, then drags the knife across her inner forearm, slashing across the cut from the broken glass, opening her flesh. She crawls on top of Theo, straddling his hips, and holds her arm above his face, watching as the blood begins to flow, dripping across first his chin, then, as she adjusts her position, his lips. At first, there is nothing, a long moment of silence that Sylvia counts along with her heartbeats.

Reaching out to touch Theo's face with her other hand, she presses her forearm against his mouth. She waits, silently praying, calling out to any gods who will listen.

Please, please, let this work. Bring him back to me.

A flutter of movement against her skin is all the warning Sylvia gets, the flash of pain as he latches on to her arm, then she is being flipped over, Theo pinning her to the bed, his body full length against hers, his mouth pulling hard on her skin. As she opens her eyes to look at him, he tosses her arm aside, face a mask of pure need, and presses against her neck, teeth sinking into her.

Then there is nothing, just the long slow pauses between heartbeats again, a sense of satisfaction as she feeds him, and Sylvia sinks into warm oblivion.

CHAPTER 22

THEO

WHEN THEO COMES BACK TO HIMSELF, HE IS LAYING ON top of someone, skin smeared with blood, body on fire with pain as it heals. He pushes up on his elbows, trying to piece together the last few moments. The memory of the demons floods through him, demons threatening his Sylvia, and he jerks fully awake, staring down in horror at the limp body beneath him.

"Oh no," he moans, searching her wrist for a pulse. He can't sense her heartbeat. "No, no, no, no," he mumbles, dropping her arm to feel her neck. Nothing. He presses his face to her chest then, eyes closed, listening with his body for the heartbeat he prays is still there. A long moment, and there it is, weak but a slow flutter.

It is enough.

He bites his wrist, pressing it to her lips, lifting her head so the blood runs into her mouth as he arranges her on his lap. "Take it, Syl," he coaxes, slipping into his native tongue as he speaks to her, calling her back from the dark.

It is a slow journey, but soon she stirs in his arms, mouth sucking the life from him, and he relaxes for the first time since awakening. At first, she simply clutches at his arm, eyes closed in furious concentration, grasping at survival. Slowly, though, the mood shifts, her hunger changing, and she sits up, tossing his wrist aside and lunging for his mouth. She kisses him fiercely, her slightly glowing body pressed hard against him, the taste of his blood in her mouth tantalizing. He holds her close, one hand wrapped in her hair, his other pulling her body atop him, finger sliding along her skin wet with his blood. His body still burns with healing, but he doesn't care, all of his attention on the living woman in his arms, her body burning like a flame as she straddles his hips, her legs wrapping hard around his back.

But Sylvia is not satisfied with mere kisses this time, and soon she rocks her hips against him, her passion increasing rather than waning as his blood takes hold, and with a strength that surprises him, she pulls back, untangling her legs to kneel atop him as she pushes him hard to the bed, pinning his hands above his head. Her eyes are open, the normal blue replaced by silver, and she stares at him with a hunger he recognizes, though not on her face. He's seen Sylvia close to that look, burning with desire, but never quite like this. He knows it is his blood, but it's more than that. He knows what tonight was supposed to be for both of them before he was called away, knows that some things are meant to happen, and he gives himself up to the fates.

Sylvia leans down, pressing her chest against him, her soaked tank top clinging to her like a second skin. Theo allows her to hold his arms down, knowing that he could push her off—probably—but she is strong with his blood, and he revels in her strength, in the notion that his delicate Syl could hold him captive. She releases her hold long enough to remove her shirt, baring all that skin and the jagged line of her scar to his gaze without hesitation. The move alone is enough to show Theo that she isn't entirely with him, not the Syl he knows, and he opens his mouth to speak, to break the moment, but then she presses her thighs against his, sliding down the length of his body, molding herself against the hard length of his erection, and he decides that he must touch her, must hold her.

He pushes against her arms as she leans down again, pressing her bare breasts to his finally healed chest, and is shocked to find that he actually cannot move her at all. His blood has given her strength beyond his expectations, and he marvels in the sensation. Sylvia grins down at him, not releasing his arms, relishing her momentary power, and she rocks her hips, pressing against him, her sleep shorts riding up as she slides back and forth.

Theo stares up at her, entranced at this beautiful blood-smeared woman claiming him, her breasts high and firm, her hair a glorious riot down her back. She pushes his arms together above his head, and Theo hears something snap, likely the futon back, but the bed stays steady beneath them. Sylvia reaches down, tearing the fabric of his pants and freeing him as she shoves her shorts aside. Theo pushes against her in earnest now, a small part of him still wanting to be sure, knowing the bloodlust has her firmly, but needing to know it is she who wants him.

"Syl," he whispers, his voice gentle in contrast to the savagery of her movement, the pure domination of her hands on him. "You want this?" he asks, voice low and somehow calm amid the frenzy, his own hips raising up to meet her body as she moves above him.

"Theo," she replies, and though she is still holding him down, still towering over him like some goddess of old, it is his Sylvia looking back at him. "I want you," she whispers, lowering herself ever so slowly onto his shaft. "Yes," she tells him, free hand cradling his cheek as she moves. "So much yes," she adds, closing her eyes to kiss him as she pulls herself tight against him. "Yes," she repeats, finally releasing him to press her palms against his bloody but healed chest, slowly riding him in a rhythm designed to devastate him. She is warm and tight and her newly touched skin echoes against his shaft in trembling desire. Theo reaches down slowly, hands sliding onto her body, holding her hips gently as she moves. After a long moment, she shudders, falling forward into his waiting embrace, meeting his mouth with fevered kisses as her body continues to rock back and forth on his hips.

"You," she whispers against his lips, then she pulls away, just far enough to stare deep into his soul with those silvered eyes, "are mine," she tells him, hips rising and falling in a rhythm to punctuate each word. As her body tightens around him with the start of another release, Theo falls into the moment, hands pulling her tight against his body as he gives himself to her completely.

"Yes," he agrees, later when she has collapsed against his chest, breath ragged and heart pounding against his skin. "I am yours."

CHAPTER 23

SYLVIA

"**W**HAT TIME IS IT?" SYLVIA MUMBLES, LIFTING HER HEAD slightly from where it rests at the foot of the bed.

"Late," Theo replies, pressing himself up behind her, both of them sticky and sweaty amid the chaos of the blankets. "Early."

"Morning?" she asks, opening an eye to judge the quality of light in the room. She doesn't move her body, not yet, still enjoying the sweet satisfaction that fills her being. Theo's blood sings in her veins, filling her with strength, not to mention the release of so much pent-up tension finally satisfied.

"Not yet," he says, lifting up on an elbow to look down at her face. "Why? You want me to go?"

Sylvia reaches down to pull his other arm tighter around her body, snuggling back into his embrace. "No way," she insists. She pauses, then adds, "Though I am starting to feel a bit gross from all this blood everywhere."

Theo nods, biting a lip swollen from her passionate kisses. "I think you need to wash these sheets."

Sylvia snorts. "I think I need to throw these sheets away." She rolls back a little, looking over her shoulder to where he lays behind her. "Is this why you have dark sheets in your apartment? To hide blood stains?"

The joy and ease on Theo's face fade, replaced by the neutral mask she dislikes. "I don't get blood on my sheets," Theo says, sitting up and sliding off the other side of the bed. Sylvia's skin is cold where he no longer presses against her. She marvels at the heat in him, her vampire filled with her blood, warming her body with his own, but he's already moving away, guilt souring the mood.

Sylvia sighs, hearing the multiple messages in his words. She flops onto her back, staring at the ceiling for a moment, cataloguing the circles of light thrown by the lamp on her night table. Theo watches her silently for a long moment, then shakes his head, mussed red hair sliding around his face and shoulders. Sylvia wants to touch it, run her fingers through it again, savor the satiny strands running across her skin.

"What do you want, Syl?" Theo whispers.

Deciding to ignore his somber tone, she smirks, tilting her head back and looking up at his towering frame at the foot of her bed. "Well, this is definitely a Taco Shack moment, but I'm pretty sure we missed the 4am closing time." She sits up, relishing the strength in her limbs, the satisfaction in her entire body. "I guess a shower comes first, though." She glances at the bed around her. "And new sheets."

Theo nods, holding his hand out to help her stand on watery legs. They pile all the stained blankets on the floor, adding her ruined clothes and his ripped pants. Sylvia sees the look on his face as they abandon the clothing, and she wonders how the vampire will get home without clothes. She has a brief vision of him flying home in her robe and can't stop the giggle that bursts free.

"What?" he asks.

"Nothing." She smiles. "Just wondering what you're wearing home."

Theo shrugs, his hair wild around his face, body still streaked with dry blood. "I'll figure it out. How about that shower first?"

Leading them into the small bathroom, he turns the water on but lets Sylvia adjust the temperature, stepping in behind her and closing the curtain. The water is pink beneath them, blood running off their bodies to circle the drain. Theo lifts the bar of soap, then raises an eyebrow at Syl. At her nod, he washes her body, hands gentle, a contrast from the fierce passion of the last few hours. Sylvia lets herself be washed and pampered, relishing the feel of his hands on her body, his fingers in her hair, massaging her scalp. When he washes her back, she leans in close, body pressed against him, and her arms wrap around his back tightly, suddenly afraid that she will lose him.

"That was bad," she whispers against his chest.

Theo's hands freeze on her back. "I thought you liked it."

"No," she says, looking up at him, water dripping into her eyes and making her blink. "That was awesome. Really great." She tightens her grip around his back. "I mean before. Earlier. That was awful."

Theo turns to return the soap to the dish, but she catches his hand, slowly running the bar over his arms and shoulders, down his chest, and over the curve of his backside. She takes her time with the shampoo, fingers enjoying all that hair. When she is done, he wraps her in his arms, burying his face in her neck. For a moment, Sylvia wonders if he will bite her again, but the thought is fleeting, and he simply kisses her neck. They hold each other for a moment, then he lifts his head and looks down at her, red hair curling around his face. "I'm so sorry, Syl."

"Why are you sorry?" she asks. "There's nothing to be sorry about."

"I didn't protect you," he says softly. "If he hadn't helped me, I would not have been able to stop them."

"Theo," she says firmly, "you nearly died tonight."

He reaches down to touch her face. "*You* nearly died tonight," he says. "And I was the one who almost killed you."

"But you didn't," she insists. "I'm fine." But she can see the guilt in his eyes, that bright gold faded now, and she remembers the lust in his eyes as he bit her. A small thrum echoes out from her belly at the memory of him like that, and she bites her lip.

"We can't do this again," he declares, shaking his head. "It's too dangerous."

Sylvia releases him, running her hands down her body to wipe away the last of the soap. She's angry again, the familiar annoyance at this same argument, and she waits to collect her thoughts before speaking. "Should I have let you die then?"

Theo looks up from where he has been rinsing his chest, eyes wide.

"You were dying," Sylvia says. "I had no choice."

Theo takes her chin in his hand and lifts her face so she can see his mouth say the words. "There is always a choice, Syl." He pauses, swallowing hard. "I am grateful, you know I am, but that was so dangerous, Syl. So dangerous."

"I couldn't let you die," she insists.

"And what about me?" he asks. Sylvia narrows her eyes, confused. "What should I have done if I came back to myself too late and you were dead?"

"But you didn't," she repeats, though her skin goes cold at the thought, the shower seeming to lose its heat. She turns around, pulling away from him to adjust the water, soaking in the heat as it warms her. For all that she is annoyed with Theo, scared and worried, her body still sings with happiness, her spirit content.

"Do you want to be a vampire?" Theo asks from behind her. "Do you want to live like me?"

Sylvia thinks of the dawn arriving soon, at the idea of having to hide away from the sun forever, of feeling the hunger she glimpsed earlier, and shakes her head. "No," she whispers. "I don't."

"I didn't think so."

They finish the shower in thoughtful silence, but when Sylvia turns off the water, Theo hops out and hands her the bigger towel, taking a moment to dry her off with his big hands. The tension between them eases, but it doesn't disappear. She dries Theo with the other towel, then appreciates that fine body wearing only a low-slung towel across his hips. A glance at the clock when they exit the bathroom lets her know that Theo doesn't have much time left with her.

He helps her remake the bed with her spare sheets, and she makes a note to buy another set tomorrow, darker colors this time, just in case.

"Do we want to talk about the demons?" Theo asks when the bed is made, and Sylvia flops across it, sleep calling her name.

"Do we have to?" she moans, putting an arm over her face. Theo sits next to her.

"We can probably wait until tonight, so long as you don't leave the apartment today."

Sylvia nods. "They can't come in unless invited, right? Like you?"

"Most of them, yes." He frowns. "Maybe you should stay somewhere else today," he suggests. "Like a hotel."

Pulling the blanket up to her chin and snuggling into her cozy clean bed, Sylvia frowns at him. "But I'm so comfortable," she groans. At his look, she grunts. "Fine! I'll just take a short nap and then get a room somewhere." She lifts an eyebrow at him. "You better be paying though."

Theo chuckles. "Of course."

A thought hits Sylvia, and she sits up, blanket forgotten. "Theo!" she says. "What about Grace?"

"She's fine," Theo assures her with a smile. "Apparently, she lost her phone yesterday."

Something in Theo's expression makes Sylvia ask. "You don't think she lost it, do you? You think someone stole it."

"The timing is too perfect," he muses, running a hand through his hair and starting to braid it. "Those demons knew you would be here ... without me." He finishes the braid, then gives her a hard look. "He's definitely hunting you, and until we have a better plan, you shouldn't be where he knows you are."

"So, what is the plan then?"

Theo shakes his head. "I'm not sure yet. I'd like to ask Oren and Harald, if that's alright with you."

Sylvia nods. "Of course. They're your friends."

"And damn fine fighters," Theo adds. "Had they been here tonight, I would not have failed."

"Had they been here tonight," Sylvia comments with a leisurely stretch, the sheet sliding beneath her bare breasts, "none of this would have happened, and I wouldn't feel so satisfied."

Theo rewards her with a warm grin, a hint of fang revealing the edge of his desire. "I am glad to hear I satisfy you," he says, leaning down to kiss her.

After they pull apart, Sylvia stares up at him. "You do satisfy me," she tells him, "now." She pauses, then forges forward, unwilling to let him go without at least bringing it up. "But what about next year, ten years from now?"

"I imagine I will continue to hone my skills," Theo replies, but she knows he is trying to distract her.

"I'm serious," she says. "What happens to this... to us? I don't want to be a vampire. How...?"

"I don't know," Theo murmurs.

"Haven't you dated a human before? What did you do?" she presses.

Theo looks away, then kisses her again. "I have never 'dated' a human before," he admits. "Not like this."

"What do you mean by that? Like this?"

Theo frowns, looking away from her to stare at the floor. "I don't do this, Syl. I don't go on dates. I don't stay the night." He runs a hand over his head, pushing stray hairs behind his ears.

"But here you are," Sylvia whispers.

"Here I am," he repeats, a sad smile on his lips.

"I don't know if that's endearing or terrifying," Sylvia comments, "and I'm too tired to decide now." She looks up at him. "What happens tomorrow?"

"Tomorrow we will plan to remove this demon threat," Theo says. "I should have done it tonight, but other things came up."

"Totally worth it," Sylvia tells him. "Demon-planning tomorrow. No problem."

Sylvia drifts off into sleep as Theo sets up the hotel room, but he wakes her long enough to force a promise. "Sylvia," he says, shaking her shoulder gently, "I need you to do two things for me today."

Sylvia opens sleepy eyes to look at him, her vampire lover. "What?"

"First, go to the hotel as soon as you can. I know you need to rest, but don't stay here too long after dawn."

"Okay," Sylvia agrees. "Will do." She gives him a lazy thumbs up. "And the other?"

Theo moves so his face is very close to hers, and she blinks hard, awake now. "*Don't die,*" he demands. "You have my blood in you, so you are strong, but you are also subject to my weaknesses. Whatever you do, do not die in the next week. Not unless you want to become a vampire like me."

Sylvia nods, a wave of cold rushing through her at the thought. "I won't," she promises, kissing him hard. When he stands up, the first hint of pre-dawn light leaking into the room, she giggles at the towel still slung around his waist. "Great look," she comments.

"Vampire morning after chic. Is this the vampire walk of shame, then?"

Theo smirks at her, the look very much male. "It's called the stride of pride, Syl."

Sylvia giggles, then rolls her eyes. "Such a guy thing to say. Won't people see you?"

Theo shakes his head. "I'll be fine." He gives the window a quick glance, as if judging his time. This is later than he has ever stayed before, but he should be able to fly back to his coffin before the sun actually rises. He still has a few minutes left. "Be careful, Syl."

She nods, tucking the blanket under her head as she snuggles back into bed. "I will. You too." She blows him a kiss. "See you tonight."

Theo leaves through the window, and Sylvia giggles once more at the towel-clad vampire fleeing her apartment before falling into a deep sleep. She wakes hours later, much later than she intended, so she quickly packs a small bag with a few overnight items. She's not sure how long she will be away, but she does her best.

Sylvia puts on the silver necklace before she leaves, feeling oddly safer with it on. She considers bringing the bag of bloody sheets down to the garbage, but the bin is in the basement, and that seems too risky given the demons pursuing her.

She walks quickly down the stairs and onto the street, feeling safer in the sunlight as she heads to the hotel, even though the bright light makes her thankful she wears sunglasses. The sun feels too hot on her skin, no doubt an aftereffect of Theo's blood. *Will I get a sunburn from a four block walk outside?* She studies the others out on the street with her as she moves. Theo never actually said whether demons could be out during the day or not—she really should have asked him. But she knows they need to be invited inside, so similar rules probably apply.

She is two blocks from the hotel's entrance when a man grabs her from behind, wrapping his arms around her body. Sylvia immediately tries to break free, but something warm and fuzzy envelops her, magic dulling her senses—then, she is swimming through a fog, distantly aware of her body sliding limply into her attacker's very human arms.

Idiot, she thinks blearily. *Demons aren't the only dangerous things in this city.*

CHAPTER 24

PILKINGTON

PILKINGTON SITS IN THE CIRCLE, PERMANENT SCOWL IN place as Charlie Wagner watches him from across the room. The demon considered standing for a moment, but he doesn't want the summoner to see the effort it would take to get comfortable with his wings in the small space. He misses the open air of Sylvia's fire escape, the wind in his face as he flew back here to deliver the required blood.

Charlie had glanced at him curiously when the demon handed him the towel soaked with Syl's blood, but the old wizard hadn't said anything. Pilkington had fulfilled the requirements of the request, so there was nothing to say. For a brief moment, Pilkington had hoped that would be the end of it, and Charlie would release him—or the magic itself would let him go.

But the dagger changes everything, altering the flow of power in the exchange, forcing Pilkington to sit in the circle and wait for his next command. Because there will be another. And another.

Pilkington has heard of demons who spent years trapped in circles, bound to the will of their summoners, but those were lesser demons, creatures of great physical strength but little magic. They had no way to free themselves without killing their summoner after a mistake was made.

Pilkington is no lesser demon, no minor imp, and he knows the only thing keeping him in this place is the deadly power of the artifact in Charlie's hand. Pilkington has to give him some credit—the man never lets go of the dagger, keeping it always in one hand, going about his other tasks with the other hand. Pilkington pushes out with his power again, pressing hard against the wall of the circle, but nothing has changed.

When he handed Charlie the towel, the summoner had simply said, "You will wait there," and instantly, Pilkington was trapped in another circle, magic as smooth as glass keeping him in place. He has pushed with all different kinds of magic—his own abilities seem non-existent in this space. The skills he inherited from his mother barely make the walls shimmer for an instant, but they solidify immediately. At Pilkington's last attempt, Charlie had glanced at the dagger in his hand, then over to the trapped demon in the circle, a small grin on his face. He looked like he wanted to say something, to comment, but he turned away instead, the years having taught him restraint at last.

Pilkington has been in the circle for hours, the night faded into dawn, the smallest hints of light trickling into the underground station through cracks in the ceiling high above, when he finally decides to try the magic he inherited from his father. He's not comfortable with that power, avoids it as much as he can, remembering how easily it rises in him, taking over and turning him into something else, a mere vessel for an otherworldly power.

He doesn't want to admit it, but the sunlight makes him decide to try. Sylvia has been protected through the night by her vampire, but with the rise of the sun, she is defenseless again. Well, as defenseless as his arusha could ever be.

Just a little, he thinks. *Just to see if it does anything.*

He pushes a tiny whisper of the power into the circle around him. The magical air shivers, and a wave slides up around him, rising to the ceiling far above him. Pilkington pulls back as Charlie turns, not wanting the wizard to see what he is doing. Charlie moves to the stairs in the far wall, seeming to wait for something.

Or someone. I don't have much time. Pilkington concentrates again, that wave larger this time, warping the circle—and the ground beneath him. He feels it then, the power within straining to break free, and he knows that with one more push, he can bring down this entire room, crushing Charlie with the ceiling. Pilkington will also be buried, but he isn't worried. He's strong. He will survive.

Pilkington braces himself, gritting his teeth and curling his wings close to his body, ready to push—then he feels something he was hoping to avoid. A familiar presence on the stairs, then carried into the room. He pulls the magic back at the last moment, incapable of risking the room's destruction if she is in it.

The tall blond man from the previous night appears on the stairs, carrying Sylvia over one shoulder, her body limp and clearly bespelled. The blond takes a few steps to the center of the room, then drops Sylvia's body onto the ground. As her head thumps onto her shoulder, Pilkington vows to end the blond's life. The man kneels beside Pilkington's arusha, retrieving zip ties from his pocket and binding her hands in front of her. He considers her legs with something like faded lust, but then he shrugs, the need for revenge stronger. Pilkington stares at the man as he pulls a long tie from his other pocket and wraps it around her face, tucking it inside her mouth like a gag. His fingers linger on Sylvia's chin a few moments too long, then he stands and moves over to speak quietly with Charlie.

Could that be Adam? The same man who dated Sylvia only a few months ago? Pilkington squints, struggling to see the resemblance. He only saw Adam from a distance a handful of times, and he was always more focused on Sylvia. It's possible—the hair and build are the same—but his reaction to Sylvia is so ... *wrong.* What had she done to Adam? He grins. *No doubt he deserved it.*

Pilkington studies Sylvia from where he sits, perfectly still, taking in the long flowered skirt that folds over her bent legs, the white tank top that doesn't cover the obvious marks on her neck even with the black jacket. She has lost a shoe, one foot still wearing a simple sandal and the other bare. Her face is calm, eyes closed, her hair braided over one shoulder and resting on the floor.

She is alive. She will remain that way.

234

Even trapped within his own circle, Pilkington notices that her scent has shifted subtly, something there last night now vanished, covered by the smell of her vampire lover, and despite the dire situation, he smiles.

CHAPTER 25

Sylvia

SYLVIA WAKES SLOWLY, COMING BACK INTO HER BODY IN fits and starts, the magic releasing her in waves. She is suddenly aware of a cottony tongue inside her mouth, and she swallows frantically a few times to wet her throat. She tries to lick her lips, but there is something stopping her, and she struggles to understand before her brain remembers the hand on the street, and she assumes she must be gagged, the cloth not tight but definitely in her mouth and wrapped around her head. She tries to open an eye to see where she is, but a wave of nausea rolls through the guts she just rediscovered, the sickness shifting into a massive headache that makes her decide not to open her eyes. Taking a slower stock of her body, she learns that she lays on something hard, likely a concrete floor, her left side cold enough to suggest she's been here for a while. She wiggles her ankles, rubs them against one another, and finds that her feet are free, but she is only wearing one shoe. She

236

must have lost the other when she was snatched on the street. The top of her bare foot is freezing cold against the floor.

She listens for a few heartbeats, trying to isolate sounds, but nothing stands out. There is no hum of traffic or honking cars, so she must be farther away from her apartment, or even Theo's, but she knows there are parts of the city that are quiet, warehouses in the industrial area near the river that bustle with activity when a ship comes in but are desolate between each unloading. But this space doesn't feel like a warehouse; it feels closed in somehow, maybe underground. The air is slightly musty too.

I wasn't that far from home when they grabbed me. I'm not sure how much time has passed, but I've been here long enough to be freezing, so I'm guessing a few hours. I don't have to pee, so it couldn't have been longer than that.

She checks the rest of her body methodically, her aching shoulder pressed against the floor, her arms bent in front of her, noting the way sensation ends at her wrists. For a panicked moment, she wonders, *do I still have hands? Is this a twinge of phantom pain surging into my forearms?* Then, she realizes her hands have fallen asleep from the awkward position on the floor. She wiggles a finger, relieved at the odd sensation of her flesh as she grazes her belly through the thin tank top.

She moves a little more, slowly, subtly, judging that her hands are bound at the wrists with something that digs into her skin.

The pounding in her head retreats, and she risks opening one eye, the one nearest the floor, hoping that whoever kidnapped her won't see she's awake right away. Loose strands from her braid fall over her face, and though she wants to push it aside, she stays still, taking in her surroundings.

So, the rumors are true. There really are abandoned subway stations under the city, Sylvia wonders. *Are there alligators in the sewers as well?*

She lays on what would have been the platform, though the area where the tracks belong has been filled in with huge blocks of concrete and stray bits of trash, rebar and metal glinting in the pale sunlight leaking in from cracks in the roof far above.

But I'm not in downtown, she realizes, studying the way the light streaks through the dark space, dust motes floating through the air shafts. *Someone would notice those holes go too deep if they walked above us. So, I must be just outside the city. Maybe along the river where the old trains used to drop coal on steamships last century.* She realizes two facts: she is too far away for anyone to hear her screams, and by the light in the room, Theo won't wake for a while.

He cannot rescue her. She is alone.

The thought is terrifying. Stimulating. And something washes through her, rage like nothing else that has come before, and suddenly her mind is clear.

She doesn't need Theo. She can do this on her own. She takes a deep breath, feeling the echo of Theo's strength in her body, not like last night, but still vibrant.

They won't expect resistance, she thinks. *They will think I am terrified.*

I am terrified, she admits. *But I will survive this.*

And if I die, the thought drifts across her mind, *I will become a vampire. So, actually, I can't die.* That thought is sobering, and Sylvia knows just how very much she wants to live, how much she values her life the way it is, and her determination to live doubles.

Sylvia freezes, hearing the shuffles of feet behind her. The feeling slowly creeps back into her hands with burning fire, and Sylvia thinks she can break the restraints once she can feel her body again.

She takes another long look around, this time with both eyes and realizes that what she took for a shadow next to the tracks is actually Pilkington, the demon sitting cross legged inside a small circle. He stares at her and shakes his head in a quick negative, his eyes cutting to something behind her and back at her. The message is clear—*don't move.* His eyes look up to the ceiling, as if gauging the quality of the fading light, and very subtly, his hand taps against the outside of his wrist, as if to note the time. Sylvia watches him for another moment, wondering if there is more to the message, but he doesn't move again. There is something odd about the space around him, the air somehow warping in front of him, and Sylvia assumes he is trapped inside that circle.

His poor wings, crunched in that small space with him.

She runs through the little she has learned about demons—searching her memory for some way to free him—but comes up empty. Pilkington must obey the summoner and can do little to help her beyond mentioning the time. She considers the light. *Maybe a half hour to sunset?*

Somehow she can sense the position of the sun, another gift from Theo's blood. She recalls the oh so human hand that grabbed her on the street. Just a man.

Maybe two of them. With Theo's strength in her veins, she can totally take them.

"It's nearly time," a voice says, and Sylvia's heart begins to pound at the sound, courage draining out of her.

No.

Her mind refuses to get beyond the word, and all at once she is a girl tied to a stone pedestal in a cemetery, Charlie Wagner invoking a demon with her blood. She knew he hunted her, knew he sent the demons, knew and understood it logically in her mind, but even so, her body's reaction to that sound is beyond her control.

"Get her ready."

A hand grabs her shoulder and rolls her onto her back, and her wide terrified eyes look up into Adam's face, and the paralyzing fear is gone, replaced by rage. She punches him without thought, the zipties around her wrists snapping easily, and she watches him fly across the room to crash into a pillar with a satisfying crunch.

Game on, she thinks.

She gets slowly to her feet, trying to hold on to this feeling of superiority before she sees him, the demon of her childhood. The stranger had shown up last time, just in time to save her from being served to some demon from the underworld, but this time, a tiny part of her hopes that she is truly on her own this time. She wants to do this alone. Slowly, she turns to face Charlie Wagner.

And there he is, just a middle-aged man with thinning hair, scrawny from years of hard living, but the dagger he holds casually is a warning. She may be strong, but she is still human, and that blade can kill her. She studies the blade—*old*, she thinks, *pre-fifth century, probably Middle Eastern.*

"Sylvia," he whispers. "How strong you are." He nods. "I thought you might have some of his blood." He gestures at something behind her, and Sylvia remembers Pilkington. "It's better this way," he says. "Proper."

Firm blue hands grip her from behind, the touch gentle, but she can feel the steely strength beneath the hold, and Sylvia knows she is outmatched. She saw what those demons did to Theo, and the vampire is far stronger than she is even with his blood, not to mention a trained fighter. Besides, she doesn't want to fight Pilkington. He's only doing what he has to do.

There has to be another way.

Then the demon holding her taps his claw against the top of his wrist in three quick motions, an echo of what she had seen before, the universal signal for time. But what does it mean? That she should wait for the right time? Or that time is running out? *I should have learned sign language.*

She looks at the light, gauging with the new inner sensor. Maybe fifteen minutes before Theo can come. She sees the circle on the floor, outlined in what must be her blood. The air warbles around it, similar to what surrounded Pilkington before, and her skin prickles as something inside her recognizes the magic. This time, there will be no stone slab, no restraints. Whatever Charlie has planned is new.

Charlie gestures, and Pilkington stiffens behind her. The demon starts to move her forward, but slowly, as if he is resisting, dragging out the moment to buy time.

Fine, Sylvia thinks, *more time. I can do that.* One thing she does remember about Charlie is his love of talking, especially about how brilliant he is.

"What are you doing?" she asks, her voice timid.

"Finishing what I started," he tells her, reaching out his hand. Pilkington moves her left arm out in front of her, huge hand around her wrist as he presents her hand palm up to Charlie. She can almost hear the demon screaming his resistance, but his body obeys his master.

"What you started?" she blurts. "You mean what that witch started—and you ran away from." Charlie's expression darkness, and Sylvia remembers her plan to get him talking, to waste time, and adds, "But how are you doing this?" She looks around the room with wide eyes, marveling as she takes everything in: the circles, and dagger he holds, the demon behind her. "When did you get so *powerful*?" she asks, knowing it will please him.

He chuckles, rough hand running across her palm. She resists the urge to pull away, not that she could with Pilkington holding her arm in place. The summoner runs the tip of the knife against the skin in the center of her hand, and for a second, she feels nothing, but then the burning starts, and a line of red appears. "This blade," he tells her, watching her face as she stares at her hand. Sylvia realizes that he expects her to be shocked at the blood, and she tries to school her expression. Clearly, he hasn't spent much time with vampires if he expects a little cut like that to scare her. "It's very special," he continues.

No shit, Sylvia thinks, but she stares at her hand, eyes wide with pretend shock and honest fear.

Charlie moves the knife and slashes at Pilkington instead, the blade slicing easily through the cloth glove that covers the demon's forearm and the top of his hands, a small piece of black fabric drifting free to fall to the ground. Sylvia sees a thin white line on Pilkington's forearm, a strange mark that disappears beneath the rest of the bracer, and she feels the demon's body tense behind her, a sudden burst of outrage bleeding into her, but Pilkington doesn't move, doesn't speak—doesn't fight back.

Something about the mark teases her memory, tickling just beyond what she remembers, but then Charlie is speaking again.

"Demons have no power against it," Charlie says. He gestures, and Pilkington is moving her, walking slowly over to the circle drawn on the concrete. "They must obey me."

"Don't they have to obey you anyway?" Sylvia asks, stalling again. "What's so special about that dagger?"

Charlie holds it up, examining the blade in the last of the day's light. "They say it once belonged to an ancient god," he whispers. "Perhaps an angel." He looks at her, eyes blazing with the edge of madness. "With it, I will summon a demon greater than anything those Tallardy bitches could dream of." He glances beyond Sylvia to the demon still holding her arm. "Oh, I know who you are, Pilkington." He sneers the name. "Not a Palici like she thought. Oh no, you are something else entirely." He smiles at Sylvia, his eyes cold daggers. "When she calls the Greater Demon Hesperus, I will control both of you—the dark and the light." Sylvia doesn't like the way Pilkington's entire body tightens at the words, isn't willing to look at the expression on the demon's face. She doesn't recognize the name Hesperus, but if it makes Pilkington uncomfortable, it's definitely something terrible.

"But what do you want with me? How do I call this demon?" she asks. "If you have some sort of magic demon-controlling blade, why do you need me?"

Pilkington pushes her into the circle, and she stumbles a little bit, catching herself on the invisible wall of air on the far side. As the demon steps away, he drags his foot ever so slightly across the line, smearing her blood just a little bit. Sylvia stands in the center of the space, arms out to feel the boundaries of the circle around her. It's like a tube of glass, but she can see and hear just fine. She runs her hands all around, and at the spot where Mr. Pilkington smeared her blood, her fingers dip out, just a little bit.

It's a hole, she realizes, *a hole in the binding circle. Can I make it bigger and escape? But he said to wait.*

Not yet.

The cut on her hand leaves smears on the wall of magic around her, and she stares over it at Charlie, not looking at Pilkington, who has retreated to his own circle across the room, hands pressing hard against one another, as if keeping himself from striking the summoner on the way by.

"Bait," Charlie Wagner tells her with a sneer. "I can control them when they come, but I can't make them come."

A shuffling groan from the pillar distracts her, and Adam sits up from where she threw him, climbing onto shaky feet with blood running down his face. He still hasn't completely healed from the beating Theo gave him a few weeks ago, and Sylvia isn't sorry to see new damage. She remembers him in her living room, a rag-doll in Theo's grip.

"Excellent," Charlie says as Adam makes his way to his side. "You'll get to see the show." He looks at the ceiling, then raises the dagger over his head. "It is time. I invoke thee…"

It happens too fast for Sylvia to interrupt, and the rest of his words are lost in the rush of air inside the circle. Sylvia gasps, trying to breathe in the sudden vacuum, and she slides to the floor, back pressed against the circle where the gap is, hiding the opening from Charlie. She looks up, watching the air above her coalesce into darkness. Soon the darkness has a shape, then there is a hulking creature in the space with her, its huge clawed feet materializing on top of her legs, the weight of it nearly unbearable. She wants to move, to pull away, but she holds herself still, not wanting to draw its attention.

Pilkington is big, but this creature is *bigger*, its body defying the amount of space inside the circle. It has massive wings that are pressed hard against its back, a huge chest and powerful arms tipped with dark claws. Its grayish-green skin is marked with dark lines like Pilkington, but they are in a different pattern, more savage where Pilkington's seem almost lovely in comparison. It has no hair, but two large horns sprout from the side of its head, and Sylvia thinks of Darkness, the villain in a movie she watched as a child—and never again after the cemetery. A long tail swishes back and forth behind the demon, tipped with a sharp claw, and Sylvia presses herself harder into the wall of magic, not wanting that thing to touch her.

She can hear Charlie speaking again, his words clear after that rush of power, and the air inside the circle has normalized. Sylvia takes a shallow breath, frozen against the wall, ignoring the pain of claws slicing into her flesh. "I offer unto thee this virgin sacrifice, oh Great Destroyer of Worlds," he says. The demon cocks its head at him, glances down at her dismissively, then back up at the summoner.

"What fool do you take me for, pretender?" the creature hisses, and its voice makes Sylvia's head ache. She expected the sound to be deeper, but it's almost a whisper, the kind of sound that could get into a person's head and drive her mad. Sylvia wants to cover her ears, but she doesn't move.

The light is fading now, sunset nearly arrived. *How long will it take for Theo to find me? Will he even be in time?*

The question seems to take Charlie off guard, and he adjusts his grip on the blade, a bead of sweat dripping down his forehead. "I would never presume, oh Great One," he says, a disgusting note of wheedling in his voice. He gestures at her in the circle with the demon. "I summon thee with a suitable sacrifice."

Again, the demon glances at Sylvia, then back at Charlie. "Suitable," it echoes. "Sacrifice." This time its voice is hard, and Adam winces, a thread of blood streaming from his nose. He takes a step away from Charlie, away from the circle. "Do you think to play with me, mortal?"

"I give you virgin blood!" Charlie yells. At the demon's awful chuckle, Charlie looks at Sylvia and back at the demon. His gaze is hard as he turns to Pilkington, the demon suddenly standing next to him, hands folded before him, the image of perfect obedience.

"But you brought her blood!" Charlie snarls at Pilkington. "You are bound to me! You have to obey me!" He raises the dagger, and the demon in the circle follows the movement, its head tilting sideways, fangs showing as it pulls back its lips in a snarl.

But Charlie doesn't see the demon's reaction. He is focused on Pilkington, who smirks, seeming not to care about the magical artifact so near his face. "And I did obey you, my lord, to the letter."

Sylvia decides she has waited long enough. She scoots to the side, revealing the small tear in the circle. "He means to bind you to him with the blade," she says quickly. "He wants to force you into eternal service." The demon snarls and shoves her aside, claws digging into Sylvia's chest as it tosses her behind it, its body suddenly dissolving to black mist as it spills through the small opening in the magic. Sylvia slides down the wall of the circle, but even before she hits the floor, she sees the demon appear outside the circle.

Charlie raises the blade to defend himself, but something is wrong. This demon isn't bound by anything except vengeance. It strikes swiftly, and Sylvia hears the scream end in a sudden wet crunch. She may have fainted for a moment because the next thing she knows is how dark and cold the room has gotten, and that hideous demon face looms a few inches from her own, dark eyes peering down at her through the warped air. It drags a clawed hand against the barrier between them, the sound a strange scraping noise that echoes inside Sylvia's skull.

"And you, little bait," it whispers in that horrible voice. "I owe you my freedom, for without you, I would be bound even now." It stares at her for a long moment, and Sylvia's hands scrabble at her chest, fingers hooking on the compass around her neck. The demon's golden eyes follow the movement, and it looks at her fingers, then its lips stretch in a hideous expression.

Sylvia thinks it might be a smile. She feels something gathering around them both, a rush of power, and there is a horrible feeling in Sylvia's chest, a zinging crunch, and she realizes that she hasn't been able to feel much of anything since the demon threw her. The feeling fades immediately, then Sylvia is just cold again, feeling very heavy as she lays on the floor. The demon nods and stands back up. It says something in a guttural tongue to Pilkington, and her demon replies in the same language. The demon makes an awful sound, a mockery of laughter, and she sees Pilkington drop into an elaborate bow before it, then it is gone.

Pilkington squats before her, smearing the blood circle with what looks like a bloody shoe, Charlie's shoe, she realizes with a shock, then he is dragging her onto his lap, huge hands gentle as he rolls her onto her back. The sun has set, and the room is so cold. The demon presses one of his hands against her chest, their fingers tangling for a moment as he moves her fingers and the necklace out of the way, and there is an awful sucking sound. Sylvia tries to look down, but Pilkington's other hand grabs her chin.

"Don't," he says. "Just lay. He'll be here soon."

Who is he talking about? Then, she just stares up at the oddly groomed demon—so different from the monster that had just disappeared into the night.

"Adam?" she whispers, surprised at how firm her voice still is despite that awful emptiness in her chest.

Pilkington shakes his head. "He ran. Coward."

"Charlie?" she asks, though she knows the answer.

"He paid for his mistakes with his life," the demon replies. Sylvia follows his gaze to where the blade lies discarded on the floor near a splash of blood.

"Why did you help me?" she asks, mind wandering as some of the heaviness begins to fade.

"I could not leave you," he tells her, and she tries to reach up to touch him, this strangely polite demon.

"Could not?" she echoes, her fingers twining with his, blood slicking their touch around the necklace she still holds. "More compulsion magic?"

"I would not," he corrects himself. "I would not leave you helpless."

"I am not helpless," she says, the lightness growing. "I am so strong."

Pilkington shakes her gently. "You are strong." He looks away from her to glance at the stairs, then back at her face. "And if your lover doesn't hurry up, you will be stronger still."

"Am I dying?" she asks, oddly unconcerned with the response.

"Not if I can help it," the demon says.

Is that weird crackling against my skin his magic keeping my body alive? Something in her recognizes the feeling, the sensation of laying in his arms as he holds her together.

"Do I...?" she begins. "Do I know you?" She squints, trying to see his face through the light growing around her.

That's odd, she thinks. *It was getting darker, not lighter.* But Pilkington's entire body seems to glow around her, a small cocoon of light in the dark space beneath the world.

"I know you," she says. "I know this ... this feeling." The demon says nothing, and a memory flashes through Sylvia, there and gone, of a man's face in the night, *I am yours, Arusha.*

"Arusha," she echoes, recalling the word Phil said to her as he left that last time. "What is arusha?"

"You," the demon says in a quiet voice. "You are my arusha."

"Oh," Sylvia says, knowing he speaks the truth, feeling it somewhere inside. "Are you mine?" she asks, not knowing why it feels like it isn't the right question to ask.

"Always," he says, and Sylvia isn't sure he spoke with his mouth, if there was any sound at all, because she is drowning in that light.

A name comes to her, and she whispers it, seeing the recognition, the acceptance in him, and she knows that no matter what happens, this demon will protect her.

Way to go, Syl, she thinks dreamily, eyes closing as she drifts. *Not only a vampire lover, but a demon protector as well.* The thought follows her into oblivion.

CHAPTER 26

Theo

THEO WAKES WITH THE BURNING NEED TO SEE SYLVIA, TO find her. He knows she is in danger, somehow feels it, his blood in her veins singing to him, calling for him, and the moment the sun disappears beneath the horizon, he is out of his coffin and into the basement beyond, cursing himself for assuming he would have the chance to grab clothes when he woke. Clad only in a towel, he uses the tunnels to head in her direction, lingering underground long enough for the last dregs of light to fade from the sky. He can travel in such light, but it will weaken him, and he has a feeling he will need all his strength to face whatever has Sylvia.

He is still weak from the fight the previous night, still drained from sharing so much blood, and when he stumbles on the man in the dark corridor beneath the building, he doesn't hesitate, attacking swiftly and gorging on his blood, feeling strength flow back into him, restoring his abilities. He shoves himself into the man's clothing, the gym shorts and t-shirt different from his normal clothing, but Theo hardly cares. Anything is better than the towel—or fighting naked.

Theo's blood tells him the moment the sky is clear, and he abandons the body, flying up a maintenance shaft into the ground floor of a building, rushing out the fire exit and bursting skyward, moving as fast as his magic will allow, not caring if anyone sees him, not caring if people point at the sky and start screaming, not caring if he ends up viral online and the Vig call for his head.

Sylvia, he thinks, only Sylvia, hunting his blood and finding it, though the call is growing fainter. Theo doesn't want to admit what that means, that Sylvia is hurt, maybe dying, and by the time he senses her below him again, he is frantic enough to consider punching through the ground and into the underground chamber she must be in. He sees the entrance a moment later, the remains of a doorway in what had been a warehouse, but now only a pile of wood and cinderblocks. He hurls himself down the stairs, feeling her get closer, but still far away at the same time.

He skids to a stop at the bottom, the scent of blood hitting him like a physical blow. *So much blood.*

Sylvia's blood. He sees her laying in the demon's lap, Pilkington's hand pressed to her chest, the other holding her hand, the demon's face close to hers, perhaps even whispering something to her. Theo ignores the flash of jealousy at the closeness of that embrace, reminds himself that the demon is likely keeping her from bleeding out, and he slides to the floor next to her, balancing on his haunches, already biting his wrist so he can press it to her face. His blood flows quickly, a gift from his last victim, and he forces it into her mouth. Sylvia's body is a disaster, her legs shredded and torn and her chest a gory mess. It looks like the wound had been worse, her shirt ripped as if bones had pierced it, but she seems partly healed. Theo assumes the demon's magic repaired the worst of the damage.

I didn't think demons could heal with magic.

He looks up at the demon, sees the same concern reflected on Pilkington's face, and though he knows what that look means, decides to ignore it for the time being. Right now, Sylvia is more important.

The vampire and the demon wait for several long moments, watching the blood drip into Sylvia's mouth, then she sucks in a long wet breath, hands clawing for his wrist. She drinks for a long time, and Theo watches the lines of ragged flesh on her legs draw together into red marks, the gouges on her chest pulling into mere scratches. He is lightheaded by the time she pauses, and he staggers, falling hard to one knee as his leg gives out. The demon's hand catches him on the shoulder. A jolt of power surges through Theo as the demon's magic gives him energy.

Just what kind of demon are you?

Theo doesn't claim to be an expert on demons, but Pilkington has shown two new abilities tonight. Theo makes a note to do more research in the future. Clearly, he knows very little about their powers.

Unless Pilkington is a special case.

Either way, Theo decides, he will look more into it.

More thought leaves his mind when Sylvia opens her silvered eyes, looking up at both of them with clarity.

She's alive. Thank the gods. She's alive.

CHAPTER 27

SYLVIA

"WHAT DID I TELL YOU ABOUT DYING?" THEO ASKS SYLVIA much later. They are still in the underground station, but Sylvia is healed enough to sit up. Her clothes have been mangled, and Pilkington conjures a coat to preserve her modesty.

"I know," Sylvia repeats, tugging the coat closer around her body, surprised by the soft material seemingly pulled from another dimension. She is no longer bleeding, but she is still covered in blood, and the night air is cool. "Don't do it."

Pilkington chuckles, and she smiles at him, the demon who had stayed with her while she tried to die. She remembers him talking to her, a white light and a sense of peace, but she can't recall his words. She isn't sure she wants to know. "Thank you," she tells him. Then adds, "I owe you." At his expression, she says, "And I know what that means, so just accept it, dammit. Seriously. I owe you one." The demon nods.

"I also—" Theo begins.

"Shut up, Muldavian," Pilkington snaps. "You owe me nothing." He looks at Sylvia. "And as for you, the only thing you owe me is a new coat. You have freed me. We are even on the life score." He looks at the floor where the magic blade still lays in a pool of Charlie's blood. "What should be done with it?"

Theo shrugs, leaning down to pick it up. He yelps in surprise and drops it just as quickly, a trail of smoke escaping from his burned hand. He studies the red mark, which does not fade right away as he clearly expects, then gives the blade a wary look. "I am open to suggestions," he says finally.

"I cannot take it," Pilkington says, his voice tinged with annoyance. "Nor can you," he looks at Theo. "We are both bound by it." He shakes his head. "It's a powerful artifact."

"Can we destroy it?" Sylvia asks, waiting for one of them to mention the fires of Mount Doom.

Pilkington shrugs, his massive shoulders rippling his wings. "I don't know," he says. The blood smearing his chest and pants reminds Sylvia of just how close she'd come to dying. The demon has repaired the cloth glove Charlie cut with the blade, a small glow marking his wrist before he hid the line up his forearm, but he hasn't cleaned himself up. Her blood is a dark smear against his blue skin, and Sylvia knows she should be horrified at the sight, but she finds herself more distracted by the strangely human muscles of his chest, the dark lines on his skin elegant like tattoos. She feels strangely close to this demon, familiar like an old friend.

It's because he was with me when I almost died. That kind of thing forms a bond. She looks away to study Theo, the vampire frowning at the blade on the ground.

"I can do more research," Pilkington says. The vampire looks up at his use of the word "more" as Pilkington continues, "But in the meantime..." He looks at the vampire, whose face is darkening, then at Sylvia.

"Well, we can't just leave it here," she says, leaning over to pick it up. "Any kid could just come in here and take it. We don't want kids summoning demons. I've seen that movie, and it ends badly for everyone." There is a sharp jolt when she grabs the hilt, like a static shock, but then nothing. She stares at it.

"We can't risk it falling into the wrong hands," Pilkington is saying. "It must be hidden somewhere."

"It's too dangerous," Theo replies, but his words trail off as Sylvia looks at him.

"I have to keep it," she states. "That's what you're really saying. I have to make sure it doesn't fall into the wrong hands." She frowns. "Keep it secret. Keep it safe." Pilkington looks amused at her words, but Theo looks simultaneously unhappy and terrified. He opens his mouth to say something, but nothing comes out. He closes it, tries to speak again, and frowns. It's not like him at all. She puts the blade on the ground, then looks at him.

"Not you!" he bursts out. "Anyone but you!"

"Who then?" She looks from him to Pilkington, around at the empty space, and back to them. She picks it up again, and Theo stops, face brooding but silent. Sylvia looks at the blade in her hand and back at both of them, a terrible thought in her mind.

Stand up, she thinks, and both creatures stand immediately. An awful look crosses Pilkington's face but is quickly replaced by a blank expression. Theo's face is stolid, a soldier ready for battle.

"Oh my god," Sylvia whispers, then drops the blade, the power it holds making her sick to her stomach. "I'm so sorry," she adds, getting to her feet.

"Don't," Theo says. "It's okay." He pulls her into a hug. Sylvia buries her face in his chest but twists to look over his shoulder at the hulking form of Pilkington standing nearby. She's not so sure he would say the same thing. She pulls out of Theo's embrace.

"Okay," she says, "a few tests, and then I'm done." She spends the next minute trying to determine how the blade works. Skin to skin contact gives her instant and complete control. Having it in a pocket but not touching her gives her some control but not complete. Not touching it at all renders her powerless.

"Plan," she says finally. She looks at Pilkington. "Can you find a way to destroy it?"

The demon nods. "I will look."

"Good." She looks at Theo. "Until then, I can hide it." At Theo's expression, she adds, "We'll guard it."

The vampire nods reluctantly.

"Others will seek it," Pilkington says. "The Destroyer knows it is here, knows that Sylvia had it, and got away."

"Why didn't it kill me?" she asks, recalling that odd feeling in her chest when it spoke to her.

"It did!" both creatures say in unison, then smile awkwardly.

"Or it tried," Theo adds.

"You set it free," Pilkington says. "It cannot kill you while it still owes you a debt."

"It did something to me," Sylvia tells them. "I felt it in my chest." She shakes her head at the looks they give her. "No, not that. After, when I was on the ground." She tries to remember the words. *What had it said?* "'I owe you my freedom,'" she repeats. "What does it mean?"

Pilkington shakes his head. "Nothing good. Once it knows you survived, it will come for you."

"Maybe we shouldn't destroy this so fast," Sylvia says, "if it can control that thing."

Both Theo and Pilkington frown; Sylvia throws her head back and laughs, the first time she has felt able to since waking up in this room. "Maybe I'll just use it to bend you to my will," she says to Theo with a wicked grin.

"It would not be the first time I had to obey a woman," he retorts, but the joke fades, and Sylvia considers the blade in her hand, the responsibility falling over her.

"We'll figure it out. For now, let's see if it can even be destroyed."

Pilkington nods. "As you wish."

Sylvia sighs, then slowly stands up. "Look, all I want now is a shower and a bed." She tucks the blade inside the coat pocket. At her mention of the word bed, Theo's expression goes warm, and Sylvia's blood stirs, an echo of the desire she feels in him. From beside her, there is another stirring, but it disappears as quickly as it appears, and Sylvia decides that she has had enough of magic and mayhem for one day.

She looks at her vampire. "Take me home?"

EPILOGUE

SYLVIA

"**Y**OUR VAMPIRE IS LATE," MR. PILKINGTON COMMENTS, sitting at Sylvia's tiny kitchen table. His human form is still big, and though something about his face tugs at Sylvia's memory, she tries not to think of it, focusing instead on the puzzle they still haven't solved.

She sticks her tongue out at the demon, comfortable around him now that she'd nearly died in his presence. If he was any threat to her, he would have just let her die. Mr. Pilkington has become more than an ally these last few weeks—he's become a friend. She still has a hard time remembering that the handsome human before her is actually a huge winged blue-skinned creature. He hasn't appeared in that form since being summoned by Charlie, arriving for their first meeting about the dagger in his middle-aged human skin. She had invited him in again, this time without stipulation, and he had accepted with a quiet joy.

"He's meeting up with Oren and Harald first," Sylvia explains. "They're coming here after they…" Her words drift off, and she looks out the window, still not comfortable with the idea of Theo feeding on a stranger before his arrival. She knows it's necessary, especially if he's going to have to feed her his healing blood every time she leaves his sight and nearly gets killed.

Theo's blood is finally out of her system, but every now and then she still has an aftereffect of so much blood in such a short time—a rush of desire, a sense of pounding hearts around her, the burn of the sunlight. Her symptoms have faded more every day, but she knows what he means now when he warns her about taking his blood—or him taking hers. It helped him find her so quickly that day though, so Sylvia isn't entirely sorry for it.

Mr. Pilkington nods, unbothered by vampire habits. "Of course." He leans forward, giving her a long look. "Can I ask you something?"

Sylvia shrugs, wandering over to sit across from him at the small table. "Sure," she says. "What's up?"

"How do you feel … after everything?"

Sylvia frowns, not sure she understands. "What do you mean? Like am I okay mentally?" She laughs a little. "Hell no. I'm completely freaked out that Adam will force his way in here again." Her mouth sets in a firm line. "But this is my home, and I won't be chased away from it. I know it's not much, but it's mine. And I like it."

Mr. Pilkington nods. "It's nice," he says, glancing around at the small room, slightly neater since she's been hosting their little meetings, but still littered with half-empty glasses and the occasional tank top. "I mean, it's small, but it suits you."

"Let me guess," Sylvia says, "you have a huge mansion in..." She laughs again. "Where exactly do you live, Pilkington? I know it's some other realm, but is it like this? Do some demons live in studio apartments?"

Mr. Pilkington smiles, always glad to answer her questions—unlike a certain vampire at times. "Some live in smaller quarters, but it's not a matter of real estate. We create our homes using magic. Some demons have less magic, so their dwellings tend to be smaller."

"So, what's your house like?"

"Huge." He smirks. "And only getting bigger. I have a great library when it's in order. I've gone through most of the books there, but there are still a few I haven't gotten to yet. Maybe they have something about the dagger."

Sylvia nods. "I always wanted a library," she says wistfully.

"I'm sure your vampire would build you one," Mr. Pilkington observes.

"I know. He'd buy me a building if I asked." She looks around the small space again. "But this is my place, and I don't want Theo's money." She has noticed that Mr. Pilkington never calls Theo by his name—only the vampire and the Muldavian. She assumes there is a reason, but she hasn't puzzled it out yet. She could just ask, but she knows he would tell her, and something stops her from prying.

"You're an interesting human, Sylvia," Mr. Pilkington says. "I understand what you mean by your own space, but not many humans would give up the chance for a building."

"I don't want a building," Sylvia repeats. "How would I ever keep it clean?"

The demon laughs, telling her a story about the soul-servant he has in his house, a spirit intended to keep the place clean while the demon is away on business, but who only manages to make it more disorganized.

Sylvia is laughing when someone arrives on her fire escape, and she turns her attention to the window, expecting to see Theo climbing inside.

Instead, she sees Oren lifting his jean-clad leg through the opening, his hair pulled back in a low ponytail that brushes his black band t-shirt. Harald follows, the shorter man wearing khaki shorts and a white t-shirt, black boots tightly tied like the soldier he would always be. Their somber faces make Sylvia's stomach clench. She waits for Theo to climb in after them, but she knows he isn't there.

"Where is Theo?" Sylvia asks, bracing herself for unpleasant news. "What happened?"

The vampires are silent for a moment, Oren sighing in frustration while Harald studies their positions at the table, taking Mr. Pilkington's measure as he always does when the demon is with them.

Oren breaks the silence with one word. "Jolena."

The story continues in Keep Me Close

BOOK CLUB QUESTIONS

1. Theo, Oren, and Harald have a strong bond forged over a thousand years. Do you have friends like them?

2. Sylvia often recalls Phil, a boy she knew when she was a teenager, comparing the men in her life to that remembered idea of a possible romance. Is this a reasonable behavior—comparing every potential partner to a guy she knew years ago?

3. Sylvia is a recovering victim of severe trauma. How well do you think she copes with the events of the novel, given her history with the supernatural?

4. Mr. Pilkington spends a great deal of time ensuring that Sylvia is safe. Though he resists the idea, he grudgingly begins to accept her place in his life. Do

you think he is in love with her, or is their connection something else?

5. Sylvia and Theo spend a good deal of time arguing about his vampiric nature. She makes her stance fairly clear: she does not wish to become a vampire like him. How would you address the long-term complications of their relationship? Do you think they can resolve their differences?

6. After they begin a relationship, Theo starts feeding on strangers before he sees Sylvia each night, an act that rouses Sylvia's jealousy and feeling of inadequacy. Should she be bothered by his actions, essentially "eating" before he comes to visit her? Would you?

7. If given the opportunity, would you want to be a vampire like Theo, never seeing the sun again and requiring blood to survive?

8. At the end of the novel, Sylvia acquires a dagger that allows her to control both Theo and Mr. Pilkington. What would you do with such power?

9. Demons in this world have a lot of power, both physical strength and magical ability, yet they are subject to a summoning if their name is known. Would you accept such power, knowing it comes with such a weakness?

10. You knew it was coming. Who is a better partner for Sylvia: Theo or Mr. Pilkington?

CALL ME FORTH

The demon known as Mr. Pilkington
was only in town to meet up with an old
friend. He did not expect to get caught up
in human drama. Between a rival witch,
a lucky magician, and a fascinating
teenage girl, Pilkington has his hands full.
This story is a glimpse into the world of
the Conjuring Fascination series!

Because demons need love too

CHAPTER 1

T HE DEMON KNOWN AS MR. PILKINGTON STANDS AT THE
edge of the pier, enjoying the ocean breeze as it toys
with the long dark hair of his human form. His body
is young this time, a teenager, and he relishes the
sensations as he always does when he returns to the
mortal realm.

He glances down at his body, noting the ripped
jeans with dismay, certainly a far cry from the pol-
ished suits he normally chooses for his visits, but the
t-shirt is acceptable, even a bit humorous, considering
the purpose for this particular engagement. Besides,
no one would question a teenager wearing a KISS shirt
when the band is set to perform nearby that night. He
will blend in with a dozen other young men, all hoping
to get a glimpse of the aging rockers as they arrive,
maybe catch some of the sound check before the secu-
rity guards start setting up and shooing them all away
to make way for the ticket holders.

The demon debates whether to make his visit before
or after the show.

Phenex might not be happy to see him at first—he never is, especially when Mr. Pilkington reminds him of his obligations—and that could affect the quality of the show. Then again, it might inspire the performer to sing his best and infuse his music with more power. The band aren't the superstars they had been in the previous decades, but they still hold enough sway to fill the small stadium on the pier. Some of the listeners will be there for nostalgia, recalling younger days and wilder ways, but there is a growing new generation of listeners. Phenex should be nurturing that new interest, grooming a younger following. Sometimes it seems to Mr. Pilkington that Phenex has forgotten himself, sinking into his identity as Paul and abandoning his purpose here.

Feeling the human body he inhabits, the demon can understand how such a thing happens. Humans are fascinating, human bodies even moreso. Phenex has been in his for several decades now. No doubt he feels himself to be increasingly more like them. A chat with his old mentor should remind him of his purpose in the mortal realm.

Or the sight of a fellow demon will upset him and put him off his game.

It has been a long time since Mr. Pilkington has been at a live show, and he wants to enjoy the experience. It is decided, then. He will wait and make his visit after the show.

The delay means he has some time to kill, so he wanders the pier and the rest of the amusement park resting atop it.

Such a strange place, he thinks, watching a young man throw darts at a wall filled with balloons. His lady friend stands nearby, face hopeful but not truly believing that he will pop one of the balloons and win her the stuffed prize. She doesn't want stuffed animals anyway, Mr. Pilkington senses; she wants more from her young man than more material possessions. She wants certain words, words that Mr. Pilkington knows the young man will never say to her.

Human desires are so simplistic at times. If only they would speak them aloud to one another, so much tragedy could be avoided. He looks over the couple, deciding that they will never say what they really want, debates whether he should just separate them now so they can start over with others who may actually give them what they want. It would be easy enough to do: a small whisper here, the slight suggestion there.

"You have the look of a devil at work," a young girl's voice says quite close to him. Mr. Pilkington nearly startles, if such a thing is possible for a demon as old as he, and he turns to consider the speaker.

A young girl stands there, maybe thirteen years old, her blonde hair straight and tucked behind her ears, her big blue eyes considering him with a seriousness that doesn't match her youth.

"What do you know of devils?" he asks her.

She shrugs, her black band t-shirt faded and loose around her small form, her feet shuffling a bit as she kicks first one foot and then the other, her sneakers battered beneath her cutoff jean shorts. "I know enough," she says. She gives him another of those too-old-for-her-face looks. "You are up to no good."

"Am I?" he asks, delighted by this small creature who dares to speak to him as though he is just another mortal. "And what do you think I'm doing?"

She glances from him to the young couple, the woman dutifully cooing over her small stuffed bear even though Mr. Pilkington knows she is disappointed. "You were going to do something, weren't you? Something to do with them?" she asks, nodding her head in the couple's direction, who have started to move along the pier to other distractions. The demon gives the girl a more serious look. She doesn't have the look of one with the Sight, nor does he sense any magic coming off her, but there is something...

He pauses, struck by the sudden need to keep this human safe. The feeling is novel, something he hasn't felt before and wants to explore. The urge is surprisingly strong, a pull deep inside. A word whispers deep inside his demon soul: *Arusha*.

Nonsense, he assures himself. It's been a while since he last visited this plane. The body is distracting him.

"What a strange creature you are," he observes, staring at the girl who has captured his focus.

"I'm not a creature. I'm Sylvia," she introduces herself, holding out her hand. Mr. Pilkington takes it, enjoying the feel of her skin against his, very aware of his human body and its teenage hormones. If he were truly the fourteen year old boy he resembles, he might want to impress her, make her laugh. The demon he is finds this desire fascinating.

"You give your name very freely, young Sylvia, and it is a true name. That is very trusting of you." He brings her hand to his lips and kisses the back of her hand before letting her go. "You honor me."

"Should I not tell you my name?" she asks, narrowing her eyes. "How would you know what to call me then?"

"I admire your practicality," he admits, "but I can call you anything you wish. Your true name is a secret. Not everyone should get to know it." He pauses, but the word spills out unbidden: "*Arusha*."

Sylvia frowns at him. "Huh?"

The demon rallies, shocked at his carelessness, and he quickly gestures at her blonde hair, wisps blowing in the slight breeze. "Yellow," he deflects, words careful after such a mistake, knowing she will think he is defining the word, though he isn't, "after the dye from the plant." Demon law allows him to claim his arusha as he sees fit, but Pilkington is not the kind of demon to snatch a child from her home. The bond doesn't have to be like that. He can see that Sylvia is confused, about to ask him more, and he interrupts her. "It suits you." He pauses, then adds, "Much safer than your true name."

Sylvia shrugs. "You're weird," she tells him, "but I think I like you. What's your name?"

"Were you not listening to a word I just said? Names are secret."

Sylvia snorts. "Not in this place." She tilts her head, considering him. "Fine, then. Be weird. What should I call you?"

The demon considers. His true name is out of the question. Those who learn it often die soon after, and the few who live hold great power over him. Being a demon comes with many benefits, but names are a weakness. He has always hated that part of himself.

"Call me…" He trails off, not wanting to give her any of his normal monikers. The silence stretches out.

"How about Phil?" she asks suddenly.

"Why Phil?"

She shrugs, tugging her long blonde hair into a loose ponytail at the base of her neck. She uses a black hair tie from her wrist to tie her hair back as she speaks. "You seem like a Phil. Maybe a Philbert... or a Pilbert... or Pilkirk-something?" She scrunches her face as her hands fall back to her sides, considering.

Mr. Pilkington stares at her. She has come dangerously close to the name he often uses among the humans, but for some reason, he doesn't want to be Mr. Pilkington to her. He wants something less formal, more friendly, more ... human. "Phil will work fine," he agrees. "I feel like a Phil this time."

"Well, then, Phil," she begins, deliberately ignoring his mention of *this time*, "are you here for the show tonight?" She gestures toward the amphitheater, the white wooden structure nearly as high as the wooden roller coaster that circles the entire pier.

Mr. Pilkington nods, not needing her to know the details. She considers him, clearly debating something. Making a choice, she grins at him. He cannot help but return the expression.

"Great!" She grabs his hand and starts walking down the pier. "I know the perfect spot to watch from."

"I thought I would hear just fine from here," he says but allows her to lead him down the pier, following her when she ducks around the corner of an old wooden shack marked Employees Only.

"Well, you can hear from anywhere," she says, sure feet leading him into a narrow corridor, "but I know a place where we can see it too."

"Don't you need a ticket to get inside?"

She grins at him again, a wicked look that makes him like her even more. "*They* do," she says, tilting her head back toward the milling people on the pier.

She leads him through a small alleyway between the edge of the pier along the water and the wooden struts that make up the bottom of the roller coaster that rings the entire pier. There is a fence, but it is broken, a space large enough for their small frames to slip through, and then they are underneath the wooden structure, the tall beams holding up the coaster far above their heads. Mr. Pilkington takes in the workmanship, noting that despite its clear age, the coaster has been well made, built to last snowy winters. It is old now but still strong. He appreciates things that can withstand time. There are so few things left like that now, seemingly fewer each time he returns to this realm.

"This way, Phil," Sylvia says, standing next to a low beam with peeling white paint. She puts her foot on it and begins to climb deftly up into the structure. "I hope you can climb!"

The demon follows her with ease, pleased to find that his human body has the strength and dexterity to navigate the beams as they climb higher and higher into the coaster. He so rarely engages in physical acts in this realm; the climb makes him think he should do more in the future.

When they are about forty feet above the ground, Sylvia walks out onto a wide beam above the amphitheater, the stage and audience spread out beneath her feet. There are enough beams around them to cast shadows. Anyone looking into the rafters will have a hard time seeing them, even though they both wear dark shirts next to the white paint.

"This is a wonderful place," the demon tells her, settling down with his back to a beam. "How did you find it?"

The girl looks away, and Mr. Pilkington senses something dark and troubling. Anger stirs in him, an emotion he rarely experiences. He may be a demon, but he's not that kind of demon.

"I come here sometimes," she admits, dropping down to sit on the beam, both legs dangling. The coaster races by above them, shaking the structure, but Sylvia doesn't seem to notice, body steady on the beam as it shudders. After it passes, the sound rolling around behind the stage and to the other side of the pier, she adds in a small voice, "I like to get away from ... things."

"What kind of things?" he pries, just a little, but he sees right away the question is too much.

"I like to be off the ground," she deflects, gaze scanning the scene around and below them. The roadies are on stage, long-haired sound guys checking the settings and giving hand signals to the people in the sound booth far below. They haven't let the audience in yet, but Mr. Pilkington can hear the hum of people gathering just beyond the gate, can even glimpse the tops of bald heads and ballcaps from their perch in the structure.

The demon considers Sylvia's words. They sit in a safe space with a clear view of the surrounding area, the kind of place someone might come to hide from someone else.

"Does this *thing* not know how to climb?" he tries, and she shrugs again, clearly a defense she uses often. "I see."

She gives him a look then, and something in her face softens. Mr. Pilkington has seen it before. She likes him, trusts him even. It is nothing new. Part of his appeal as a demon is the way humans react to him. They are drawn to him. They just can't help it. He is surprised that it has taken her this long to soften.

Normally, he would use this moment to tempt her, offer her something irresistible in exchange for something she isn't using at the moment—a future favor is one of his favorite bargains, but he's not above the usual lot: first-born children still fetch a high price back home and innocent souls could be bartered for a great deal more in the right company. But Mr. Pilkington lives comfortably back in his realm—he has no need to make this trip about gaining anything more than a reaffirmation of Phenex's loyalty. The old poet just needs a gentle nudge now and then.

He studies the girl's face, trying to get a sense of her desire, an easy enough feat whenever he is around humans, but Sylvia is oddly blank. Sitting there high above the crowd, Sylvia is content, wanting nothing more in the world than to stay where she is. Narrowing his eyes, Mr. Pilkington studies her more closely—the bags under her eyes from lack of sleep, the scuffed knees, details he can dismiss as the normal wear and tear for a girl near the end of summer. However, the thin line of her lips as she studies the crowd below, as if searching for a specific face, tells a different story. Her fingernails are ragged, some knuckles scabbed over, and the demon scans the structure they sit in, seeing how easily she could injure her hands if she climbed in a hurry—as if trying to get away from someone.

She notices him staring at her and turns her attention to him, those blue eyes totally focused on his face. Mr. Pilkington freezes, soaking in the novel sensation of falling under another's sway instead of the reverse.

He likes this Sylvia, her lack of desire beyond the immediate moment, her simplicity, her blue eyes. He remembers her fingernails, then he allows the slow burn of anger to fill him, no doubt amplified by the teenage hormones racing through his human body. He wants to hurt anyone who would harm this creature.

"Sylvia," he says quietly, "who hunts you?" He puts power behind the question, knowing she won't answer easily. He doesn't want to force her—not yet.

Sylvia's gaze falls, skipping away from his face to skim the crowd below. "It doesn't matter," she answers quickly. "He won't find us here."

"*Who* won't find us here?" he tries again, but she cuts him off, seeming immune to his suggestive power.

Of course it doesn't work on her, a tiny voice in his mind whispers. *She's your arusha.* Pilkington immediately ignores the voice. He can call her that because nicknames are safe, and she'll never know what it means.

"I don't want to talk about that," she declares, glancing back at where he sits in the shadows beside her. "Tell me about you, Phil. I don't think I've seen you around before."

Mr. Pilkington leans back, settling himself more firmly against the wooden post at his back, letting one leg swing freely as he tugs the other up, bending his knee and creating a small barrier between them. The anger subsides as he sets it free. It doesn't matter. He is here now, and he can keep her safe from whatever hunts her. "I'm not from here," he tells her.

Sylvia nods. "Figures. How long are you in town?"

The demon shrugs. "Not sure." He looks down, watching the audience mill about, forming lines at the bar and merchandise table. "I'm just here to see a friend."

"Oh, is she at the show?"

The demon looks up, letting a slow grin cross his human face at the seemingly innocent question. "I'm meeting *him* after the show," he says, noting the small red flush working its way up from the collar of her shirt.

Human beings are fascinating, he thinks again, relishing the response in his own body. *How do they ever get anything done with bodies like these?* Not that his demon body doesn't experience pleasure—it does—but it seems much less pressing. Perhaps that is a result of the careful negotiations required to share such moments with fellow demons; none of them are trusting by nature, always expecting the other to find a way to exploit the agreement, re-imagine the contract. He knows that the way Sylvia had been leaning in to him a moment before means something to her, a connection he can only grasp in the abstract.

This body understands it though.

"Oh," she says, looking down, then quickly back up to sneak a glance at his face, and then immediately away again. "Cool."

"Indeed," he says, noting that her gaze seems less focused now, no longer scanning for a specific stalker in the crowd. She settles, body relaxing as she leans back against the support opposite from him, mirroring his position, one foot on the wooden beam a few inches away from his own while the other swings freely back and forth over the empty air.

They say nothing for a few long moments, Sylvia occasionally sneaking glances at him when she thinks he isn't watching her. The demon doesn't look away. He can follow the general motion below, his superior senses allowing him to take in the entire area without much trouble. Even limited by the human body, he retains much of his power. This is a sanctioned visit, after all, an official meeting with a minion, not some impromptu conjuring. Mr. Pilkington retains his free will, beholden to nothing except the requirement to remind Phenex of his purpose in this realm.

The opening band sets up on the stage below, the powerful wave of live music replacing the radio over the speakers, and the demon feels the surge of adrenaline from the crowd below. It's not the band they are here to see, but it is enough for the moment, the music feeding their eagerness and anticipation. Mr. Pilkington's human body tingles with the combination of sound and emotion, and he looks over at Sylvia, sharing a moment of joy with the human girl. For the next few hours, he allows himself to focus on the experience, everything else in his existence slipping away.

When KISS finally does hit the stage, he finds himself grinning foolishly along with Sylvia, the two of them sitting up to face the stage, thighs and shoulders brushing as their feet dangle above the crowd. They sing along to the songs they know—Sylvia's voice surprisingly pleasant while the demon's human voice occasionally breaks into a croak. He laughs even harder at those moments, knowing his normal voice is quite good—it's one of his strengths when coaxing others to do his bidding. He wonders idly if this feeling of freedom is because of the body, his normally sensible disposition overrun by human emotions and sensations, and then decides that he doesn't care. He is always interested in different experiences, new feelings in particular, and he surrenders to the moment as only a demon can.

He leans against Sylvia, suddenly very aware of her body next to his, the way her hand rests on her leg, palm up, fingers open and relaxed. He reaches over and takes her hand in his in a smooth motion, glancing at her face to make sure she doesn't object. Instead, she grins at him, wrapping her fingers around his, and they turn back to the concert, the music taking them away from everything else in their worlds.

As the last song ends, the crowd's cheers dwindling as the pier's overhead lights turn on, the demon looks at Sylvia, then down at their still linked hands. Sylvia smiles shyly, coming back to herself, then slowly pulls her hand away and stands up, easily balancing on the beam with no sign of worry that she hovers high above the ground.

"I should go," she says, tilting her head toward the path they had used to climb up. "You staying here for a bit?"

"Maybe I should walk with you," Mr. Pilkington says, recalling her unnamed fear. "It's late."

A tiny smile flits across her face, quickly subdued as she turns around, heading for the way down. "Okay," she agrees. "I'd like that."

They climb down in companionable silence, and when they join the few remaining stragglers leaving the concert, she takes his hand again, a casual gesture—just two friends holding hands as they walk slowly down the pier, passing shabby wooden structures holding rigged games and cheap merchandise. Mr. Pilkington's gaze darts to the Ferris Wheel, a construction he has never actually ridden before, despite his many trips to this world over the years, and he narrows his eyes at Sylvia, a small tug on her hand to get her to look at him, and then a quick head tilt in the direction of the huge wheel. "Want to take a ride, arusha?" he asks, not willing to let go of his time with her just yet.

"On the Ferris Wheel?" she asks, smiling at the nickname while biting her lip. "With you?"

He nods, and suddenly he can feel her desire, the first hint of anything beyond her cool acceptance of each new moment since he met her hours before. Sylvia *wants* to go with him, *wants* to feel the cool night air in her hair while he holds her hand, and for a split second, there is something more—the wistful desire for a first kiss—but it is gone just as quickly, replaced by that sensation of wind again.

Mr. Pilkington frowns, wondering why she would dismiss her desire for him—not just him, but an experience with him that he assumes most human girls would wish for. She still holds his hand, and he can tell she enjoys being near him. He promises himself that he will not behave like a foolish human teenager and try to kiss her, though now that the idea has crept into his mind, he has a hard time letting it go.

"Sure," she agrees, and they walk in that direction. A few other concertgoers have the same idea and linger in a short line. A middle-aged woman joins the line behind them, tucking her short blonde bob behind an ear as she smiles at the young couple.

They reach the front of the line and the attendant lifts the bar, moving aside to let them slide onto the metal seat. The demon lets Sylvia sit first, tucking her into the side where the bar attaches and then settling in beside her, careful not to lean against her, watching as the attendant presses the bar closed and locks it with his special key. He steps away to the podium where the machinery is located, and then they are moving backward, facing the short line slightly below them. The blonde gets into the seat below theirs, sitting in the center of the seat, clearly enjoying the ride alone.

Mr. Pilkington senses something, there and then gone, a hint of danger, and he sends out his power in an expanding arc, seeking the source. At first, he focuses on the woman below them, the closest human to him, but senses nothing. He sends the magic out farther, seeking that twinge of ... something.

"You okay?" Sylvia asks. He turns to see her studying his face. "You can't be afraid of heights," she says, taking his hand. "Is it old machines that worry you?"

"What makes you think I'm worried?" He aims for reassuring, a tone that clearly fails. Sylvia's suspicious expression forces him to abandon his search.

It's nothing, he tells himself. *Just this human body giving me nervous jitters.* They bump up another few feet, then stop again, and this time their feet dangle against the metal footrest a few feet above the blonde's head. She seems to be watching the line in front of her.

The demon lets out a long breath and smiles at Sylvia. "Forgive me," he says, words carefully chosen. He doesn't plan to extort anything from Sylvia, but such a promise is too precious to ignore the opportunity.

Sylvia doesn't give the satisfaction, and his human heart swells a little bit. "Forgive you?" she repeats. "I have no reason to forgive you." She smirks at him. "You planning to do something you need forgiveness for?"

Mr. Pilkington thinks of his purpose in visiting the human realm, knows that while he isn't breaking the word of his mission here, he is certainly flouting the spirit. Forgiveness isn't something he normally deals in, the deception required to gain a human's trust only to bargain for forgiveness always makes him slightly uncomfortable. He will never say he is a demon with morals—but he does consider himself a demon with standards—and sitting on this ride with this human girl is quickly sliding beneath his decency.

No children, he reminds himself. *Never bargain with those so young.*

Sylvia is still staring at him, and he studies her face, the youthful bloom in her cheeks, the smooth skin, the way she is biting her lip. She isn't a child, but she's young. Too young. Then he sees those eyes again, too old for her face, eyes that mirror his own when he catches a glimpse of his human forms now and then.

I will not take this from her, he decides. *I will not steal her first kiss.*

He moves away from her, a slight readjustment of his body so she isn't so close to his face. He catches the pull of Sylvia's desire, the wish to have him closer to her, so he settles for leaving his hand in hers but making no move to snuggle.

The cart moves up another few feet and then stops, swinging a little in the breeze. A tendril of Sylvia's hair comes free from her ponytail, curling around her face. She smiles, and he knows that her desire has shifted again—focusing on the wind again—that feeling of freedom with the cool air brushing her skin.

They lurch again, and this time, they continue moving up, cresting the top of the wheel and then falling gently back to the ground. Sylvia's hair blows, and her face lights up as they move. The demon watches her, savoring her enjoyment, relishing the novelty of a human's joy that has nothing to do with his actions. She laughs and he joins her, sinking back into their comfortable new friendship, soaking in the sensations of the wheel's movement in the night air. The lights of the pier glow, the hulk of the roller coaster outlined against the sky before the darkness of the water beyond. The wheel is quieter than he expected, and he can hear everything else—the distant screams from the coaster, the background susurrus of the ocean waves against the beach far below, the bells as someone manages to win a prize at one of the water pistol games that line the edge of the pier. Sylvia gasps as they crown the wheel again, eyes wide as she takes in the scene revealed.

"It's beautiful," she says, then laughs as they begin to descend again, more of her hair blowing into her face now as they slide backward past the attendant on their way back around.

"It is," he agrees.

They enjoy the few remaining trips around the wheel in silence, grinning broadly at one another. When the cart slows to a stop halfway up to let the first riders off, Sylvia turns to Mr. Pilkington.

"Tell me something," she says, voice more serious than he expects.

He nods. "Anything." The word is out before he can stop it, his fool's head caught in the blue of her eyes, the joy of the moment, and everything in him freezes, the blood in this body draining in a rush of cold.

You bloody imbecile.

But it is done, the promise given, and he can't take it back.

Sylvia senses the change in him, and whatever she is about to say dies on her lips. Her mouth moves a few times, frantically trying to find a replacement, but her words fail. The spell drags out, the enormity of what he has just done sinking into the demon's essence, and she simply stares at him instead. They move up one space, pause, and then move again. They are almost at the top, the perfect spot for the quick image he had spotted in her when they first approached the wheel, but Mr. Pilkington can only stare at her, waiting for the question he must answer.

They move forward to the top spot, and she looks away, a soft sigh as she longs for a cool breeze, but the air is still. The demon pushes with his power, and the air obeys almost too much, a chill wind whipping past the car, blowing her hair into her face and then back again. She shivers, the breeze cold, and the demon puts an arm around her unconsciously. She ducks into his side, tucking her body against his, the moment intimate and yet still friendly, comforting.

She stays tucked under his arm as they move forward and down again, slowly moving back to the platform on the ground.

When the attendant opens the bar, the demon stands first, reaching out to tug Sylvia free, and she smiles at him. They hold hands as they walk away. Mr. Pilkington glances back once to see the blonde woman get off the Ferris wheel, but her expression is unreadable as she heads in the opposite direction.

"That was nice," Sylvia says, looking down at her shoes as they walk slowly to the entrance of the pier.

"It was," he agrees, still waiting for her question. Until she asks, she will hold power over him. Mr. Pilkington is horrified to find that part of himself does not want her to ask him anything at all so that she will continue to hold power over him after they part, giving him a reason to see her again.

It's this damn body, he tells himself. *I will never be a teenage boy again—complete fools.*

He follows her gentle lead away from the pier and down the main street, then walks with her into a smaller residential area. He assumes she must live nearby by her knowledge of the under coaster special seats, and he is proven right when she turns down a small street filled with cozy old bungalows, homes from when this had been only a summer retreat for the city's elite, now rundown and battered with age. From here, he can see the lights of the pier in the distance, and if he listens very hard, he can hear a distant shout from the coaster.

"This is close enough," Sylvia says, letting go of his hand and stepping away from him. He sees the way she glances nervously around, checking the street for anyone who might be watching.

"Are you certain?" he asks, determined anew to find this threat in her life and persuade it to find other pursuits.

She nods a little too forcefully, then smiles at him, her fear forgotten for the moment as she looks at him. "Thanks," she says.

He frowns. "For what? I've done nothing." Normally he would be trying to get her appreciation, to gain a favor, but he accepts the words without invoking his power, without making them mean anything more.

"For good company," she says. "It was really nice meeting you."

"You too," he says truthfully, suddenly wanting to hold her hand again.

She stares at him, words poised on her lips, but then she closes her mouth, gives him a broad grin, and turns away. "Good night," she says, words echoing on the night breeze as she moves quickly down the street.

"Good night," he whispers, wondering when the last time he had wished a human well and actually meant it. When her slim form turns down a driveway and disappears around the side of a small white bungalow, he turns away, heading back to the pier and his meeting with Phenex, the feel of her hand still on his skin.

CHAPTER 2

MR. PILKINGTON IS ALREADY BACKSTAGE, MAKING HIS WAY to the noisy room that must be the afterparty, when he feels the summons. At first, he assumes he can ignore it—he's on official business at the moment, not privy to the normal rules of engagement for his species. But the second wave brings him to a halt, his entire body freezing in place, unable to take another step away from the call.

"Hey man!" A slurred voice erupts from behind as a drunk man bumps gently into him, uses his shoulder as a grounding post, then weaves his way around the frozen teenage boy in the hallway.

Mr. Pilkington opens his mouth to reply, to excuse himself for stopping so suddenly, but his lips don't respond, his body unable to do anything that isn't obeying the summons.

What in the hells is this?

He's a demon—summonings are literally the bane of his existence. He can no more resist a summoning than he can change his secret name: a name currently being spoken aloud in a ceremony not far away. He takes a jerky step to the side, spinning around in the hallway and heading toward the call. Now that he is officially obeying, he has more control over his body. He slows his steps, refusing to reach the summoner one moment before he has to. If he'd been home, he would have appeared in the summoning circle instantly, unable to resist being pulled through the dimensions and subject to his summoner's demands.

But how can they summon me? I'm on official business in this realm.

Mr. Pilkington is always very careful when he visits the mortal world—wording his requests to his superiors specifically to cover all angles, allowing him the maximum amount of free will for the duration. No one should be able to use his name to call him while he is already in this world; technically, he is under the command of a Greater Demon to complete a task and he has not finished yet. Such trips are common enough. If demons on a mission could be summoned, nothing would ever get done. The geas should supersede any other calls—which means he has two problems: someone alive knows his true name, and that same someone can overpower a compulsion from a Lord of the Realm.

As his feet make their way away from the stage and along the pier, the demon considers his options. He is a powerful being, commander of superior magic, but when summoned, he has very little agency. A bigger problem, however, is the human body he inhabits—it is weak. In his true form, he can easily overpower a human given a split second's opportunity, but in this form, he has nothing in his favor beyond his charming smile and washboard abs. He thinks it unlikely the summoner will appreciate such features, but spares a moment to be grateful that Sylvia is no longer with him. In this state, he cannot control his actions; she would have questions—and he is bound to answer the next one she asks. He doesn't want to think about what will happen if she discovers his true nature. Part of him wants to think he can protect her, but he is not a naive demon nor in the habit of deluding himself.

Humans who discover a demon's identity do not live long.

His body moves to the edge of the pier, locating the small staircase that leads down to the rocky beach below. He used the same stairwell when he first arrived one the beach hours before, but he knows the summoner isn't on the beach.

There is still time to formulate a plan, though the demon knows his options are limited. He's more annoyed than worried. Mr. Pilkington is not a young demon; he has seen summoners come and go, fools and geniuses both. His existence is not in danger.

It may take some time, but he will kill this summoner, destroy anyone else who still knows his name. He's done it before. It will be difficult in this body, but he can be patient. He may have to wait until the next time he returns—and he decides that is acceptable. Once the summoner realizes he or she has power over him, he knows the summons will continue, generally getting more and more sloppy until the demon can strike. And the next time he is summoned, he will be in his normal demonic body.

A loose plan forms as his feet walk along the beach, the rocky shore sloping up from the water in a sharp break. Following the path upward, he soon finds himself on the edge of a cliff, the water crashing on the rocks far below, and he knows where the ceremony is being held.

The old cemetery dates back to the 18th century, gravestones of humans long dead, their descendants moved on or forgotten, the old stones jutting out of the rocky soil atop the cliff in this forgotten corner of the town. The surroundings are familiar—he's been summoned to similar places all over the human world. The language may change, the clothes of the summoner shifting, but the routine is always the same—they give the command and he has to obey.

Except normally, he appears inside the circle, only released to do the summoner's bidding. As he draws closer, hearing the words with his human ears as well as feeling the call in his essence, he wonders if he will find himself inside the circle or if this time will be different.

It has to be different, he admits. *This summons calls me away from a powerful geas.*

Squaring his shoulders, he enters the cemetery, weaving through the jagged stones as the spell commands. When the figures come into view, he lets out a long breath.

He did not suspect this—but he should have.

Standing in front of a concrete slab is the blonde from the Ferris Wheel, only instead of flashing him a friendly smile, she stops speaking at the sight of him, lips curling in a look that he knows well.

She thinks she has me. And she's right. For now.

Standing to her right, on the far side of the concrete slab from where he approaches, is a dark-haired man, face rough and reddened from years of hard

living. Some power, but tiny compared to the witch—
and nothing compared to Mr. Pilkington's strength.
The demon decides the minor magician will die first.
He takes in more details, seeing how the man's hand
rests casually on a human limb, and the demon realizes
there is a person tied down on the slab, a small blonde
girl that he recognizes with a start. He keeps his face
impassive, but it's too late—he knows the witch who
summoned him felt his reaction.

The demon sends out a small brush of power, confirming that only three people occupy the cemetery
with him—the witch, the man, and the girl. Glancing
around, he does not see the familiar circle. The ground
behind where his summoner stands has been cleared
of debris, the scrub grass and dirt flat, but there is no
salt line to hold a demon defenseless. Seeing the girl
laid out like a sacrifice, he knows they plan to draw the
line in another medium.

He stops a few feet away, able to control his body
now that he has fulfilled the summons and reached the
summoner. She hasn't told him what he has to do yet—
but he already knows. He forces himself not to look at
Sylvia, but he can feel her terror, her need to be free,
to get away from both of these monstrous humans, run
and never stop running. For a moment, Sylvia is glad
to see him, wants her new friend to rescue her, but
when he simply stands there, her joy turns to confusion and despair and then to anger.

He doesn't speak, waiting to see what his summoner will demand, ancient senses sizing up the situation. She will have to be very careful with her request,
and she knows it. Witches don't summon demons of

his caliber—overriding official geas in the process—without knowing how the arrangement works.

But how did she do it? He scans her appearance, the simple soccer mom outfit, the well-worn sneakers, eyes settling on the dagger held aloft in her left hand, a few drops of blood still dripping from the blade to run into her hand. He doesn't recognize the weapon, but he can feel the power.

It's not her, he realizes. *She's no more powerful than any other witch in this realm. But that blade...*

Mr. Pilkington doesn't deal in magical weapons, so his knowledge is limited. He can tell that she has cut herself with the blade, officially binding it to her—and him to her for the meantime. Focusing his senses, he determines that the power is coming from the blade, not from the summoner herself. It must be the blade that allowed her to summon him. The demon doesn't generally fear weapons—death in any world except his own only results in banishment back home—but something about the feel of the weapon's power makes him hesitate. He has a feeling that getting killed by that weapon might end his existence permanently.

New plan: separate her from that blade. Don't get stabbed in the process.

He stares at her, face blank, running through possibilities as he waits for her command. He is about ten feet away, too far for her to lash out with the blade and cut him and just far enough that throwing it would probably miss. The demon moves very fast, even in this human body. Unless she's a championship knife thrower, an unlikely skill given the amount of time she must devote to her witchcraft—summoning demons is not easily learned—she should miss him at this distance.

He tries to get a sense of her desires: there is the usual arrogance and lust for power, requirements in any summoner, but he dives deeper, needing something more.

Anger bordering on rage.

That will do, he decides.

"I knew you would come, demon," she says finally, a proud smile curving her lips.

As if I had a choice? Mr. Pilkington says nothing, nodding his chin once in acknowledgment.

"I told you it was him," she says, this time addressing her companion.

The man scowls, hand casually squeezing Sylvia's ankle where she lays tied to the slab, eyes wide and mouth covered by several pieces of duct tape. "I didn't doubt you," he says. Even Mr. Pilkington can tell it's a lie.

The moment's glance at the man, seeming to listen to his reply, gives the demon enough time to take in the details of Sylvia's predicament. She is tied by a combination of rope and duct tape, her hands bound at the wrists by tape and tugged high above her head, several coils of rope running between her arms and wrapped around the entire slab. She struggles but can only move a few inches from side to side, unable to pull her hands down. Another coil of rope holds her shoulders to the slab and another just below her waist. Her feet are taped together at the ankles, only one coil of rope tying them around the slab.

She still wears the same clothes he saw her in—they must have grabbed her right after she left his side. He wonders if the man is the one she was hiding from. The way she flinches from his touch on her ankle, trying to twist her body away but unable to move very far, could be a normal reaction to a kidnapper's touch, but there seems something more familiar there.

Mr. Pilkington does not like the way she is tied, the open expanse of her torso, the carefully spaced ropes and the thin line of her stomach he can see between the top of her jean shorts and the bottom of her worn t-shirt. The empty space behind the witch suggests they plan on having a circle—and the demon knows that some circles must be drawn in innocent blood. This is a summoning, but not of him—it's a trap for a stronger demon, a Lord of the Realm, perhaps.

But what does she need me for?

He still says nothing, not sure if she knows how much free will he retains. She doesn't seem surprised that he hasn't spoken; maybe she thinks he cannot say anything. Such would be the case if she willed it while summoning him the traditional way. But other than his body obeying the summons, the demon still retains his powers—and hopefully the ability to use them. Until she demands otherwise, Mr. Pilkington can do anything he wants here. He does not want to inform her—or remind her—of that fact.

He waits and watches.

"Imagine," the witch says, reveling in her control, "conjuring one of the Palici. Bound by my word to do my bidding."

Heat floods the demon's body at the title she gives him, rage such as he had not known in centuries.

Those. Lying. Bastards.

Mr. Pilkington is not one of the Palici, twin water spirits known to punish those who break their vows, valuing oaths and truth above all things. He has, however, spent many long nights in their company, often indulging in drink, cards, and occasionally women. They had vowed revenge for that last game, when he'd had a lucky streak to rival the gods, an actual, legitimate lucky streak—Mr. Pilkington prides himself on never cheating at cards—but that had been ages ago, long enough for them to forget. He never thought they would return his luck—which was looking less and less lucky each passing moment—by passing off his true name as one of their own, allowing him to be summoned in their stead.

Mr. Pilkington stops imagining the various ways he will return the favor, focusing instead on how he can use this to his advantage. The name is his, so he is bound to obey her commands. But she thinks him a Palici brother—a spirit who can't lie.

The demon prepares his defense, readying a clever web of falsehoods to save his arusha. He is a demon— he is made for lies, for subtle temptation. Surely he can outwit a mortal witch.

My *arusha?* Mr. Pilkington rallies. He has not claimed a human in a very long time—and he isn't claiming Sylvia, he assures himself. But he will not let her die in this place. *Not today.*

"Demon," the witch says, addressing him in a tone that forces his essence to respond, body poised to obey her next words. "You will aid me in summoning your master."

Mr. Pilkington nods in obeisance, not sure what she means. His master? It isn't as if he has a supervisor back home. He serves the Greater Lords, like all demons of his rank.

But she thinks I'm a Palici—

Oh hell no.

The Palici brothers are fundamentally water demons, like him from a certain perspective, though Mr. Pilkington's origins are far more complicated, and like all water spirits, they fall under the domain of the Marquis Forneus. Mr. Pilkington risks a glance at the open sea beyond the cliff that edges the cemetery, the low stone wall only a few feet beyond where they all cluster, then looks back at the small cleared space intended for a circle. The true form of Forneus is a creature of the deep ocean, a leviathan beyond imagining, but the demon's preferred form is that of a elderly human male—one prone to lectures on rhetoric if given a chance.

This insane witch means to summon a Lord of the Deep—which means the dagger she holds is no ordinary magical weapon. Mr. Pilkington isn't a huge fan of mythology—and he probably would have doubted its existence if he didn't find himself under the weapon's sway in this cemetery—but there are old tales of artifacts that could command creatures.

Mr. Pilkington's desire to save his arusha slides underneath a new priority—getting that blade away from the witch at all costs. Forneus is generally an easygoing demon, one that Mr. Pilkington enjoys interacting with when he requests his visits to the mortal realm, but if the Marquis is actually summoned like a regular demon, and Mr. Pilkington is anywhere nearby when it happens, the Lord will not be so forgiving.

"Speak your master's name," the witch commands.

"I do not know his name," Mr. Pilkington replies truthfully, and the witch scowls, another drop of blood falling from the blade in her hand as she lowers her hands to her side.

"Dammit, Esmerelda!" the man exclaims. "I told you he wouldn't know!"

The witch glares at him, no doubt more angry at his use of her name than his words. The demon only knows of one witch named Esmerelda who could have summoned him.

A hell-cursed Tallardy witch. The Tallardy family has produced powerful magic users throughout the centuries. Mr. Pilkington has never dealt with one in person, but he has heard enough stories to be cautious. *That definitely explains the rage, though.* Long ago, a demon wronged the family; generations of Tallardy witches have been taking their revenge out in demon blood in the centuries since. *I can use this.*

"It doesn't matter, *Charlie*," Esmerelda declares, clearly using the weaker mage's name to mark him as he has marked her. "I don't need your master's name." She holds up the knife. "I have this." Glancing back at Mr. Pilkington, she gestures with the knife, the implication clear. "Come over here."

The demon's human body obeys, clearing the ten feet between them to stand on her right side beside the stone slab across from Charlie. Mr. Pilkington deliberately avoids looking over at Sylvia's face, the desperation in her wide blue eyes, the angry sputtering he can hear through the tape covering her mouth. Her body writhes on the slab, but she cannot break free of her restraints. The demon stares across the stone at the man instead, blank face easily unnerving the witch's companion. She may be a Tallardy witch, but Charlie is a coward. After a brief moment, he looks away, unable to hold the demon's gaze.

Charlie's desire for domination fades, replaced by a slightly stronger urge to flee.

Yes, Mr. Pilkington thinks, *run away, fearful one*, pushing subtle waves of power across the slab.

Charlie's body tenses, his hand gripping Sylvia's ankle just above the duct tape, his thumb brushing against the tops of her socks. Mr. Pilkington wants to grab his hand, wrench it away from Sylvia's skin, and toss the man over the cliff to the rocks below. He holds back, waiting for the right moment.

He wonders if the witch means for him to use the magical dagger to sacrifice Sylvia. That's what he assumed when he first arrived, but the ritual has become more complicated. If the Tallardy witch means to summon Forneus, she could theoretically use Sylvia's virgin blood combined with the death of a demon to do it, but he doesn't think she will surrender control of that weapon to him, even though he is under her power. The demon is glad of that—the idea of touching the blade makes his human skin crawl, everything in his essence recoiling at the thought.

He promises himself that he will research magical weapons more diligently when he gets home this time. *Because I will get home.*

Probably.

"Call your master," the witch commands, and Mr. Pilkington stiffens, unable to comply because he doesn't know what she means.

"My master does not have a phone," he replies quietly, knowing it will annoy her, and annoyed Tallardy witches easily become enraged Tallardy witches—and angry witches make mistakes.

"Call your master to you," she says instead, revising her request.

"My master does not come when I call," the demon replies, unable to avoid thinking of his one true master, not Forneus as she assumes. Technically, he could consider Forneus his lord, his superior because he approved Mr. Pilkington's visit to the mortal realm, but this time, the magic knows what she means, and his essence responds to that command. It is true that the one in his mind would not come if he called, but not for the reason she assumes. She is getting closer to the right command—he knows his time is almost up. "He will certainly not come for one like you," he adds conversationally.

"He will this time!" she snarls, and before the demon can react, she lashes out with the blade, slicing Mr. Pilkington's human arm to the bone. Blood sprays in an arc across the slab, coating Sylvia's legs. Agony streaks across his body, followed by frightening numbness. Mr. Pilkington's knees wobble, body weakening, and he feels part of his power draining out of him with the blood that runs freely down his hands, puddling on the floor near his feet. He is far too affected for a simple wound, but then he understands. Esmerelda holds out the dagger, and Mr. Pilkington watches as it glows, absorbing his magic, his strength.

Wonderful, he thinks slowly, mind trying to understand what has happened. *I was right. That blade will unmake my existence. First it will drain my power, imbuing the Tallardy witch with my strength—and likely my knowledge—and then I will be no more.*

Knowledge. Like who I really am.

The words spark in his mind, and he rallies, jerking hard to steady his body. Before he can even see her gloating face, he already knows.

"Well, well, well," she breathes, "not a Palici after all." She bites her lip, considering, then brings the bloody dagger to her face, the tip of her tongue slipping out to lick the blade, tasting him.

Bloody Tallardy witches. No wonder that demon tried to kill them. Insane power-hungry fools.

Mr. Pilkington glances down at Sylvia, taking in her wide blue eyes, wet with tears yet still filled with concern for him. She will survive for a few more minutes here. She has to.

Because he has to leave her for a moment.

The witch has to die, and her companion, and he can't do that in this body, certainly not now with that blade sucking out his power. And there is a very easy way to return to his realm.

He lets his knees go weak, making it look like he is about to swoon, falling backward. Instinctively, the witch reaches out to catch him, and the demon ducks down and sprints past her, pushing the body to its absolute limit and beyond as he moves to the cliff's edge. He feels something give in his knee as he clears the short stone wall, then glorious weightlessness and the woosh of cool air against his face as he falls to the rocks below. He thinks of Sylvia's hair on the top of the Ferris Wheel, and then he connects with something hard.

By some miracle, he hits the water, the cold enveloping his body, and for a split second he is irritated— *Can I not even kill myself properly today?*—but then the water seeps into his open mouth and down his throat, the cold pressing hard against his body, and he closes his eyes, surrendering to the inevitable.

CHAPTER 3

MR. PILKINGTON APPEARS IN WHAT HE CONSIDERS HIS living room, though he knows this is the human word for it—his fellow demons would call it the main room. He is naked, still chilled from his encounter with blade and water, but he is dry and unharmed, the familiar dark skin of his arm perfectly formed again, the lines of his birth markings clearly outlined again. He stares for a moment at his arm, sure he can see a hint of the line the dagger made on his human body. The wound is there and then gone again, a problem for another day. He stretches, relishing the feel of his true form, extending his leathery wings to their full expanse, running both hands through his long dark hair. He breathes in the familiar air of home, then closes his eyes, preparing to return to the human realm. Normally, this requires time and another trip through the proper channels to obtain clearance, but Mr. Pilkington is still under orders to complete his first mission.

He never actually spoke to Phenex.

Getting killed and returned home before completing his objective is supposed to be an inconvenience, a pit stop before he can return to fulfill his orders. He can return, and immediately, to the place he originally appeared—beneath the pier.

Opening his eyes, he finds himself again on the beach below the pier, the sounds of the humans much subdued at the late hour.

Damn, he thinks, seeing the all too human arms of the middle aged man he often wears. He begins running immediately. He had hoped to return in his true form, but the magic won't allow it, certain that any visit to Phenex among the humans requires a human body. This human body, however, is much more effective than the teenage form he used before—a form he has decided to retire.

His legs are long as he runs along the shore, retracing his steps from earlier when he'd been compelled to answer the summons. Tight dark pants hug his legs, and a dark shirt covers his torso, the color blending into the darkness of the night. His feet are bare, his preferred method of hunting, and as he runs up the slope to the cemetery at the cliff's edge, he makes no sound. He slows when he approaches, scanning the area with his magic, his power strong though not yet fully recovered from the wound and subsequent death.

Now free of the witch's control in this body, he can do as he wishes. But if she sees him and has enough time to say his name, she can easily ensnare him again.

His geas may allow him a speedy return after one death, but another in such quick succession would be suspicious, and there may be questions before he is allowed to return a third time. His arusha does not have that kind of time. He must be careful.

He senses only the three of them as he approaches on silent feet, ducking behind the old gravestones as he creeps closer. He can hear the witch and Charlie talking as they stand over Sylvia's still-squirming form. She has moved to stand where he stood only a few moments before, her feet standing in his blood still soaking into the ground.

Mr. Pilkington lets out a breath as he ducks behind the gravestone directly behind the witch.

"I just don't understand how you're going to summon Forneus without the actual demon to do it," Charlie says in what is clearly an argument he has been making since the demon ran off the cliff.

"Just be glad you have me here to do the actual work," Esmerelda snaps. "We don't need him anymore." She lifts the blade over Sylvia's body, pointing it at the sky. "We already have his blood."

She begins to chant, and though the demon feels the power in the ritual, it is not made to summon him, so his essence ignores the call. Mr. Pilkington shifts his weight, judging the distance and planning his timing. If he moves too soon, she will turn. It may take her a moment to recognize him in the new body, but if she manages to say his name, he will be under her control again. He needs her to be deep in the magic.

The chanting becomes more powerful, and Mr. Pilkington's human body shivers. A quick glance out to sea shows a darkness massing out in the ocean, a call to his true master beginning. It is one thing to consider the problems that would arise if they manage to summon Forneus, a Marquis of the Realm and a Greater Demon;

it is quite another to consider what will happen if they actually succeed in summoning his father.

Now.

Mr. Pilkington's timing is perfect. He slams his body into the witch, knocking the dagger from her hand as he drives her to ground beside the concrete slab. He feels her try to resist, but she uses her body instead of her magic, her considerable power still caught up in the ritual summoning, and her physical strength is nothing compared to his. He crushes her beneath him, using both his magic and his hands to squeeze her chest, destroying her heart and snuffing her life in an instant.

He stands quickly, ready to release Sylvia, and finds Charlie standing over her, the blade shaking in his hand as he stares at the demon. Before Mr. Pilkington can react, Charlie rams the dagger down into Sylvia's stomach, blade tracing a line of destruction across her flesh. He drags it out of her with a spray of blood on his side of the slab, then turns and flees.

Mr. Pilkington prepares to leap over the slab to give chase, but the scream and wave of blood that pours from Sylvia's stomach stops him, and he climbs atop her body instead, pressing into the wound with his large hands as he calls on his power to heal her. The dagger and death have weakened him, and he expended more energy than he should have in killing the witch, but his magic is enough to slow the bleeding. She will need human help, though, to heal her insides properly.

Keeping one hand on her belly, he uses the other to break the ropes around her shoulders and hands, breaking the tape on her wrists easily. She watches him in confusion, tears covering her face as he pulls the tape from her mouth in a swift motion. A soft groan escapes her, a pitiful sound that is somehow worse than the scream of pain he heard through the tape moments before, and her hands reach for her middle, clenching in pain.

"You will survive, arusha," he promises, and her eyes narrow in confusion. He scoots down her body, releasing her belly and pressing both of her hands to her stomach, the pressure enough to hold the skin together for the moment, the blood only a slow leak. The restraints on her ankles tear free, and then he slides her into his arms, cradling her gently against his chest. He scans the cemetery for any sign of Charlie or the dagger, but both seem to have vanished into the night. Glancing out to sea, he confirms that the deeper darkness gathering there has faded, replaced by the normal color of the night sky.

He begins walking swiftly out of the cemetery and back toward the lights of the town, knowing the hospital isn't far. He is careful not to jar her as he moves, aware that his magic is enough to keep her from bleeding out, but the hold is tenuous and her body is fragile.

"Who..." A faint voice whispers, and he looks down at Sylvia, her eyes still too old for her face, her lips frozen in pain. "Who are you?"

He feels the need in her, the desire, but he knows that he doesn't have to answer her completely. She is asking him a question, and the magic binds him to tell the truth—*Anything,* he had sworn—but she is delirious, likely swimming in and out of consciousness in his arms, and while he knows he can cheat the spell—reply with nonsense and be done with her, the technical letter of the promise fulfilled—he doesn't want to. He moves more quickly, not willing to run and risk reopening the weak line of her skin again, but knowing that every moment is precious.

"Who...?" she mumbles again, and he decides that he will reply truthfully, but this will not fulfill his promise to her. She will have to collect that debt in the future.

Because she will live, he promises himself. She will live a long and happy life free of demons and sacrifices.

"I am yours, arusha," he replies, feeling the oath bind him as surely as if he were a Palici.

"Mine," she agrees. "You are mine," she repeats, voice slurring as her eyes drift closed, that vibrant blue disappearing beneath her eyelids. She mumbles another word, a sound he never expected to hear from her lips, and he freezes, nearly tripping and dropping her completely.

My name. She knows my name.

Everything in him screams that she needs to die. Humans cannot be allowed to know his name and survive. This entire mess could have been avoided if he'd been more cautious—and avoided card games.

But then Sylvia would have been sacrificed along with some other demon instead, and her light would be gone from the world. He wonders if he would have noticed, then starts moving toward the hospital again, knowing that he cannot allow her to die.

It doesn't matter if she knows my name, he decides. He has been hers since the moment he fell into those blue eyes.

Leaving her at the hospital is easy enough. The doctors on staff are confident, already barking commands to their underlings, their human medicine enough to save her. Just in case, he imbues the place with enough underlying fear to be sure they will do everything in their power to keep this girl alive. Satisfied that she will live, and that no one will remember the tall, gorgeous man who brought her in, he leaves the building behind.

It may be some time before he can return to this realm. There will be many reports to give to his superiors about the powerful weapon and the Tallardy plan to summon a Marquis of the realm. The information will certainly earn him more trips back here, not to mention the goodwill of a Greater Demon, but he knows enough to complete the task he was appointed before he returns home.

Sighing, he coaxes a shirt off a jogger, the man deciding that he should run bare chested anyway, enjoying the cooler weather. He washes off Sylvia's blood in the water below the pier, then trades out his bloody shirt for the only slightly sweaty jogger's shirt. Making sure he looks presentable enough to blend with the rest of the humans, he heads up the stairs to the pier.

Phenex probably won't be glad to see him, but it will be nice to visit with an old friend. Perhaps they will even sing a song or two together as the night wanes into morning.

Mr. Pilkington hopes for a love song.

AUTHOR BIO

J M PAQUETTE IS THE AUTHOR OF *THE KLAUDEN'S RING Saga* and the *Conjuring Fascination* series. When she isn't writing fantasy and paranormal romance novels, she can be found teaching English to college students as Dr. Paquette. Her areas of expertise include the history of the English language and the intricacies of grammatical rules as well as guidelines for effective writing and communication across disciplines. (If you've ever wondered why English is a crazy language, watch her video series on YouTube under Editor JMPaquette!). She enjoys editing manuscripts for both academic and creative writers and loves being a guest co-host for the podcast Drinking with Authors (even though she doesn't drink). Check out JM Paquette at authorjm-paquette.com and 4horsemenpublications.com and as Author JM Paquette on Facebook and Instagram.

Discover more at
4HorsemenPublications.com

10% off using HORSEMEN10